HOT IRON

A CACHE IRON MYSTERY

ALEX BLAKELY

COPYRIGHT

This is dedicated to all the people like me who love a good mystery.

1

"Man, I got to get laid," Cache Iron said as she looked to the passenger beside her.

"Well, don't look at me," Vanny replied.

"I can't believe I just said that out loud."

"It's okay, we've known each other forever; I'm not sure anything you say can shock me anymore. Listen, there are so many cute guys around where I live, I want you to drop me at the airport, go back to my place and raid my closet, find the tightest, shortest dress that I own— I think it's emerald green— and go to the bar at the end of my street, and don't come home until you have found someone to help get that dress off."

"I wish you didn't have to go. This week was all about us catching up. I haven't seen you in person since you flew out to Italy to visit."

"I know and I feel bad. I had booked this week off work, my boss okayed it months ago, it was going to be you and me, sun and surf, and oh yeah, those galleries you want to visit. This new client we got is a major piece of work and when he called me and begged me to fly to Pittsburgh, I... I just couldn't say no.

He did so much for my career, when no one else would take a chance on me."

Cache looked at her with the sad smirk she made when she was disappointed. "It's okay, I understand."

"Don't give me that look, I hate it when you give me that look. I'm hoping to be gone for only a few days. You have the keys to my place; you and Duke enjoy the surf and go visit those galleries you want to visit, because when I get back we are going to party like it's our last days on earth."

Traffic was busy at five o'clock in the evening as Cache drove her truck toward the departure drop-off point of Los Angeles International Airport. Vanny had thrown her bags in the back of Cache's truck, and Cache had to circle the departure area twice before she could spot a place to pull up and drop Vanny off. A man at a station screamed at her that she couldn't park there but then headed in a different direction to deal with another issue. Cache looked at Vanny and smiled. The two of them hugged it out; after all, they hadn't seen each other in almost six years, so what were a few more days going to hurt? Cache held up her smartphone to take a picture of them, Vanny holding up two fingers in a peace sign behind Cache's head as Cache stuck out her tongue for the photo. A quick picture, a few more hugs with lots of promises of what they would do when she got back and an enormous wave from Vanny, and she turned toward the sliding doors and disappeared. Cache could see the airport attendant coming at her, yelling that she couldn't park there and she would need to move her vehicle. She apologized for the incident. He seemed to be taken back by someone saying they were sorry and Cache jumped back into her truck. Cache scanned her photos and posted one to her social media accounts with the hashtag *#livininLA*.

Cache and Vanny had left Duke to guard the beach house. This place was confusing; cars whizzed by her and honked at each other. Cache could spot cabs darting in and out the moment a break in the traffic occurred. She grabbed her phone, put it into the phone cradle, and turned on the ignition. She had just started fumbling with the GPS app that would navigate her way back to the beach house when she got a text from an old friend, Angelo Malone.

"Hey, Cache, see you're in LA, or are you going away somewhere? If you're here, call me, I would love to talk to you."

As Cache made her way back to the beach house, she realized that driving in LA was more about patience and grit. With assholes everywhere either cutting her off, drifting into her lane because they were on the phone and not paying attention or driving up and then slowing down to check her out or her truck, this was a lot different from back home. Los Angeles seemed to be a place where you were either wealthy or not, and everyone was crowded in together, all hankering for the California lifestyle. She thought about the land back home, the refreshing smell of mountain air, emptiness as far as the eye could see; that was God's country. She wasn't sure what he would think of LA. She had spent the past forty minutes listening to the radio as she made her way up Interstate 405, and between rocking country tunes the newscasters kept talking about another victim found off of a rural road about thirty minutes away from where she'd last been seen alive. The victim was an elementary school teacher, last seen a few days ago, out celebrating with friends. All the radio announcer would say was that there were signs of trauma and the victim had been found gagged and tied up. The police asked anyone with information to call them.

Another thing I don't like about LA, too much violence, she thought as she pulled into Vanny's driveway. Vanny's car was parked in the garage and Cache's small trailer was wedged up against the garage door. A classic California car, a Porsche 914 from years gone by. Porsche didn't even make them anymore, but her car was still considered a baby when compared to Cache's '48 Whiticker long bed. She put the truck in park and looked at the message from Angelo Malone. She had met Angelo a few years ago, shortly after she was discharged from the army. Her skills as a tracker and former military police officer had proven invaluable to him as he hunted for the escaped Bolden Brothers during a fierce snow storm.

Cache replied to the text, "In town visiting a friend for the week, would love to see you, if you have the time." Send. Cache jumped out of the truck and slid her phone into her pocket. There was a cheerful face waiting to see her at the door. Duke's snout was pressed against the glass, leaving a steamy impression on the door, as he wagged his tail.

"Man, I hope he doesn't set the alarm off." Cache looked down at the door lock, a number keypad on the frame. "Why don't people use keys anymore?" she muttered to herself. "What was that code? Oh yeah." Cache remembered who Vanny's favorite celebrity was. "Now, what was his birthday? Oh yeah." She keyed in the code, and the door lock turned green and sprung open to a happy and probably hungry dog.

Cache spent the next several hours poking around Vanny's house, pulling open cabinets, rummaging through closets, looking for the dress she'd talked about and feeding Duke with the food that she had in the trailer. She opened the big French doors off of the living room that led onto the deck and smelled the salty air of the ocean. It was not mountain air, but Cache could see the appeal of living on the beach. She found herself a bottle of wine and a glass, and she and Duke went out to sit on the deck and take in the evening air. As she sat there, she closed her eyes and listened to the sound of the waves crashing on the beach. This is relaxing, she thought. Not entirely what I came for, but up there. She felt a vibration in her pocket and pulled out her phone. Another text from Angelo.

"Lunch would be perfect, but it has to be tomorrow," the text read.

With no formal plans, Cache texted back and said, "Sure, but don't know LA well, I'm at a friend's beach house in Santa Monica." A few minutes passed and the three little bubbles appeared from Angelo.

"Perfect, I'm in Venice Beach, I'm only about fifteen miles away." Three more bubbles showing that Angelo was texting something. "Let's meet at Donovan's Tiki Bar, it's in Santa Monica and probably close to you, noon?"

Cache texted back, "Sure, sounds good, look forward to seeing you."

She put her phone down and looked at Duke. "I wonder what he wants," Cache said to Duke. Duke didn't offer much response. She had done some work for Angelo back in Montana a few years ago. They'd stayed in touch ever since. The case Angelo had been working was his last for his department before he retired. Angelo had given up on the Montana winters to move down to California to enjoy his later years. He'd been almost twice her age when she met him, closer to her daddy's age than hers, but they'd gotten along well, even though they were dealing with a tough situation. Angelo had been with his police department for almost thirty years and was divorced. In that line of work, it was often difficult for some people to separate work life and personal life, and sometimes work life won out. The odd time, Cache had picked up on the vibe that maybe he was interested in being more than colleagues, but he'd never acted on it and she was glad she didn't have to deal with that awkwardness.

"Duke, you don't think this is a date, do you? I'm not sure how I should dress. Should I cancel? Should I go? What if he makes a move? Will I let him, or will I stop him in his tracks? Well?" she asked. Duke just looked at her like she was talking crazy talk and plopped his head down on the deck.

Cache thought about where her personal life had taken her over the past few years. At 34, she'd thought she would be married with a kid and maybe another one on the way. Life had decided that was not the direction for her. There had only ever been one boy for her; while many had tried in college, nothing had ever taken, and that boy from back home had decided that there were other pastures he wanted to explore and living the rest of his life in Montana didn't seem like a direction he wanted to go in. For Cache, Montana was home: it was where her family was, it was where her roots were, and the thought of living permanently anywhere else terrified her and almost nothing terrified her. She closed her eyes and listened to the waves crash along the beach, seagulls giving out their high-pitched squawks as they tried to look for that evening's meal. Maybe I should make a move on him, she thought. It's been a while since I had sex. Would it be that bad if we hooked up? She pondered the thought and shivered at contemplating having a relationship with someone old enough to be her father. But then, who would know? It's not like I'm thinking relationship, marriage, she reflected. It's just sex. She sipped on her wine as she pondered what her strategy was going to be. Was it going to be casual, seeing an old friend, or was it going to be forbidden candy with the goal of getting out of the restaurant and getting between the sheets somewhere?

Cache woke the next morning with a cold, wet nose in her face. The sun had come up over the beach. The cyclists and runners were making their way up and down the boardwalk as people wandered onto the beach to survey the area for the best location to park themselves for the day. Cache opened the upstairs doors in Vanny's bedroom and walked onto the deck. The older woman next door waved to her, dressed in a rainbow-colored sundress, and Cache waved back. I guess this is what beach people do, she thought. They get up, sit on their decks and watch people. She wandered back to the bedroom, glanced at the clock and realized she had a few hours before she would meet Angelo for lunch. She went through her morning routine, showered and took Duke for a walk along the boardwalk, stopping to talk to other dog walkers, while little kids came up to pat Duke on the head or pull at his ears. Duke always had a friendly disposition. Nothing seemed to bother him as long as he was where he wanted to be. She had concluded, after a good night's sleep, that friends was all she and Angelo were going to be. If she wanted someone that badly, Cache would throw on that tight emerald dress she'd found in Vanny's closet. The one that would allow her natural elements to be on parade for everyone to see. She could then make her way to one of the local beach bars to see what she could catch for the night.

Cache took a cab to Donovan's Tiki Bar, concerned that she would get lost and end up late. She had a pet peeve about being late for things. "Better to be thirty minutes early than five minutes late" was her motto. The one thing the army ensured was you were always on time or there was hell to pay. She had decided to go comfortable that day. A pair of running shoes, a pair of shorts and a plain white tank top that clung to her chest. Her cab pulled up outside of Donovan's. The bar had a Hawaiian theme to it, with two large tiki heads about five feet in height, each with glowing eyes, greeting the guests next to the hostess stand. The bar had a small patio, with silver railings and glass panels and an open area that led into the bar. Lilies were on prominent display throughout in white, orange and red, creating a sweet floral scent in the air that her nose scooped up. Large palm fronds clung to bamboo poles hung from the ceiling, rotating, providing a gentle breeze that tantalized her skin.

She walked up to the hostess at the front door. "I'm meeting someone here," she said.

From across the room she could see a hand waving. An

older man with a white beard she didn't remember and the loudest Hawaiian shirt anyone had ever seen.

"I see him," she said to the hostess, and smiled as she wandered past the other patrons in the restaurant.

"There you are," she said, smiling at Angelo.

"You found the place, I see," he said.

"Yeah, I took a cab just to be safe, didn't want to get lost," she said.

"Well sit down, let me look at you, it's been a few years."

Cache checked him out and thought, No, definitely no sex, don't need the therapy.

"It has been a few years; do you regret trading in the Montana winter for the California surf?" Cache asked.

"You know Montana is home. It was home for most of my career. Of course, I'm a New York boy, born and raised, but you know I don't miss the weather. It's nice to wake up to the smell of the ocean every morning."

The waitress came by and introduced herself and provided them with the menus.

"Would either of you like something to drink?" she asked.

Angelo gestured to Cache. "What would you like?"

"I think I will start with a glass of white, a pinot grigio if you have it," Cache said.

"And for you, sir?" the waitress asked.

"Just a ginger ale for me," he responded.

The waitress left, and they flipped open the menus. There was a wide selection of seafood, Italian and good old American beef. After a few minutes the waitress returned and took their order; Angelo chose the fettuccine and she decided on the Santa Monica burger. The waitress said it should be about twenty minutes and left the table. Cache noticed through the ordering process that Angelo seemed fixated on her chest.

"So, I'm glad you texted me. My friend that I came to visit had to go out of town, so I was thinking I might just get back on the road and head for home. What did you want to talk to me about?" Cache asked.

Angelo looked like he was lost in thought, though Cache noticed that, given the air temperature inside, her nipples had firmed up and could be seen under her top.

"Angelo, what did you want to talk to me about?" she asked again.

"Oh, oh, um, um, oh yeah, it's important. I don't know if you know this, but I didn't retire when I moved down to Los Angeles. I opened up a bail bond agency, you know, with my background in law enforcement."

Cache said, "I remember you mentioning it in one of your emails to me."

Angelo continued, "Well, a couple of weeks ago I posted bail for this guy who was accused by his girlfriend and her roommate of rape."

Cache responded, "I would have left his ass in jail."

"Would have been best, but to hear him talk about it, it sounded like his story had some level of plausibility to it, so I posted two hundred thousand dollars for his bail. Last week he was to appear before the judge for a preliminary hearing but was a no-show. The judge issued a warrant for his arrest; police go to where he was living and he wasn't there, hadn't been to work in a few days, so it appears he is on the lam."

"So, what does this have to do with me, Angelo?" Cache asked.

Angelo once again seemed fixated on her plain white tank top.

"Hello, Angelo, are you there?"

Angelo came to attention and realized she had caught him staring. "You know, there is a brilliant invention you might want to check out some time—it's called a bra. I hear they are huge with women."

"Yeah, I hear that too. Funny thing is, I wore one for years and I don't see an undershirt under that flowery top of yours," Cache said.

"They're uncomfortable, I don't enjoy wearing them," Angelo said.

"Neither do I," Cache answered, "for the same bloody reason. I like the girls being out and free."

Angelo asked, "Were they out and free in the army?"

"No. If you want to know, we had to wear a sports bra, but I'm no longer in the army and my boobs can do what they like. It amazes me how a set of nipples can reduce grown men to fourteen-year-old boys, and I have to say it gives me great pleasure to watch men squirm at even the hint of them. So did you want to have lunch to talk about my breasts?"

Angelo said, "No I don't want to talk about your tits—I mean, your breasts." Angelo's face had become flushed with just the brief conversation about her nipples. The waitress brought their food to the table and made sure they had everything before she parted company with them.

"So I ask you again, what does your rape-loving client have to do with me?"

Angelo began laying out his idea. The police had gone to all of his client's known haunts, but there was no sign of him. Angelo said that his client, George Wilkes, had a brother near Grove Meadows, Arizona. They were estranged, and he had spoken to the brother, as had local law enforcement; he was adamant that he had not talked to or seen his younger brother for years. George had been a disgrace to his family according to his brother, Jack, but Jack was the only family George had. Angelo said he had a gut feeling that the brother knew more than what he was saying and that he might open up to a pretty brunette with stunning breasts. He offered Cache 10 percent of the bail, which would be twenty thousand dollars, if she could find George and return him so that Angelo wouldn't be out the two hundred thousand dollars he had posted as his bail. While she appreciated the offer, she reminded Angelo that she wasn't a bail bondsman, or bail bondswoman, to be politically correct, but he countered by saying her six years in the military police was the best training she could get. Cache agreed to go and talk to the brother. She had never been to Arizona, and with Vanny not here to act as the designated tour guide, it would give her something to do and put a mini adventure in this vacation. They finished their meals, caught up on other things in their lives and parted ways. She told him she would head out later that day. Cache had no formal commitments and thought she might as well go back to Vanny's, hitch up the trailer and grab Duke. Cache would call Vanny to let her know that she was going out of town for a few days but would lock up and set the alarm.

———

The drive along Interstate 40 was peaceful. She had the windows rolled down on both sides to allow the fresh air in. She could feel the rays of the sun searing her left arm, which rested on the edge of the door. The air coming into the cab felt parched. Cache would rotate the knobs of the old radio to see what stations she could pick up. She had thought about upgrading the radio in this old 1948 truck more than once, but it didn't seem right. It had been her grandfather's; he'd passed it on to her when he died, and she didn't like the idea of altering it too much. Originally the truck had been a dark green, but it now had faded spots all over it. The logo of the Iron & Sons ranch on either front door had peeled away after many years of use, and only an outline from where the sun had baked the logo into the door panels could be spotted if the light hit the doors the right way. The drive gave Cache a chance to think about where her life was going. Her mini trailer, in tow, had enough room to accommodate one adult and one dog inside.

The small galley kitchen opened up in the back. She had installed solar panels along the roof, with her brother Cooper's help, that would charge the batteries. Cache thought about Jake, the one that got away. He was working in Los Angeles now, the first boy she had ever slept with. Maybe *slept* was the wrong word, but she thought about him along the drive as she and Duke headed to Arizona. Angelo had given her a copy of the warrant in the event she had to prove that George was a wanted man. Angelo hoped Cache could bring him back to Los Angeles if she were to find him, but if need be, turning him over to the state police might be a good backup plan. Cache looked at Duke. He would periodically stick his head out of the window and then pull it back in to look at her. Cache went over her plan for the next couple of days with him. They would arrive near Grove Meadows this evening and would look for a place to park the trailer. Tomorrow, they would find Jack Wilkes's bait and tackle shop, called Jack's Tackle, and pay him a brief visit. Ask a few questions, see if she could get any answers, and then assess the situation. If it looked like something that might pan out, she would touch base with Angelo and go from there. If his brother didn't know anything, maybe they'd make a drive to the Grand Canyon and then plot a course back to Montana. See a couple more states in the process.

They'd been driving for about five hours when she reached the California/Arizona state line. They stopped a short bit at the Arizona welcome center to let Duke stretch his legs and get some water. The woman at the welcome booth was bubbly, probably some previous winner of a local beauty contest who'd hoped to get into the entertainment industry one day and ended up at a booth greeting people from California. Cache made some inquiries about places to camp around Grove Meadows and asked about their fishing. The woman laughed and told her that the fishing was at Lake Havasu, so any fishing stores around those parts were for locals on their way to the Su. She suggested Cache try the Sunny Side RV Park. It was about fifteen minutes outside of Grove Meadows, so hopefully they'd be familiar with Jack Wilkes's tackle shop and could point her there. Cache got back into her truck and headed back onto the highway.

Cache pulled into the Sunny Side RV Park at around eight o'clock in the evening. The campground was of a fair size with several trailers parked randomly through the area. There were new trailers, old trailers, and a few that looked more permanent than mobile. The roads were mainly gravel and kicked up dust as she drove over them. She could see several residents huddled together in little packs outside of various units, on beaten-up lawn chairs, drinking beer or soda. Some trailers had awnings, some flamingos or garden gnomes in the front yard. All in all, it was your traditional trailer park.

The park was owned by a retired husband and wife, William and Sally Bean, a nice old couple who pointed her to lot twenty-three, where Cache could park her trailer and connect with a power hookup. While filling out their registration forms, she inquired about Jack's Tackle; they both knew Jack well and gave her directions on how to get there. They exchanged small talk, and they asked about Duke and how long she had had him. They favored cats and had several in their trailer, which was attached to the small log cabin office they had created. Cache told them she was down this way for the fishing and to catch up with an old friend of the family. The Beans were genuinely surprised that Cache had left Montana for fishing, but Cache made it sound like the trip was more to catch up with Jack.

Cache pulled her trailer into spot twenty-three and disconnected it from the truck. She plugged her trailer into the electrical hookup, opened up the small galley kitchen and turned on both the exterior and interior lights. She fixed up some dinner for herself and Duke. Cache set up two small folding chairs that she carried with the trailer and a tiny plastic table, and relaxed after the long drive. The smell of barbecue was in the air; it smelled like ribs, and she could hear televisions coming from the open windows of a few trailers that surrounded her. After dinner she shut the external galley kitchen and locked it up, and she and Duke crawled into the small trailer and locked the door for the night. She popped open the vent in the ceiling to allow some fresh air in. Cache grabbed her laptop from one of the storage drawers inside the trailer and used the time to read all she could about George Wilkes and the crime he'd been accused of. She flipped through the files Angelo had provided her so she understood the situation. After a couple of hours of research, she put the laptop away and set her alarm for six o'clock a.m. No point in just hanging around, she told Duke. They would stop into Jack's Tackle, talk to Jack, see if she could learn anything about his brother. Then she would make a judgment call, and if it turned out he didn't know anything or didn't want to share anything, then they might just get on the road back to Montana.

2

The morning sunshine peered through the blinds of the small trailer. Duke was resting to the side and Cache pulled open the blinds. Cache unzipped her sleeping bag and reached for her duffel bag to retrieve some fresh workout clothes to pull on. She grabbed her trail running shoes.

"Hey, Duke, feeling like going for a bit of a run?"

His ears perked up at the word *run*, and his tail wagged away furiously. They crawled out of the trailer and found a small trail in the RV park. She leashed up Duke so he wouldn't be tempted to go out and explore on his own. The trail she'd found wound down behind the campground to a few hills that provided a challenge to get up. Even that early in the morning, the heat had already started for the day. The taste of salt from her own sweat rolled its way into her mouth as she wiped her forehead, dripping with perspiration. The sweat that found its way into her eyes stung. The air felt thick to breathe as they continued to run along the dirt path for about thirty minutes, with patches of dry grass and rock on either side of the dirt trail. They ran up a hill, slowing their pace to more of a walk as the terrain became steeper, until they reached the peak. Cache found herself on top of a smooth, rocky ledge perched high above the valley below, where she could see the surrounding countryside for almost 180 degrees. This would be a great place to do her morning yoga routine and clear her head, she thought. Duke stretched out on the rocks and rolled over on his back, paws up, while Cache went through her morning routine. Downward-facing dog, triangle pose, warrior II, bridge pose, upward-facing dog, bow pose, and finishing with boat pose. After thirty minutes of yoga, she felt energized for her day.

"Smell that fresh air," she said. "It's beautiful here. One could just stay here forever, but we have a job to do."

Once Cache finished up her set, she ran back to their camping spot. The campsite had a small area for showers that Cache took advantage of to hose the sweat off of her skin, then she threw on the clothes she planned to wear that day: white leather running shoes, a white cotton thong that would rise just above the top of her jeans, a pair of old beaten-up jean cutoffs and a plain white tank top. It was now just past seven thirty a.m., and William had said that Jack opened up shop around eight o'clock. Duke hopped in beside her, and they drove out of the campground and made their way to Jack's Tackle. I figure this will only take a few minutes; I'll ask a few questions and let Angelo know what I find out, Cache thought. Jack's Tackle was on the north side of the road. While the store had only been open for fifteen to twenty minutes, when she pulled in she saw that there were already several pickup trucks and cars in the parking lot. Cache pulled into the last parking spot, farthest from the door, and checked herself in the rearview mirror.

"What do you think, Duke, ponytail or no ponytail? I think ponytail." She threw on an Iron & Sons baseball cap. She looked down at the girls—they seemed quite perky this morning—and squeezed them through her tank top.

Cache wandered into the tackle shop. Little bells above

the door clanged together to announce her arrival to the other occupants. She noticed a bearded gentleman talking behind the counter at the front of the store to two elderly men. The store had aged linoleum throughout, dark scuff marks in certain places that no amount of scrubbing would get out. The walls were covered in wood paneling that looked like it belonged in the sixties, with a yellow hue to it. The air was musky, even slimy, which Cache attributed to an area in the store where Jack had live bait for sale. Fishing rods covered the back wall; the displays that created three rows to the back had lures, hooks, nets, waders and an assortment of other items. Along the wall closest to the door was a small magazine rack with magazines about fishing and hunting and a few men's magazines where the models on the cover were likely fishing for something else. Beside the magazine rack sat an old red cooler with part of the words *Coca-Cola* still painted on the side, which seemed to hold sodas and an assortment of frozen treats, Cache noticed as she walked toward the fishing rods at the back of the store. The walls displayed various species of fish mounted on pieces of driftwood and stickers with some reference to fishing. She looked at the different fishing rods, lifting them up out of the rack and examining them, and it was clear from the glances over her shoulder that the men in the shop were all very strongly aware of her presence. Cache heard a few low-volume comments and snickers from the older men, which she surmised were about her. She drifted through the store until the last of the patrons had either checked out at the cash register or left the store after rummaging through the merchandise.

"Can I help you, miss?" the gentleman shouted out behind the counter.

"No, just looking," she said. "I understand the best fishing around here is at Lake Havasu?"

"Well, that is one spot. You can also go up to Dolan Springs."

"Do you have anything for fly-fishing?" she asked.

"No, not that big around here," he said.

Cache continued to roam through the store and grabbed a couple of sodas and went up to the cash register.

"I think I will just get these then," she said, smiling at him.

"You're not my usual patron, you new around here or just passing through?"

"Just passing through, from Montana originally."

"Ah, that is why you wanted fly-fishing. I hear it's pretty country up there."

"We like to think it's one of God's best-kept secrets," Cache said.

"I like your tat, definitely catches the eye."

"Which one?" she asked. Cache showed the inside of her left arm, with a Latin phrase, and her right upper shoulder, with crossed flintlocks and a nasty-looking skull in the center.

"Definitely the shoulder ink; I have no idea what that says." He pointed to the inside of her left arm.

"Personal joke, but the flintlocks are because I like the pirate lifestyle. Being free, sailing the seven seas, gold, fighting off fellow pirates—it all sounds so romantic, doesn't it?" She leaned in and cocked her head to one side and smiled, her long brunette hair falling down her back from her cap, which was raised up on her head so he could see her beautiful eyes, the gap in her neckline falling open.

Jack smiled at her and said, "Bullshit!"

"What?" Cache asked, trying to act offended.

"You heard me, I said bullshit. I spent over twenty years in the armored division, you don't think I've had run-ins with people who had a similar insignia? Was that your MOS?"

Cache looked at him. "MOS? What is that?" she asked, hoping to defuse his questions. She had read up on him before coming here, and from what little she could find on the web, Jack Wilkes was a former soldier who had served with distinction before being discharged after a combat-related injury. While she thought Angelo had assumed a pretty face with great jugs might get him to open up, she suspected it was their shared sense of service that might open his lips.

"Lady, I don't have time for games. MOS. Military occupational specialty. I'm assuming you were or are military police?"

Cache decided that the jig was up and that being honest might better get the answers she was looking for.

"Yep, I was in the military police for six years."

"Were? Why did you leave?"

"I spent six great years in the army, met many people I have a great amount of respect for, saw the world—no active combat, but at the end of six years I decided that it was time for me to head back to Montana to start the next chapter in my life, whatever that might be. And you, how did you end up owning a tackle shop in Arizona?"

"Well, I was out on patrol, we got ambushed and they killed part of my platoon. I lost a leg and wasn't sure I could still do what I did to the best of my abilities, so I retired."

"I'm sorry to hear that," Cache said.

Jack rolled up his right sleeve to reveal a tattoo of several dog tags that he explained were the names of his friends who were killed that day, as a constant reminder.

"So, what really brings you here, as if I don't know?" Jack asked.

"I am looking for your brother, George. He is a bad dude and needs to be found before he hurts anyone else."

"Like I told the police, I haven't seen him, we are not that close, I have no idea where he is and don't care. The cops said he raped somebody and jumped bail?"

"Yeah, it's a little more than that. You see, your brother had a date with a woman named Judy. They went up to her place to make out, but that is as far as she wanted to take it. So he started smacking her around and eventually found some packing tape in a drawer and put her over a table, taping her arms and legs to each table leg. He then tore her clothes off and raped her. She pleaded with him to stop, and then the room-mate came home. He held a knife to her throat and told her to stay quiet. The roommate walks into the kitchen. Sees what is occurring and starts screaming at the top of her lungs and runs for the doorway. Your brother, George, was a little quicker and grabbed her by the back of the head just as she reached the door.

"She told police that he asked her where she was going and then told her she had a party to attend and, while holding the back of her head, smashed her face into the rear of the door a few times. He then dragged her kicking and screaming into her bedroom while she begged for him not to. She was engaged, had never had sex before and was saving herself for her fiancé, Brad. From what I read from the survivor accounts, that seemed to turn him on more, and he beat her senseless and raped her too. He took turns raping those women for several hours, threatening to kill them both. The only reason they survived is the noise roused a neighbor who called the police. While the police knocked on the door, Judy figured they were both dead anyway and cried out for help. The police kicked the door down and your brother made a departure via the fire escape outside one of the windows, but the officers caught him and dragged his ass to jail. So now you know what your little brother did, if you ever hear from him."

Jack looked horrified at hearing the full story. "How do you know this is true and not some tale made up by these women?"

Cache looked at him. "The bail bond guy asked me to come down and see you in person; I guess he thought with us both being ex-army that maybe you would talk to me. Jack, from what I read about you, you seem like an honorable guy, but I saw pictures of the victims and I have some experience in dealing with sexual assaults from my time in the military; they were telling the truth. Look, if you don't know anything, there is nothing you are going to be able to tell me, but I'm guessing this isn't your brother's first assault and won't be his last. If you hear anything, do your brother a favor and call the police. At some point, they may just look at him as the animal he is and put him down. No court, no jail."

With that, Cache told him it was nice to meet him and saluted him and made her way to the door. She could tell the news had shaken him, and he stood quietly behind the cash register. Cache opened the door. The small bells above the door clinked together and she was about to leave when she heard, "Wait." She turned to him and walked back to where he was standing.

"Look, when the police asked me if I had heard from him, I hadn't heard a thing from him for years and was fine with that. The other day, I got a call from him and he said he was in trouble and needed some money. I asked him about the charges against him that the police had shared with me. He said that he met a girl at a bar; she was engaged to some rich dude and they hooked up. The fiancé found out about it, had her press rape charges against him so he could save face with his family, and her roommate was backing her up in the claim because she was part of the wedding party."

Cache asked, "Why not go to court then? Why jump bail?"

"I asked him that. He said because of who the family was, he was going to be found guilty before the trial even started and he feared that their reach would even extend into the prison to silence him."

Cache asked, "So he said he needed money. Did you guys agree on a location? Is he coming here?"

Jack said, "I'm meeting him this afternoon at one o'clock at Benny's Burgers. It's a small diner just up the street. I told him I would meet him there, give him some money, and then I didn't want to hear from him ever again. So, I bet you think I should call the police."

"If I asked you not to, would that come as a surprise?"

"Yeah, a bit—dangerous animal, needs to be locked up, isn't that what you said?"

"It is, and normally I would tell you to call the police and let them handle it, but my friend Angelo stupidly put up two hundred thousand to bail your brother out. If I can get him back to Los Angeles, it will help him out, plus I have more than enough experience working with dangerous people."

"So, what do you want me to do?" Jack asked.

"Just meet with your brother. I will be at the diner and will try to take your brother into custody without any innocent people getting hurt."

"And you won't hurt him?" Jack asked.

"I will try not to, but when dangerous animals get cornered, all bets are off. I will try to see if I can get him away from the rest of the people in the diner."

"And how do you plan on doing that?" Jack asked.

"Your brother has proven he likes pretty things, and I happen to be a pretty thing. I'm sure he will be more focused on my boobs than anything else."

With that, Cache thanked Jack for his help and told him she would be in the diner, watching. Once Jack had made the delivery and left the diner, she would take over. She walked out of the tackle shop and climbed back into her truck. It was now nine thirty a.m. and she had a few hours to kill before she needed to be at the diner. Cache stopped at the local gas station and fueled up the truck. She picked up a map. The attendant, who was probably sixteen, was a bit surprised that anyone still bought them, and she asked the boy behind the counter if there were any out-of-the-way areas around these parts. He told her there were some old mines to the north and then just farmers' fields around town. Once you left the main street, there was pretty much nothing. Cache took the time to look at the map and study the places where she might be able to lure George. She pulled up beside an old phone booth and hopped into the back of her truck. She'd had a lockbox manufactured for this old truck, the only modification that she'd made when the truck passed down to her. Diamond plated steel, it was thin, so as not to take up much room, and sat behind the window of the front seat of the cab. The lockbox had a biometric lock on it, and it would only open for Cache's palm print. Inside the box were various tools that might be needed on the ranch. On the underside of the lid was a Marlin rifle. As she packed for her trip, she had forgotten to remove the weapons from the back of the truck. Only realizing it when she got to Vanny's. Cache planned on leaving them at her place as they toured the area, but she was now happy that she had them with her. Welded to the bottom of the container was an ammo box that she opened with the key on her key chain. She pulled out a clip and reached for her Beretta M9, which was in a holster hanging on the right side of the lockbox. Cache slid the clip in and tucked the gun into the back of her shorts. She would put it in the glove box for the time being. Cache had over six years' experience using this style of handgun, both on the range and in real-life scenarios. She rummaged through the box and pulled out a pair of handcuffs and leg irons that Angelo had brought with him to the restaurant, just in case she needed them. He must have been certain that she would say yes to his proposal, or at least he had hoped. Those would need to come up front with her, so they could be quickly accessed when needed. She rubbed Duke's face and grabbed a plastic water dish she kept in the back and filled it up with cool water that she had purchased for him along with the map.

She lowered herself into the bed of the truck and laid out her plan for Duke. Unfortunately, whether he thought the plan was wise or not, he wouldn't say, but talking it out aloud reaffirmed in Cache's mind how best to handle the situation. After Jack left the diner, she would approach George and turn on the charm. She would suggest they go somewhere private to get to know each other better. Cache figured he was probably hungry for his next encounter but might be lying low to avoid any chance of interacting with the police. But someone who wanted to have sex with him, how could he pass on that?

Getting him away from town so no one could come to his aid seemed like the best idea. No innocent bystanders with little chance for escape. With the hardware she was packing, she figured she should be able to get him cuffed without an ounce of sweat on her forehead. Once she bagged him, she would call Angelo, get the trailer and get this rapist back to Los Angeles. She went through the various steps in her head over and over again. It all just seemed so simple. How could anything go wrong? This would be the easiest money she'd ever made; maybe this would be the start of her next career.

3

It was about twelve fifteen when Cache entered the diner with Duke. She saw a sign on the window that said dogs were welcome. She liked that. Cache hated leaving Duke in the truck, though she could have secured him to a hitch on the lockbox. The sound of bells clanking together as she walked in to Benny's Burgers caused a few people to glance up from what they were doing and look at the door. There was a long counter with stools underneath that sat in the middle of the room. A cash register from an earlier time sat on the counter portion closest to the door. An opening in the wall gave a view into the kitchen, where two men moved back and forth wearing white aprons and hairnets. A stand of pies under a glass dome sat on the counter next to the register to keep them from being consumed by the flies that buzzed around her head. Above the pass-through to the kitchen, a small old color TV sat on a shelf above the door that led to the back with a porthole window in the middle of it. Booths lined the wall closest to the window. A group of men sat in the booth closest to the door on her right-hand side. Another man sat facing the door in the last booth on the left-hand side. A waitress was serving coffee to her right. She was probably in her midfifties and wore running shoes, a blue top with a skirt and a heavily stained white apron wrapped around her waist. She had dark hair with a touch of gray and black-rimmed cat's-eye glasses; she looked at Cache.

"Sit anywhere you like, sweetheart, I will be with you short-ly," she said as she glanced down toward Duke. "Is he friendly?"

"Yes, very."

"Okay, he can come in then."

Cache walked to her right, convinced that the men in the booth weren't her target. The counter ran in an L pattern and she found a spot against the wall at the counter that would allow her to survey the room. She noticed that the man in the back was wearing a ball cap and spent a lot of his time looking at the menu, then looking around the room. Opposite him toward the back were signs for the washrooms and telephones. How many places still have pay telephones? she thought. The waitress walked up to her and asked her what she wanted to drink and gave her a two-sided laminated menu sticky to the touch.

"What's good here, Paula?" she asked as she read the wait-ress's name tag.

She smiled and said, "Everything is good. If it ain't good, you didn't get it here."

Cache laughed.

"What can I get you to drink?" Paula asked.

Cache smiled and said, "Can I start with a coffee, two creams, two sugars?"

"Honey, you know how hot it is out there and you want coffee? Boy, girl, you must like the heat."

Cache said, "Just old habits."

Cache surveyed the diner. The men in the booth closest to her were talking about farming, occasionally looking up to yell at Paula to get her opinion on whatever they were discussing.

The man in the back with the baseball cap only looked up on occasion and seemed fixated on playing with the ketchup bottle and saltshaker on his table. From this distance, it was hard to determine if that was George Wilkes. His fidgety movements may have suggested someone waiting eagerly for someone or just complete boredom. She glanced at the wall and noted that it was now twelve thirty. Provided Jack didn't change his mind, he should be here shortly. The man tended to glance over at the clock frequently and therefore Cache assessed that it was probably indeed George waiting for Jack to arrive. From her angle, he appeared to be nibbling on a piece of pie and drinking a glass of iced tea.

At about twelve forty, the diner door opened up and the bells rang, announcing a new visitor to their little gathering. A voice shouted as a man came through the door, "Hey, Paula, hey, Jason, can I get two slices of your apple pie to go?"

"Sure thing, Fred, how are things down at the police station?" Paula asked.

Fred was about mid-to-late twenties, brown pants, brown short-sleeve shirt, black boots, pistol on the hip with a shiny star sitting on the upper left-hand side of his chest. He had mirrored shades hanging from his right breast pocket. He was clean shaven, with bleach blond hair that didn't protrude much from under his hat.

"Pretty quiet today, Paula. Thought I would sneak down to grab a piece of pie before the sheriff gets back. Hey, who owns the old truck out in the parking lot?" he asked her.

"Around here, old truck is pretty much everybody. Anything special about it?" Paula asked.

"Yeah, it's a '52 Whiticker truck," he said.

Cache, overhearing the conversation, spoke up and said, "It's a '48."

"So that's yours out there, Montana plates?" the deputy asked as he made his way closer to Cache, eyeing her from top to bottom. Guys always think a woman can't tell when they aren't looking at their eyes. Cache had been blessed with a lot of cleavage, and her preference for tank tops always gave a bit of a show to those tempted to look anywhere but her eyes.

"You're a little way from home, aren't you?" the deputy asked.

"We're just passing through on our way to the Grand Canyon."

"We? Oh, is your husband or boyfriend with you?" He readjusted his glance to first check out her finger for a ring and then focused his attention on her face. Cache pointed below to her feet, where the deputy glanced down to see Duke lying on the floor.

"So, what's your name, fella?" the deputy asked.

Cache looked at the deputy and with a slight flick of her hair said, "His name is Duke."

"Oh, so he's royalty," the deputy said.

"Sort of," Cache said. "My dad named him Duke after his favorite western star, John Wayne."

"I have to agree with your dad. Now, that was an actor. I can totally relate; my parents watched all the old westerns when I was growing up." The deputy's eyes caught the television set above the door and he asked Paula to turn up the volume. I noticed over his shoulder that George had grown more impatient with a law enforcement officer in the establishment and was checking out the window and then looking back to his pie.

The TV news anchor was reporting on the remains of a murdered teacher found a few days ago in Los Angeles. Police had held a briefing that morning to suggest that evidence found at the scene was very similar to that in the case of another victim, Gabriela Perez, who'd been found dead two months ago. They'd found both victims with similar markings on their body and other evidence on their persons. The local media was reporting that sources inside the department were indicating this seemed to be the work of the Pinup Killer.

The deputy told Paula that she could turn the television down and that it offered nothing more than what law enforcement already knew.

Cache said, "That's tragic, but who is the Pinup Killer?"

"The person they are referring to as the Pinup Killer has been stalking young women over the past few months in Los Angeles. They call him or her the Pinup Killer because they leave a vintage pinup card depicting something similar to the victim on the victim's remains."

"I'm not familiar with pinup cards, what are they?"

"They were popular in the 1940s; it's art involving a female in a sexy pose that a person might pin to their wall. Back then I guess that was provocative, not like what we have today on the web. You can find details about the killings on the internet. I think the first victim was a public librarian. They found her strangled, and there was an old pinup card of a librarian holding books with her skirt up in the air. The second victim, Gabriela Perez, was a housekeeper, and they found her with a card of a French maid. I'm not sure what card they found the teacher with, but I imagine it will be all over the web in the next few days."

He spoke to Cache and Paula, informing them they'd never had a serial killer around these parts. In larger cities maybe it was more prevalent, but not around here. Cache thought, staring past the deputy at the man in the far booth, You may not have a serial killer in these parts, deputy, but you have a serial rapist. The deputy collected his pie, said goodbye to Paula, tipped his hat to Cache and left. As he walked out the door, he bumped into Jack as he made his way into the diner. From the exchange of pleasantries, they obviously knew each other. Jack surveyed the diner and waved hello to Paula. He spotted Cache at the counter and their eyes met for a few seconds before he saw she was looking past him. He followed her glance to the gentleman in the last booth, who was looking up right at Jack. Their eyes met, and Jack made his way to the booth and sat down opposite George.

Paula wandered over to ask Jack what he wanted, but he appeared not to have ordered anything as she topped up George's iced tea. The four gentlemen in the booth next to the door waved Paula over to get their bill. They sat there for a few minutes discussing the bill, pulled out their wallets and left some cash on the table, and got up and left. The front of the diner was now occupied by her and Duke, Jack and his brother, and Paula going back and forth to the kitchen.

From Cache's position she couldn't hear the conversation, but it seemed heated from the look on George's face. She then watched as Jack slid an envelope over to George, which George picked up, looked inside and tucked into his jeans. Cache thought she should make sure that the money found its way back to Jack. Jack stood up and said something to George, then turned and left without glancing at her, waving at Paula.

If Cache was going to make her move, she would have to do it quickly, while few people were here in the diner. She looked at George, who was checking out the window to see who was floating around outside, then got up and headed to the back. From the sign up on the wall, he was either heading for the washroom or going to make a call. Cache looked down at Duke and told him to wait there. She thought, Here goes nothing, as she walked to the back of the diner, where George had disappeared.

Cache noticed that there was an old phone against the wall and not in use. To her right the men's room, to her left the ladies'. She went up to the ladies' room and opened the door. There were two stalls with the doors open and no one in sight. She closed the door behind her and put her ear up to the men's room door. Cache could hear someone inside. She turned the handle slowly and walked inside. The men's room was filthy. A small white porcelain sink was to her right, with chips in the porcelain. There was a mirror above the sink that looked like no one had wiped it clean in days. To her left was a toilet stall with the door open and a rotting, foul smell coming from inside that she didn't want to know the cause of. To the right of the toilet stall there was a urinal.

George had his hand down toward his crotch as he stood up against the urinal, his left hand bracing him against the wall.

"Is it big?" Cache asked.

Surprised to hear a woman's voice in the men's room, he turned to look over his shoulder.

"Hey, lady, I think you're in the wrong place, the women's washroom is next door."

She smiled and said, "I'm not looking for a woman. I need a man, and this seems to be the place to come find one; that's why it's called the men's room."

He said, "Why do you need a bunch of men to help you with whatever problem you have?" He finished his business, zipped up his pants and walked over to the sink. He eyed her up and down. White leather running shoes, long tanned legs, a tight pair of jean shorts. A plain white tank top hanging down over a pair of firm breasts and nipples protruding under the fabric. Her long, straight brown hair was tied in a ponytail poking through the back of her baseball cap.

"What can I do for you?" he asked.

Cache knew she needed to take control of the situation. She needed to get him away from the diner so no one could come to his aid, and she needed him to want to go with her.

"I'm horny, I need someone to give me a good fucking. Are you man enough for the challenge?"

She could see the wheels spinning in his head. She knew people like him had an itch. An itch to do the wrong thing. He had probably been wanting to scratch that itch since LA but feared getting caught while the police were looking for him.

"You're not my type," he said.

Cache thought, Yeah, because I'm not saying no. "Look, if you're not man enough for the job, I get it, sorry to waste your time."

"Really? How about I screw your brains out up against that wall?" he said as he looked to the wall beside the urinal, which smelled like piss. "Broad like you probably needs it rough, am I right?" he asked.

"It's filthy in here. Sorry, if you want this very fine piece of ass, we need somewhere a little cleaner than this. I have a pickup truck. Ever do it in the back of a pickup truck?" she asked.

"Many times," he said. "Okay, well you lead the way."

The two of them exited the men's room. George walked up to Paula and asked her what he owed her and settled his bill. Cache approached her to do the same and told Duke to follow her. George seemed put off when he saw Duke.

"Hey, you didn't say anything about a dog."

"He's harmless," Cache told him. "Probably will sit in the front seat and watch, but it's me you want to fuck, right?"

They made their way outside toward Cache's truck. "Whoa, that's nice," he said. "What year is it?" he asked.

"'Forty-eight," she said. He grabbed her by the waist and leaned in to kiss her. He smelled like he hadn't bathed in days and he was already sticking his tongue in her mouth. She pushed him back and said, "We are not doing it in the parking lot of a diner, we need to find somewhere secluded. Any ideas?"

George thought for a moment. "There are some old mining roads to the north we could drive up to. The mines haven't been active for years; you could yell at the top of your lungs and no one will hear you." He then thought for a moment and smirked. "Is that what you're looking for?"

Cache responded with her hand flat on his chest. "I don't know, do you think you can make me scream?"

George said, "Sweetheart, I can make you scream your lungs out." He ran his fingers up over the tattoo on her right shoulder. His touch gave Cache a shiver, feeling like a slimy slug was crawling up her arm. "What's this one about?"

"What can I say, I like pirates."

"Should have had two swords, not pistols, and you should have had a pirate flag; that would make this look somewhat cool." He looked down at her wrist and he turned her palm outward to show the tattoo on the inside of her left arm. "What does that say?" he asked.

She said, "It's personal, you don't need to know."

"Honey, I'm going to fuck your brains out, isn't that personal enough?"

Cache said, "That's sex, it's not personal. So do you want me to follow you?"

George pushed back from Cache and said, "Yeah, that sounds good. That's my bike over there, try to keep up if you can," as he walked over to his bike and fired it up. His bike looked old and beaten; it was composed of mismatched parts and needed some love.

"Hey, what's your name?" she yelled over the sound of the bike.

He thought for a moment. "Barney, what's yours?"

Cache thought, Barney my ass, maybe I should say Jackie. "It's Cache."

"So, Cache, do you think you can keep up?"

Cache said, "I don't think you want to lose this piece of ass," as she walked over to the side door of the truck to let Duke in and then made her way to the driver's side. She leaned over and opened the glove box to make sure her gun was there. "Yep," she said, and closed the box. Cache then felt underneath her seat for the handcuffs and leg irons. "Check."

She backed up her truck and followed George out of the diner parking lot. They drove down the main drag for three-quarters of a mile and continued up a gravel trail for about twenty miles. Cache pulled out her phone. The reception bars were becoming smaller. She realized as she drove following George that he might end up taking her to a dead zone where she could not call for help.

4

George drove along the gravel road; he knew the ideal spot for them to go. It was about two miles from the Lucky Dust mine, which had closed in the early 1900s. No one for miles. He could do with her what he wanted and no one would come to her aid. He thought about her tattoos and the insolence of the bitch when she'd refused to answer his questions. She'd obviously never had a proper master in her life. He drove, checking his rearview mirror to make sure she was still behind him. In a short time, it would be him behind her, tied up and vulnerable. Maybe he would kill her dog in front of her, or maybe he would just be mean to the beast to see what she would be willing to do to spare him any agony. She wanted to scream, he thought. She was going to scream, all right; she would cry, she would beg and if she resisted even slightly, he would beat her into submission and take what he wanted.

George could call some friends he had met a few days ago and maybe offer them each a turn with her in exchange for some favors. There were people he could sell her ass to who would take her over the border; she might fetch a good price.

He glanced down at his saddlebag; he had the right thing to shove in that mouth of hers. The more he thought about hurting Cache, the more he was getting turned on. The itch that was hidden behind the surface was back, it was hungry and it needed to be satisfied. George would keep going with her until she was limp, with no more energy left to fight, and then he would just keep going. In the end he would likely kill her, drag her naked body into the woods where animals could feast on her remains for days. Maybe he would leave her severely wounded so she would think she might have a chance, but he knew the animals would win. His bike could go in the back of the truck and he could get a sweet ride out of this adventure. He thought about dragging her to one of the trees and lashing her wrists to the branches, so they were out wide. George would then take the long bowie knife that he had in his saddlebag and cut her out of those shorts. The thick black leather belt he was wearing would make an excellent whip, and he would hand out the lashes until she did everything he wanted her to. She must have a bank card on her, maybe credit cards. This could mean even more money to him. He drove for another twenty minutes, making a right and then a left to take them into the middle of nowhere.

George pulled up in a small clearing three-quarters surrounded by trees. Most of the trees were long since dead, many pulled from their roots by nature, leaning on one another for support. The smell of the decay of the forest was in the air. He could see small slivers of light through all the trees. The area George pulled into was covered in dry grass that would have begged for any moisture to quench its thirst. He looked around at the decay. No life in sight. This was the ideal place to hurt someone, he thought. Cache brought her truck to a stop about twenty feet away from his bike.

———

As Cache drove along the highway following George, he consistently looked back to make sure she would not get lost. Like a spider trying to attract its prey, someone like George would not miss the opportunity to satisfy his cravings with someone like Cache. While following behind, Cache reviewed her plans with Duke, who was harnessed in the front seat for his own protection. She knew this was a risky endeavor, despite the fact that she had been trained most of her life to deal with guys. There was always the risk that George could get the upper hand. She had reviewed the files of his victims and knew that whatever he had in store for her would not be pleasant and might not be something she could walk away from unscathed. However, she knew she was better prepared to deal with him than the next woman who might become his fixation.

The other alternative was to involve the local police. The deputy had seemed to take quite a shine to her, though she couldn't help but notice it wasn't her eyes he'd spent his time staring at. No, it could be problematic for Angelo if George was to be transferred between states, based on all the paperwork that would be involved. Her best chance of helping out her old friend was to bring George in on her own. After about twenty minutes going down the paved highway, George turned onto a dirt road that had seen better days. The old truck bounced up and down as the tires found the divots in the road put there by mother nature. They kept bouncing away as she tried to stay close to George's motorbike. She could see him watching her in his mirror, probably looking like a wolf with his tongue slithering down his face as he thought about the little lamb he was going to have for dinner.

Her stomach turned as she continued along the drive, part adrenaline rush and part fear of the unknown. The last thing she was going to do was have any physical contact with this creep. Eventually George signaled to turn right, and Cache followed along for another ten minutes until they pulled into a small wooded area. This place was definitely remote. She yanked out her smartphone but noticed she had no reception bars; if she needed help, she was going to be out of luck. She pulled up about twenty feet away from George's motorbike and watched him climb off of his hog, throw his black helmet on the handlebar and start poking around in his saddlebag.

"I wonder what he has in there, Duke," Cache said. She reached into the glove box, grabbed her handgun and slipped it down the back of her shorts. She grabbed the handcuffs and put them into her back pocket and left the leg irons on the seat beside Duke. Cache kissed Duke on the snout and exited the vehicle.

"So, what do you think?" George asked as he extended his arms and twirled around. "Good enough place to get your brains fucked out?"

Cache smiled at him. "The only person getting fucked today is you," she said.

"Trust me, you will enjoy what I have in store for you; some might even say you will beg for more."

Cache looked at him and put her hand on her gun. "The problem with being out here, George, is there's nothing to tie my legs to, like you did with Judy."

George looked at her. "Hey, wait, who the fuck are you?" he asked, the tone of his voice heightened and agitated.

Cache pulled her gun from the back of her jeans so George could see the automatic sitting in her right hand.

He pointed at Cache, his hand shaking, as he said, "Listen, that bitch lied, she wanted it rough, she told me so."

"And what about her roommate? Was she looking for some fun too as you dragged her into her bedroom, pulling her along the floor by her hair like you were yanking a wet sack of cement?"

"Lady, you got it all wrong. That lying piece of shit came home and saw what Judy and I were doing, and she got horny, you know, holding off sex until she was married. She wanted me inside of her, she begged me to take her into her room and do the nasty."

"Please, I saw the photos. She went crying and screaming."

"No, that is what she said to make her fiancé happy. She couldn't tell him the truth, that while he was waiting all this time for her, she was living out her sexual fantasies with a stranger. He couldn't have it, so he told her to make up a story about being raped. You don't understand, I am being framed."

"Well I'm here to bring you in. You can tell your story to the judge, which you could have done if you'd chosen not to run."

"Really? And do you think with the fiancé's rich family and their friends that a judge was going to be impartial? The verdict would have been decided before the trial ever began."

Cache looked at him and shook her head. "It's easy to rationalize horrible things, isn't it? But what you are going to do for me is turn around, get on your knees, interlock your fingers behind your head and cross your legs over one another."

"So you can shoot me in the head?" George asked.

"If I was going to shoot you, I would shoot you where you stand and drag your body off to the woods. No, you have a date with the courts back in Los Angeles and my job is to get you there. Now do what I said."

George turned around and got on his knees but scooped up a load of gravel and dirt in his palm. He crossed the back of his legs but kept his hands in front of him, out of Cache's line of sight.

"I said put your hands behind your head," Cache demanded as she grasped the handle of her gun with both hands. No reply; he just kneeled there in silence.

"I said, put your hands behind your head. I'm not playing games with you." As she approached him slowly, she scanned the surrounding area for anything that could be used as a weapon against her. She walked closer to him and pressed the barrel of the gun to the back of George's head.

"Put your hands behind the back of your head."

George spun around quickly, throwing the dirt and gravel into Cache's face, disorienting her. He leapt to his feet, drove his shoulder into her rib cage and pushed her back hard against the front of her truck like the offensive line in a football game. Her gun dislodged from her hand and flew out of it. Duke began barking but was unable to move from the position that he was in. George stood back and slapped Cache across the face with the back of his hand, drawing blood from her lip. Her back was in pain from being slammed against the metal grille. Cache's training kicked in without her thinking. She shoved George off of her by first hitting his face with the inside of her palm and then landing a punch against his ribs. He staggered back. Unlike his brother, he was thin and short and seemed to lack any muscular build. She grabbed him by his shirt—she could see the rage in his eyes—and she drove her knee into his groin, causing him to drop to the ground. He reached around her legs like he was hugging a bear, pulled them together and yanked her to the ground.

"You fuckin' little cocksucker, I'm going to teach you some manners," he said as he pulled her underneath him so his legs were straddling her waist. He threw a punch that landed across the right side of Cache's face; she felt like a speeding train that had hit a brick wall. George grabbed at one of her breasts like he was planning on tearing it from her body and continued to backhand her across the face a few more times. The fight was leaving Cache, and she knew if she didn't do something, she would be raped and tortured in these woods, never to be heard from again. She made one last play and punched him in the throat. He grabbed his throat with both his hands like his head was going to come off and he needed to keep it attached to his body. He struggled to breathe as Cache reached up to his face with one of her hands, dug her fingernails in and tore the flesh from the bone. He screamed in pain and fell over on his side, trying to recover. The adrenaline was pumping again for her as she got to her feet.

She kicked him in the rib cage. "You like pain, don't you, George?" she said. Cache then kicked him again, letting her rage out. "This one's for Judy, you piece of shit."

As she continued to deliver an onslaught of punishment to him, she surveyed the area until she noticed her gun was lying under the truck by the front right tire. She stopped kicking him and made a run for the gun. Sliding along the gravel like a baseball player sliding into home plate and tearing the skin from the outside of her leg, she grabbed her M9 and fired a round just by George's leg. He stopped his movement and looked up at her. Her top was torn and blood dripped down from her mouth and nose onto her chest. Her hair was messy, and she was covered in dirt, but he could see the rage in her eyes. George was too much of a coward to accept death, though he could only guess what fate waited for him back in Los Angeles.

He put up his hands. "I give up."

"You know, maybe I should just blow your fuckin' balls off, just to ensure you hurt no one again."

He swallowed. "Please don't, I promise I will behave."

"Then roll over and do what I said in the first place, and if those fingers aren't on the back of your head, I'm going to keep putting lead into you until you comply or die!"

Cache sat on the back of his crossed legs, pushing them up into his back. She cuffed his first hand and brought it down to his side, cuffed the remaining hand. Cache went to the back of her truck and opened up her lockbox. It had been designed so two slats could be pulled open on top and round loops could be pushed through, allowing you to tie something into the back of the truck. She fished around for some loose chain she had and two padlocks. Cache padlocked the right corner of the lockbox so it couldn't be opened while they headed back to LA; she would use the other padlock to secure a chain run behind George's locked arms to ensure he didn't try to jump from the vehicle while in transit.

She picked up her M9 and tucked it into the back of her shorts. Cache looked down at her top, torn and bloody. It was exposing a little more than even she liked to show in public. She would need to change when they got back to the campground before heading back to LA. She got George up into the back of the truck. When he refused the first time she asked, she found that a knee to the groin drove the point home, and she could do that all day. The second time he was more cooperative, and she ran the chain through the back of his arms and padlocked it to the top of the lockbox. Cache grabbed the leg irons from the inside of the truck and rubbed Duke's head to assure him that everything was all right. She attached them to George's ankles, confident that he wasn't going anywhere until they got to where they needed to be.

He looked at her and said, "You expect me to ride back here? Put me up front and put your dog back here."

Cache looked at him and told him she valued the life of her dog a lot more than his, and he would stay back there until they got to their destination. She looked around to see if she had forgotten something and then looked at George's motorcycle. Shouldn't let it go to waste, she thought, and she reached down into his pockets to find the keys. She pulled out the envelope of cash and opened it up. "Ooh, look what I found, finders keepers."

This elicited no reaction from George. She fished around in his other pocket and found the keys to the bike. Cache hopped down out of the truck bed and latched up the back gate. She glanced over at the motorbike and focused in on his saddlebags. What was he looking at before? she wondered. Cache went to the glove box in the truck, pulled out a pair of leather gloves that she kept in there and tucked the envelope of cash into it. She would ensure Jack got his money back. Cache walked over to George's bike and put the keys in the ignition. Maybe someone in need of a bike would come across it and find some use for it. Cache opened up his saddlebag and rummaged through it. In the bag were a long bowie knife, several leather ties and a stick that Cache pulled from the bag. The wooden stick, which measured eight inches long, had a hole bored out of each end with leather ties running through them. The center of the stick was chewed up, with numerous teeth indentations in the wood. Cache surmised that there had been other victims and that maybe this had been affixed to their head to prevent them from screaming as he unleashed what he had in store for them. She returned it to the saddlebag, tightened the straps on it and pulled it from the bike. Maybe the Los Angeles police would find the contents interesting. Cache walked back to the truck and put the bag on the floor of the passenger side.

She looked around, realized how much danger she had put herself in. The rush sometimes prevented her from seeing it beforehand; afterward she was always thankful luck had been on her side. She walked around looking at George.

"Hope you enjoy the ride."

George, not looking too happy, said, "It's not the ride I was expecting."

Cache got into the driver's side, opened up her glove box and put her M9 in it. She put her cell phone in her phone cradle, but it still had no bars. Cache turned on the radio, but the signal just went in and out. She drove back to the main road, retracing her steps. Just as she approached the intersection of the gravel road and the main street, her cell phone lit up. She drove back to the RV park, changed her clothes and had begun hitching her trailer up when Sally walked over to see who was in the back of the truck. Cache explained to Sally who he was and what he was wanted for. She thanked her for her hospitality and paid the bill. Prior to her departure, she called Angelo on her cell phone to give him an update.

"Hello, Angelo, it's Cache. I got him."

"You caught that son of a bitch?" shouted Angelo.

"Yep, I've got him secure in the back of the truck. It's four o'clock now and I am about to head back to your place. Can you arrange transfer to the police?"

"Yeah, I will call them. Look, if it's easier for you to hand him over to the local authorities, do that, I don't want to put you at any risk," said Angelo.

"The risky part is over; this shouldn't be too much of a problem. If I turn him over locally then the states have to work out all the paperwork; if I bring him straight to the LAPD, we avoid that."

"Cache, you saved my ass; I don't know how to say thank you."

"Just make sure I can hand this jerk over to someone; I want to part company with this scumbag as soon as possible."

"Okay, let me make some calls and I will call you back. Cache, thanks again for doing this for me, I just had a hunch you would get more from his brother than I did."

"Jack was a good guy. He fell for the crap that his brother was spewing, but when I set the record straight from one service member to another, he knew he had to do the right thing." With that, Cache said her goodbyes, waved to the Sunny Side RV Park and headed for California. She figured the sun would just be setting as she arrived in Los Angeles. She'd been driving for about an hour when she crossed the California/Arizona state line. Shortly after that, the sight of a man in the back of Cache's truck caught the attention of two highway patrol officers on motorbikes. Cache noticed, in her review mirror, the flashing lights and signaled that she was pulling off to the shoulder. She came to a stop and could see the officers parking behind her and talking to themselves for a few minutes. One officer walked up to Cache's window and spoke to George, who said nothing back. Cache rolled down the window as the police officer asked where she was coming from and why the gentleman was in the back and chained up. Cache told the officer who George was and why he was wanted. She provided him with paperwork that she had on her front seat, and the officer glanced at it and walked back to his bike. Cache rubbed Duke's head as she saw the officers talking and talking on the microphones on their bikes. After about fifteen minutes, as cars whizzed by them on the highway, the officer approached Cache again and handed her back the paperwork.

He turned to George and said, "Mr. Wilkes, on behalf of the governor of the state of California, I welcome you back to our fine state. I've spoken with my superiors and the LAPD have arranged suitable accommodations for you, which include a bed and a metal toilet." The police officer turned to Cache and told her she was to drive directly to the LAPD headquarters in central Los Angeles, where she would meet Detectives Murphy and Johnston, who would take possession of Mr. Wilkes, and that her friend Angelo Malone would meet her there. Cache asked the officer for directions, as she was not familiar with the geography of Los Angeles, but the officer told her not to worry as they were to provide an escort for her. The officers returned to their bikes and lit up the lights, and Cache followed the first officer for the next few hours with an officer riding behind her until they navigated to the Los Angeles Police Department's headquarters.

Upon arrival, she met Angelo, and he gave her a warm hug. Detectives Murphy and Johnston introduced themselves as uniformed police officers took possession of George Wilkes and led him inside toward central booking. The detectives were extremely thankful for her apprehending him; his escape had caused alarm in the community given the seriousness of the crimes he was charged with. Cache remembered his saddlebag, which she had stored in the front seat for safekeeping, and handed it to the officers, hoping the contents would aid them further in their investigation. They parted ways, and Angelo suggested she come by his office tomorrow around noon so they could settle everything up. He thanked her again for what she'd done for him, and she told him she just wanted to go back to the beach house and try to get any remnants of George's scent off of her skin.

ache woke in her bed, Duke flopped on her legs. She reflected on what had transpired yesterday and hoped to never hear the name George Wilkes again. The sun was beaming in through the windows and she was happy to be alive. She shuddered when she thought about what he'd had in store for her; had things gone differently, he could have left her naked body in those backwoods. Cache may never have been found; her family would have wondered what had happened to their only daughter, their only sister. She reflected on what her absence would mean to those in her life that she cared most about. Cache rubbed the furry head of the dog, who seemed to think this was the perfect time for a belly rub and proceeded to lie on his back, paws up in the air. Cache obliged him. He was part of her strength through yesterday's encounter. She'd known she had to survive it to protect the both of them. She got up, showered for the second time in twelve hours. When she'd arrived last night, she'd immediately gone into the shower with a scrub brush and tried to scrub George's stench from her skin. She grabbed a fresh set of clothes and made breakfast for the two of them. She called Vanny to tell her she was back at the beach house and filled her in a bit on what had happened over the past few days. Vanny seemed to react as if she had missed a glorious adventure, not fully appreciating how much danger she might have been in. She and Cache talked for about an hour.

"I think I might tour some galleries while I'm still in LA before I head home."

"Well, I think I'm only going to be here a few more days. Please don't go home yet, we have so much to do and my boss has promised me the next two weeks off paid—uninterrupted free time for us to catch up."

"I'll think about it. After all, it's you I came to see."

"Go visit the art galleries while I'm stuck here—that's more your cup of tea than mine—and when I get back, we can hang, go to the bars, shop."

"Hmmm, well, I have always wanted to go visit the Getty and the Hammer Museum—oh, and I believe there is a Mayhem Gallery in Beverly Hills."

"What's that place you always went on and on about when we were in college?"

Cache thought for a few moments. "Oh, the Bradley House."

"Go there, check it out, have fun, take an item off your bucket list."

"I would love to. Do you have the governor's private phone number in your directory?"

"Why do you need to talk to the governor?"

"The Bradley House has been closed to the public for years. You only get in there by special invitation and I don't see one coming my way any time soon."

"Well, piss on the Bradley House, go to the other places instead."

Cache glanced down at her watch. "Oh, Vanny, I have to go, I'm meeting Angelo at his office in Venice Beach in about an hour and I have to unhitch the trailer and leave provisions for Duke."

"Okay, but promise you won't go home until I get back."

"I promise."

"Love ya, bye."

"Love you too."

As Cache departed the beach house, she could see Duke's face pressed up against the glass window closest to the door. He would be safe here. He had plenty of food and water and could stretch out in front of one of the bay windows in the back and feel the warmth of the sun. It took Cache about forty-five minutes to get to Angelo's bail bond office; even with the GPS, she seemed to have made a few wrong turns.

Angelo welcomed her into his office with a big hug and once again thanked her for everything she had done. It was a small two-room office with flashing neon signs in the window advertising bail bonds. The front room held filing cabinets and a couple of beat-up old chairs. There was a desk where an assistant might work, but there was no assistant there. Along the walls were pictures of Angelo from his days in the Quinn Police Department, commendations, letters of recommendation, photos with fellow officers, mayors and police chiefs, and one with the governor. There was even a group shot with Cache in the middle, Angelo beside her and three other officers, from when they'd hiked the backcountry a few years ago looking for two escaped prison fugitives.

Angelo had originally tried to hire Cache's father for the job, but a friend of the family had impressed upon him that Cache was better suited for the task, given her knowledge of the backcountry and military training.

Angelo ushered Cache into his back office, where she sat

down in a vinyl chair that was peeling at the edges and seemed to have one back leg that was shorter than the other, causing the chair to wobble as Cache shifted her position on it.

The office, she hated to say, looked run-down. If Angelo was successful, the profits from the business weren't going back into it. The paint was peeling, the varnish was coming off the old wood paneling and the desk held a phone, a laptop and stacks of papers a foot or more high.

"So, twenty thousand, that is what I owe you," Angelo said. "I hope you can take a check; I don't keep a lot of cash in the safe."

Cache looked at him. He was a friend from back home, and the Irons had been raised to help their neighbors, not take advantage of them.

"Angelo, tell you what, cut me a check when you can for ten percent of the amount and send it to me in Montana; I don't need it now. That should cover the gas and the campsite charges with a piece for the danger I was in. Then with the remaining amount, you donate whatever portion you think is fair to a charity that helps battered women, maybe an organization that would help people who have encountered people like George."

"Cache, that's righteous of you. I like that; that is a deal."

She said, "It's just good karma. I think hopefully good things are in your future."

Cache looked around the office, and something on top of Angelo's desk caught her eye. A ticket, black with silver foil print, with a picture of *People Mourning* by Sergio du Jant. She picked it up and stared at the photo. She flipped it around to look at the details. It was an invitation to an event tomorrow night at the Bradley House.

Cache held it up. "Angelo, I never took you for an art connoisseur."

"I'm not; some councilman in my district was selling tickets.

That ticket there is five hundred dollars to go look at a bunch of ridiculous paintings, and there isn't even a dinner. I'm more of dogs-playing-poker type of guy, if you catch my drift."

"This picture here, *People Mourning*, that is by Sergio du Jant; he was a master. How can you not feel moved by this? Oh, I think you're going to have a good time, if you just open yourself up to new experiences. If you had two, I might even be your date."

Angelo leaned back in his chair, and a loud squeaky noise came from the hinges. He thought of himself walking in there with a pretty young thing on his arm, but the idea of shelling out another five hundred killed that desire as quickly as a bucket of ice water being poured over his head.

"Why don't you go? I have no interest in it, you seem to and you did me a big favor bringing in George Wilkes while on your vacation. Take it as my gift to you."

"I couldn't take it."

"Yeah, you could, and if memory serves me, if it wasn't for you, I wouldn't be alive. Please go and enjoy it."

Cache thought about it. The Bradley House, with its incredible history, was one of the places she'd always wanted to go. How she loved the art world. Four years at Dartmouth had taught her to appreciate beauty at a new level.

"I will tell you what, I will take this ticket off of your hands, provided you deduct the cost from the amount you're going to send me. Sound like a good idea?"

Angelo leaned forward in his chair and extended his hand. "Sounds good. Let's shake on it."

Cache didn't need his money but would give it to her parents to help with the ranch. Getting an exclusive invitation to the Bradley House was the real prize.

Angelo cleared his throat. "I should tell you, it's black tie, so while I enjoy what you wear, as I'm sure most men do, you might need to throw on a dress for tomorrow night."

"That shouldn't be any problem, I'm sure Vanny has something in her closet I can borrow. Oh, I am so excited."

She stood up, kissed him on the cheek and reminded him to call her if he ever found his way back to Montana. She thought, If only he was thirty years younger... He had been handsome as a young police officer, but now he reminded her more of her father. Cache left and returned to the beach house, where she spent most of the day decompressing with Duke. A day lounging in the sun, the two of them jumping in the Pacific Ocean, let her get all the feelings from her encounter with George Wilkes out of her system. The ocean water felt good against her skin, part of which remained bruised from her fighting for her life. Her back, which felt stiff, seemed to feel more normal in the waters of the Pacific.

That night she talked to Vanny, who was more than happy to lend her wardrobe to Cache for a highfalutin evening out on the town, though she said she wanted pictures of whatever she decided to wear. Cache and Vanny were almost the same size, pretty close in height and shoe size, though Cache's chest was a bit larger than hers. After dinner she raided Vanny's closet, figuring that if she couldn't find anything, she would have to go shopping tomorrow morning. Many of the outfits she tried on were a little tight in the chest, exposing a healthy dose of side boob. While she modeled them in the mirror, she was confident she could get a date in one of these outfits, but they didn't seem appropriate for the event she was going to. She was about to give up when she spied in the back of Van's closet a black formal jumper. She pulled on the outfit and it seemed to fit her right without showing too much of anything. Her arms would be bare and everyone would see her tattoos. Nowadays everyone had tattoos, so it shouldn't seem too out of place. Cache rummaged around in the shoe organizer to find a black pair of stiletto heels. The heels seemed to heighten her tush, and she looked at the back and front of the outfit. She found two sapphire drop earrings that would look nice with this solid-black outfit. Her long brown hair fell behind her head and reached the midpoint of her back. Cache had always been a diamond in the rough. She had grown up as a tomboy, with two older brothers, a younger brother and a family heritage of ranching. Most of the guys in her class were either too intimidated by her or just plain scared, except one boy, who could see past the dirty jeans and cowboy boots. When the dirt rubbed off and she put on something more like what a girl might traditionally wear, boys' mouths dropped; how could they have missed her?

She had the outfit and took a couple of snaps on her phone to text to Vanny. Vanny texted back that she had forgotten about the jumper. She had purchased it, never worn it and originally planned on returning it, and it had found its way to the back of her closet. She told Cache she was stunning in it; she would be beating the guys back with a stick. Cache never lacked for confidence—some would say she was fearless—but still, a compliment went a long way toward helping her feel good at this point in her life. Tomorrow she would plan out her route to the Bradley House, ensure she had enough for parking and make sure Duke had plenty of company throughout the day and plenty of food and water so he could look after himself until she got home later that evening.

The next day flew by quickly. Before she knew it, it was late in the afternoon and she was getting ready. She kissed her favorite friend goodbye and headed out to an evening of glamour and art. She drove her truck with the windows down, and a slight breeze pushed its way into the cab. It was a full moon, and everyone seemed to be out, going between shops and bars as she pushed her way into Beverly Hills. Soon the streets were lined with single-stand light posts with hand-blown glass globes, like something from a different era. The neighborhood was surrounded by manicured lawns and big black iron gates leading to properties beyond. She came upon a stone wall and a driveway leading up into the hills. Attached to the wall were gold letters spelling out *The Bradley House* as white floodlights illuminated everything around the entrance. A security officer stood at the gates inspecting tickets as a line of Jaguars, Maseratis and Ferraris all waited their turn. Cache's somewhat rusted 1948 truck didn't seem to fit the company of those other vehicles. She approached the officer and rolled down her window.

"Sorry, miss, you will have to turn around, this is a private event."

Cache smirked and handed her ticket to him. He glanced at it and said, "All right, then, just continue up the drive and there is a valet up there that will look after you. You have a good night."

She drove up the path, which had antique light stands every ten feet with tall manicured hedges behind them preventing anyone outside from seeing what vehicles were making their climb to the top. When she reached the peak, there was a set of stairs heading up to the right, and a young blond-haired surfer guy in dark pants, a white pressed shirt and a red vest awaited her arrival at a small stand where visitors were dropping off their cars. There were security men and women in all directions in black tie, earpieces and noticeable bulges under their jackets, talking into their shirt cuffs. Cache drove forward to the young man and leaned out her window.

"How much for parking?" she asked.

"It's complimentary."

She put it in park, grabbed her clutch and stepped from her vehicle. He promised that he would look after her truck. It was a classic and he would ensure there were no scratches on it. Cache looked at him and wondered if she could drag him back to her place later so they could put scratches on each other.

Cache marveled at the architecture of the Bradley House as

she proceeded up the stairs, which were covered in red carpeting, to the entranceway. She had only ever seen pictures of this art museum in books and on the web. The house had originally been built by Harvey Bradley, a pioneer in the motion picture industry in the early 1900s. Consisting of red brick and a copper roof that had turned that lovely shade of green, the house and its accompanying facilities were over ten thousand square feet. The red carpet flowed up to the main entrance, a set of twelve-foot oak doors with solid brass lion door knockers in the middle. On either side of the doorway were two men dressed in black tie and tails, their white-gloved hands holding silver trays of crystal champagne flutes that guests picked up as they moved inside the main house. Cache had never acquired a taste for champagne and preferred rye whiskey, but given the environment that evening, she picked up a flute, thanking the server, and walked inside.

The house had a large foyer with a grand marble staircase in the middle leading to the second floor. An easel standing at the main entranceway held a sign thanking everyone for their patronage of the Bradley Foundation, which supported troubled youth. It also listed the artists being featured that evening and the respective locations of their works in the house, above a map of the premises marking out where each location was in relation to the main entrance.

Cache noted that artist Sergio du Jant was being featured in the drawing room and made her way there, pushing her way through the crowds of people admiring the art and one another. The guests for the night ranged in age; there were well-to-do older couples, men in tuxedos and women in long gowns with lots of diamonds around their necks, wrists and ears. There were men in black tie with young women who may have been trophy wives, nieces or secretaries on their arms, usually half their age, wearing the least amount of fabric one could wear in public without suggesting they were naked.

Waiters surfed the crowds, offering champagne and bite-size appetizers to the guests, who seemed to be more fascinated with each other than all the beautiful oil paintings that hung on the walls. The main drawing room was the shape of a hexagon, with paintings on all walls and several standalone walls positioned in the room to feature more paintings. Marble statues were positioned throughout the drawing room as a string quartet in one corner played classical music.

Cache estimated that there were over a hundred people at the event, excluding staff and what looked like an army of security. Photographers wandered through the groups of people taking staged and candid photographs; where they would ultimately end up was anyone's guess.

Wouldn't it be something if I ended up in the newspaper? Cache thought. Mom and Dad said have fun, but they would never have guessed I would end up here at this type of event. As she mingled, she noted more young women than older women at the event. Blondes, brunettes, redheads, shaved—there was an abundance of young women all trying to stand out from the crowd. Some wore long gowns with slits running up each side, so everyone got a good look at their long legs as they moved around the event. Mothers back home might have been horrified if their daughters walked out of the house like that, but here it was almost the norm. Sheer tops seemed to be the rage tonight as well; Cache didn't know why she'd worried about side boob when it was clear that many of the women were happy to show off what they had. While she was no fan of wearing a bra, a fact others often commented on, she always kept them covered up.

A young waitress walked up to her. "Would you care for a glass of champagne?"

"You know, would it be possible to get a rye on ice?"

"Absolutely, I will take care of that."

Cache looked around the area, trying to size up the room.

There was more skin being shown by the guests than the subjects in many of the works of art. She knew what she wanted to see most was somewhere in the building. She wouldn't realize until much later how the love of one painting would change her life forever.

6

A fter a while of bumping into people and apologizing for it, she found herself in front of the piece she had been eager to see. It was called *People Mourning* by Sergio du Jant; a picture of it had been used on the face of the ticket she had acquired from Angelo. As she walked up to the picture, there was a tall redheaded woman standing there, holding a flute of champagne in her left hand. She had red gloves on that went to her elbows and a long red gown that fell to the floor and complemented her hair color. From her face Cache put her in her late forties, maybe early fifties, though she was striking. Her skin had a slight tan and very few wrinkles. Her figure was remarkable, especially for a woman her age, and she was giving a lot of the young ladies at tonight's event a run for their money. She wore a ruby and diamond necklace that plunged down into her cleavage. Cache stood beside her and took in the beauty of the painting. The heavy brushstrokes in oil told the viewer what the artist had felt as he brought the piece to life.

Cache noticed the woman beside her glance at her and she

thought she overheard her say something about candy, but she could have been mistaken.

"What do you think of the painting?" she said, looking straight ahead at it.

Cache said, "I think it's a lot of pretty circles, wouldn't you agree?"

The woman sighed and took a deep breath as she turned to her and asked, "Who are you here with, which of these older gentlemen is yours?"

"None," Cache said, "I came on my own."

"You mean you purchased a ticket for five hundred dollars to come to an exclusive event and all you have to say is 'pretty circles'?" she asked.

Cache said, "Well, I could tell you that the different circles represent the different ethnicities found in the world, and the fact that all the circles are the same shape—no ovals—was the artist's attempt to tell the world that everybody is the same, that we are all part of one race. The lines throughout the painting in various thicknesses, and the heavy brushstrokes here and there"—Cache pointed to different spots on the painting—"are the artist's attempt to show the despair that we all suffer through in one form or another daily. Was that more of what you were looking for?"

She smiled and had a quiet laugh. "You've embarrassed me. I'm sorry, I thought you were one of these young so-called nieces here with their uncles." She pointed to all the half-dressed young women that Cache had observed as she walked throughout the house.

"No, I love art, I studied it in university. It's always been a passion of mine. I saw some of du Jant's work when I was living in Italy."

"Where did you go to university, if that is not too intrusive a question?"

"I was at Dartmouth for four years studying art history."

"Oh, a Dartmouth girl. I was a Harvard girl myself."

"Well, there you have it: two Eastern gals in a Western gallery."

The woman introduced herself as Kathryn Jamieson. She was a cosmetic surgeon practicing in the Los Angeles area. She and Cache spent the next half hour standing there in front of the painting, talking about art and the East Coast. Kathryn pointed out a number of guests at the event, explaining who they were, what they did, what they didn't want others to know about them. They talked about the different galleries they'd each visited. Kathryn was also a world explorer, having gone to Egypt to see the pyramids a year earlier, and Cache told her she'd seen both Italy and Japan because of Uncle Sam. The reference went over Kathryn's head and she asked questions about Cache's uncle, until Cache cleared up the misunderstanding by explaining that she'd been referencing her time in the army. The waitress found Cache and handed her a crystal rocks glass with her rye and ice. There was instant chemistry between her and Kathryn, as if they had known each other their entire lives, and yet Kathryn was at least a decade older than Cache. She reached down and grabbed Cache by the elbow and led her around the room as if Cache were her new puppy dog. They stopped at different pieces and discussed their opinions of what the artist was thinking when he painted the subject matter. Kathryn told Cache that she dabbled in art acquisitions herself and would always try to find interesting pieces when she was away from home.

They eventually left the drawing room and found themselves in the music room. Kathryn and Cache were both art scholars and attempted to outdo one another with their knowledge. They found themselves in front of an oil painting by Brazilian artist Lucas Barbosa entitled *La Elegancia de la Monja*. The painting depicting a nun in full makeup looking like a fashion model.

"What do you think the artist was thinking when he painted this?" Cache asked.

"Don't you know the story behind Barbosa?"

"I know he was a Brazilian painter who liked to paint erotic pictures featuring nuns."

"That's his work, but as the story goes, he was an orphan in a Brazilian orphanage run by nuns. These were the only older women around him, and when he reached puberty, he started wondering what they did in the evenings when they weren't looking after the kids."

"Well, I never thought a nun would do that," Cache said, gesturing at the painting.

Kathryn touched Cache's arm as she laughed, but her laughter turned cold as her eyes fixed on something over Cache's shoulder.

"Hello, Dr. Jamieson, how are you?" A late-twenties, bubbly blonde in a short silver sequined dress approached the two of them. She was tan, with sparkling white teeth and long blond hair down to her shoulders. "It's nice to see you this evening."

"Hello, Jillian. We must pay you more than I thought if you can afford to come to a place like this."

"John—I mean, Dr. Armstrong—insisted that I come. Have you seen him?"

Kathryn took a deep breath. "Yes, he is here and so is Rachel. After all, she is the cochair of the foundation hosting the event."

"Oh, of course. For some reason, I was under the impression that she couldn't attend. Silly me."

"Yes, silly you."

She looked at Cache and held out her hand. "I'm Jillian Douglas. I'm a nurse. I work with Dr. Jamieson and Dr. Armstrong at Dream Design."

Cache looked over her shoulder. "Dream Design?"

"It's my practice; I'll tell you about it later."

Cache extended her hand and shook Jillian's. "My name is Cache Iron. It's nice to meet you, I love your shoes."

Jillian moved her foot so Cache could appreciate them more. "They're paisley brocade stitched. My parents bought them for me when I graduated nursing school; they spent more than they should have on them. I look after them carefully and only wear them out on special occasions, like this."

"They're nice," Kathryn said.

"They're more than nice," said Cache. "They are gorgeous. Mine are borrowed; unfortunately I'm more comfortable in running shoes and cowboy boots, but if I was going to buy a pair of expensive shoes, those are what I would want."

"That's kind of you to say." She touched Cache's arm and excused herself, heading out of the room.

"Sorry about that," Kathryn said.

"Sorry about what? She seems so sweet."

"You're not from LA, are you?"

"No, Montana."

"I knew there was something about you I liked. I was born in Kansas."

"So, what is wrong with her?"

"Nothing, everything. She works with my partner; he is floating around here somewhere. Fawns all over him, laughs at his jokes; his jokes aren't funny. I mean, she is an excellent nurse, I will give her credit, but the flirting that goes on, it's just too much, so I don't have her on my team."

They walked out of the music room and made their way to the back patio. A small jazz band was playing as some guests danced in the courtyard, while others gathered around small iron tables and chairs covered in white linens with lit candles in the centerpieces.

The women were facing each other as they discussed the music when Cache spotted another blonde behind Kathryn making a beeline for her.

"I think someone wants to talk to you."

"What makes you think that?" Kathryn said as Cache pointed behind her.

Kathryn turned to see Rachel Armstrong making her way to the two of them.

"Can you believe she is here?" Rachel said.

"Nice to see you too, Rachel, how are you?"

"I would be a lot better if you didn't hire sluts and then parade them around events like this."

"Calm down," Kathryn demanded, "you're making a scene and you cannot do that at an event like this."

Rachel reflected for a moment and said, "You're right, you're always right, I just don't get why she is here."

"Are you referring to Jillian, or is there someone else who has you all flustered?"

"Of course I'm talking about Jillian. Why, is there someone else I should know about? Kathryn, we know each other well, you have to tell me." Her eyes stared directly at Kathryn, as if she were trying to communicate something else hidden in her words.

"There is no one else, at least as far as I know, and Jillian's being here—you have to talk to your husband about that."

"Fine." All of a sudden Rachel realized that there was someone else standing beside Kathryn. "Excuse me, this is a private conversation, whoever you are."

"This is my new friend Cache, and we were having a lovely talk before you barged in."

Cache extended her hand. "Hi, I'm Cache Iron."

Feeling a little embarrassed, Rachel shook her hand and introduced herself as Rachel Armstrong. She was married to Dr. Jonathan Armstrong, Kathryn's business partner.

"Oh, I love your hair comb. Is that gold?" Cache said, admiring a gold hair comb with what appeared to be Egyptian markings on it.

Rachel smiled—she desperately needed a compliment—and touched the back of her head. "It was a gift from someone very special to me."

"Well, you are a lucky woman."

"Thanks. Sorry I came off as a bit of a bitch."

"A bit?" Kathryn asked.

"You know how she makes me feel. I have to go check on the caterers; our work is never done. Kathryn, we will talk later; Cache, it was nice to meet you." And with that Rachel drifted off into the main house.

"What was that all about?"

"Short version, Jillian is what Rachel was a decade ago. She came to California, pretty blonde, white sparkling teeth, big boobs, and landed herself a doctor. As she has gotten older, and as she sees young things around her husband, she becomes needy and insecure and drives Jonathan up the wall. I think he does it on purpose, just to make her crazy."

"It's things like that that make me happy I'm not married."

"Me too." Kathryn clinked Cache's glass.

They found a table close to the jazz band as they played into the evening. They topped up their drinks as Kathryn asked Cache what she thought of Lucas Barbosa's work.

"It's interesting. The work is captivating, and the subject matter makes you think."

"Did you ever hear of a piece called *Monja de Medianoche*?"

"Yeah, I've seen it in art magazines; I think it sold last year at auction in New York. Didn't it go for some crazy price, like a million dollars?"

"Eight hundred thousand to be exact. I know because I wrote the check."

"You bought *Monja de Medianoche* ? Well, that must get a few comments."

"I have it in my house in Bel Air. Do you want to see it?"

"Now?"

"Not now, but you should come by this week. I would love to show it to you. Most people don't get art; it would be nice to share with someone who would appreciate it."

"That would be wonderful, if it's not too much trouble."

Kathryn reached over and touched Cache's arm. "I don't have a lot of friends out here. It would be nice to have someone over who has shared similar experiences."

Cache thought, What is with all this arm touching that goes on here? Everyone wants to touch my arms.

"There you are, why are you hiding?" a deep voice said from behind as a man walked to their table, borrowed a chair from the table beside them and sat himself down. He must have been about six foot one or two, with a slender build, gray hair with a slight beard from probably a week's growth and a few wrinkles around the eyes; Cache estimated that he was probably in his mid to late fifties. He wore a black tuxedo with a starched white shirt, gold buttons and cufflinks, and black bow tie.

"Oh, hi," he said as he looked at Cache, eyeing her from the chest up.

"Don't hit on her, John, not everything is a plaything for you."

"I wasn't hitting on her, just being friendly."

"Fine. Cache, I would like you to meet my business partner Dr. Jonathan Armstrong. This is my new friend Cache Iron."

"It's nice to meet you."

"It's nice to meet you. I met your wife earlier, she seems lovely."

That forced him to laugh, though Cache didn't mean it to be funny. He pointed at Cache and said, "I like her."

"John, what were you thinking? I mean, inviting Jillian here; wouldn't it have been easier to run around with lit dynamite?"

"It seemed like a good idea at the time. Besides, I had a spare ticket, it was already paid for."

"John, you could have given it to Mike, Greg, Donna, Julie or any number of people on our team, but you gave it to the one person who will drop her dress the moment you sneeze and will drive your wife insane."

"So, what do I do? You're the one with all the answers."

"That's because I've been bailing your ass out since medical school."

He grabbed Kathryn's hand and rubbed the top of it. "Then help me now."

"This is winding down; get your wife and get the hell out of here and don't go near Jillian."

"Sounds good, thanks, chief, I'll see you tomorrow."

Jonathan said his goodbyes to the ladies and walked toward one of the open French doors that led into the courtyard.

The patio filled with a group of older men and their young female companions. Cache asked what is with all the May-December romances in LA. "I mean," she said, "back home you might see one couple with a significant age difference, but here it seems to be the norm." Kathryn explained that out here, young women were all hoping to strike it big in the entertainment industry, but Los Angeles, like other big cities, was expensive to live in. So, they'd find a rich guy who wanted a pretty young thing. They'd parade around in skimpy clothing. "Many of the women here will go home with their companions tonight," Kathryn said. "The guy will fall asleep, and in the morning, she will tell him he was a stallion in bed last night. He won't remember a thing because nothing happened, but he will welcome the praise.

"I mean, I shouldn't complain. We get a lot of these guys bringing their companions in to us, wanting to take an A cup and turn it into a set of double D's, like they're adding a spoiler to their sports car."

"So, what you're telling me is, men are dumb?"

"Not all men, but too many think with their cock and not

their head, or they think with their other head is maybe a better way to phrase that."

"I need to find the ladies' room, are you in need?"

"No, you go ahead. I will keep our table from the vultures. I believe it's just as you come in, off the main hall."

Cache walked back into the house. The crowds had started to thin out for the night. What had once been a hundred or more people was probably down to around thirty as more were departing. She found the ladies' room, which was surprisingly empty, and when she came out, she started to make her way back through the drawing room toward the back patio. She had stopped to look at *People Mourning* one more time when she noticed off to the side, slightly obscured, Dr. Armstrong and Jillian appeared to be having a conversation. Maybe he was telling her it was a bad idea for her to be there; maybe he'd realized the trouble it was causing his marriage. Cache noticed his rubbing her arms—again with the rubbing, what was it with all the arm touching?—and then he pulled her in close to him and planted his lips firmly against hers. Cache ducked behind a wall to stay out of sight and left the drawing room to find another way back to the patio.

The rest of the evening flew by as Cache enjoyed Kathryn's company. As the evening came to an end, a young twentysomething surfer-style guy with streaks in his hair and a chiseled physique approached their table wearing a black suit. Cache looked at him and had a pretty good idea what she was planning to do with the rest of her evening.

"Hey, Mom, are you ready to go? You said eleven o'clock."

Kathryn said, "Yes, it is about that time, thank you for being punctual. Cache, I would like you to meet my nephew, Freddy."

Cache extended her hand and shook his. "I thought you called her Mom, or did I mishear you?" she asked.

Kathryn smiled at her. "A long story for another time." She reached inside her clutch, pulled out her business card and wrote her phone number on the back. "Call me this week and we will set up a time for you to come over and look at the painting."

"That would be great."

Kathryn stood up; waved goodbye; locked arms with her nephew, Freddy; and left the patio. The band was putting their instruments away, as Cache seemed to be the only one left on the patio. She sat there and stared at the stars in the sky.

"Pretty, aren't they," a female voice said to her.

"Hi, Jillian, sit down."

"Kathryn still here?"

"Nope, she just left with her nephew."

"He's hot."

"How are you doing?"

"Feeling a little foolish."

"Why?"

"I don't know. I came because I thought he liked me—I mean, the signals were all there—but I just saw him leave with his wife. Holding hands, being affectionate."

"Dr. Armstrong?"

"Yeah. I mean, he keeps making promises to me and I wait, and then nothing. After a while you realize it's just empty words."

"It can be a lonely path when you're the other woman."

She sat there staring down at her lap. "Thanks. You're probably the nicest person I have met in a long time. You even asked me about my shoes. I know they're only shoes, but they're important to me."

Cache reached over and took her hand in hers. "It will be okay." Cache opened up her clutch, grabbed a small piece of paper, wrote her cell phone number on it and handed it to her. "If you ever need to talk to someone, call me."

"You don't know me."

"Of course I do. You're nurse Jillian with the beautiful shoes;

the rest is just pieces that we can fill in later. Do you need a hug?"

Jillian nodded, and the two stood up and Cache gave her a strong hug like she was trying to squeeze the stuffing out of a pillow.

"You take care, okay?"

Jillian walked off into the house.

Cache sat in the back for another forty-five minutes, finishing off her last glass of whiskey. One waiter came up to her and told her that the gallery would be closing in the next fifteen minutes and the remaining guests were out front gathering their vehicles.

Cache got up and walked around the gallery one more time. She knew she would probably never get a chance to come back, and she soaked it all in one last time as she exited out the front. There was only one valet left, and he told her it would be a few minutes before he could get her car. Cache handed him her ticket, collected her keys and had him point her to where her truck was parked. The parking lot for the gallery was on the far side of the house. As Cache walked, she pulled off her heels, thinking that bare feet might be easier. She had left her running shoes in the truck and now she was eager to throw them on. Everyone was gone, security was no longer outside, and as Cache approached the parking lot, she could see her truck backed into one spot with only one other car in the parking lot. Walking to her truck, an object caught her attention in the light of the full moon, something shimmering in the darkness. Cache walked toward it and bent down and picked up a woman's left shoe with a paisley brocade pattern. She knew this shoe and looked around, but there was no one there.

"Jillian?" she called out, but no answer came.

She walked toward the car at the far end of the parking lot. It was an old MGB convertible, a combination of red paint and rust in certain spots. The California vanity plate on the front of the car suggested it was Jillian's. Cache looked around the car, but there was no sign of Jillian. She went to her truck, threw Vanny's high heels in the front and yanked on her running shoes. She pulled herself into the bed of her truck, placed her palm against the biometric lock on the lockbox and opened it up, hunting for a flashlight. When she found the one she wanted, she hopped down and flipped it on and surveyed the area around the car.

There was nothing, no sign of Jillian.

Cache yelled out one more time, "Jillian, are you here?"

Everything was quiet. Cache shone the flashlight beam around the area and noticed a gap in the ten-foot hedge that surrounded the parking lot, about fifteen feet away from the parked car. Cache thought about going and getting her gun, but she was too eager to see where the path went. She stepped forward through the hedge when her flashlight beam caught sight of another shiny object. Cache went to it and examined it; it was Jillian's other shoe. Cache didn't like this. She noticed the path descended into darkness along the hill that she'd driven up to reach the gallery. As she crossed over a ridge, her light bounced off Jillian's sequined dress. Jillian was lying flat on the ground headfirst into the dirt, barefoot. Cache ran down to her, almost twisting an ankle, and yelled, "Jillian, are you okay?"

There was no movement from Jillian. Cache reached the body and turned her over. Her dress had been torn in pieces. Her breasts were exposed and a black mark the size of a quarter appeared over her heart. Cache looked down at a black thong that was now exposed with a card of some sort protruding up from underneath the silk. Cache felt for a pulse but there was none; there were marks around her neck. She leaned over, but there was no sound of breathing. Cache ran back to the truck to grab her cell phone from her clutch, which she'd left on the front seat along with her high heels. She called 911 to report a body found.

The police arrived on the scene within twenty minutes of Cache's phone call. They taped off the area and searched the ravine, looking for clues. The medical examiner arrived shortly afterward and moved down to Jillian's body to perform his work. Cache had been asked to wait by her truck until detectives arrived on the scene. As she rested against the hood, a black unmarked police car pulled alongside of her and two familiar faces got out.

"Ms. Iron, we meet again," said Detective Murphy.

"Wish it was under better circumstances."

"Were you the one that called it in?" asked Detective Johnston.

"Yeah, I found her down in the ravine, checked for a pulse, listened for breathing, and then when I realized she was dead, I came up here, grabbed my phone and called you."

"What were you doing here, were you here for the function?"

"Yeah, Angelo Malone had a ticket that he purchased for tonight's event and gave it to me for helping him out."

"Had you met the deceased at all?" asked Detective Murphy.

"I did, I met her among a few different guests tonight; we even sat and talked a little while ago."

"How long ago was that?"

Cache looked down at her watch and then thought for a moment. "Maybe an hour and a half."

"So, within two hours of talking with you, she ended up dead?"

"I can see where you're going. First, I hadn't left the building. You probably have close to fifty million dollars in artwork in there and security everywhere, cameras in all the corners; if you check you will see I was inside the whole time."

The police continued to ask her questions for the next hour. They asked about what led to the discovery. Asked about the deceased's employers and what they had talked about. Given that Cache had had very little exposure to Jillian, there was little that she could tell them. She did mention to the detectives the kiss she'd observed between Jillian and Dr. Armstrong. They said they would look into it, but Cache asked if they could leave her name out of it as she had made a friend of his business partner and didn't want it getting back to her. Cache still wanted to see her painting.

7

She arrived back at the beach house at two o'clock in the morning, still a little shaken from her discovery, to the sight of a friendly face and a wagging tail. Instead of just retiring for the evening, she jumped onto the couch with Duke, opened her laptop and searched for murders and pinup cards. She had known not to disturb Jillian's body until the forensics team got there, but the sight of the card protruding from underneath her thong had gotten the better of her curiosity, and she'd found a stick to lift the edge of the thong so she could get a good look at the card.

The card showed an illustration of a nurse holding a needle; she seemed to be busting out of the top of her dress, her skirt higher than expected, revealing her white garters underneath. The police hadn't shared any information with her and had asked questions until they were satisfied that she had shared everything she knew about the deceased. As Cache searched the internet, related stories that appeared included the murders of Heidi Larsen, a librarian; Gabriela Perez, a housekeeper last seen at a bus stop on her way home; and a schoolteacher, Emily Peeters, who had been out with friends.

All had been found strangled and dumped along paths that were frequented by joggers, pinup cards found on their bodies. The media could show no connection between the women, except they were all young and attractive living in the Los Angeles area. When she grew tired of reading the media's accounts of the events, she searched the internet for the works of Lucas Barbosa and in particular his painting entitled *Monja de Medianoche* . The work had been painted in the late 1950s and showed a door swung open to a room, revealing a nun, still in her veil and nothing else, with one of her sisters in bed, a joint in the lips of one nun and bottles of booze on the table. The artist trying to show the secrets one can find on the other side of the door. One wondered if this was the artist's fantasy coming to life in one of his works or a childhood incident re-created on canvas. Before shutting down, she couldn't help but search for Kathryn Jamieson. The search results showed various articles written about the doctor, where she'd grown up, where she'd gone to school, and her work locally with various charitable groups supporting women in need. She shut down her laptop, looking at her watch. The sun would be rising in the next few hours and she needed to get some rest. She wanted to call Kathryn to see when would be a good time to go and check out the painting but also didn't want to appear too eager or pushy. As she put her head onto her pillow, a question that she had been wrestling with since she decided to come to Los Angeles kept popping into her mind.

Her mother, in her not-so-subtle way, had reminded her that Jake worked in Los Angeles. Jake was the boy who'd gotten away. They had started dating in the ninth grade—though Jake had said she had caught his eye at a much younger age—and graduated high school together. Her fearlessness was not some-thing that you overlooked but it took a bit of courage, given Cache's two older brothers, Tommy and Cooper, for a boy to ask Cache out. When they graduated, Jake went to school on the West Coast, while Cache took a year off to work on the ranch and then went to school on the East Coast, the same school that her mother had attended.

While they'd tried to make it work, the distance was an impediment they couldn't overcome. Jake joined the FBI and was initially stationed on the East Coast, but Cache had joined the army and was deployed first to Italy for two years and then to Japan for another two. By the time she returned home to the United States to work on base in North Carolina, they had transferred Jake to the Los Angeles field office. While they followed each other on social media, Cache knew from recent photos posted to Instagram that there was someone special in his life. Her mom had suggested that she reach out to him while she was here. His mother had passed away a few years ago and his father had moved out of state. The odds of his coming home to Montana were slim, and the fact that Cache was there in Los Angeles was an opportunity that her mother felt she shouldn't pass up. At three forty-five a.m., she bit her lip and sent him a text.

————

In Los Angeles this week
   Would love to get together
   for lunch/dinner, if you're available
   C xx

————

She looked at Duke. "Come on, boy," she said, "we'll see what that brings, if anything."

Cache woke the next morning around ten o'clock a.m. The weatherman on the radio suggested that rain was expected later that day. She sauntered down to the kitchen, grabbed her

smartphone from the family room table and noticed an indication on the lock screen that she had received one new message.
She unlocked her smartphone and went to her text messages.
Jake had responded that they should have dinner tonight, if she
was free. She fidgeted and all of a sudden felt butterflies in her
stomach. What had she done? Dinner tonight, she thought.
What should I wear, what am I going to say? Duke wandered
into the room, looking at her and wagging his tail. She thought
for a moment, paused and took a deep breath. She had
forgotten for a second all the chasing he had done to try to win
her heart. If anyone should have been nervous, it was him.
Cache sent back a text: "Dinner sounds good. Do you want to
meet me somewhere or pick me up?" A few minutes went by
and Jake responded with a text asking where she was. She
texted back that she was staying at a friend's place in Santa
Monica. They exchanged texts back and forth for the next half
hour and agreed that Jake would pick her up at seven o'clock;
they would go for seafood. She also shared with him that she
was going to be out that afternoon looking at some art.

She had thought about the Barbosa painting that morning
as she was showering. Why was she waiting? In a few days
Kathryn might have forgotten who she was, and she might lose
the opportunity. She grabbed Kathryn's business card from her
clutch and dialed the number on the back.

"Hello, Kathryn Jamieson here."

"Kathryn, it's Cache, we met last night at the Bradley
House."

"I'm not forgetful. How are you this morning?"

"Tired. Some events happened after you left last night."

"I'm guessing this has something to do with Jillian?"

"How did you know? Was there something on the news?"

"Could have been. We had the police at our offices this
morning asking questions. Poor girl. I mean, she wasn't my
favorite, but for something like that to happen to her is tragic."

"I guess this would be a bad time to come over and check out your painting?"

There was a pause for a few seconds.

"Kathryn, are you there?"

"You know something, that might work out fine, I don't think I can get any decent work done here today. How about I meet you at my place around two o'clock?"

Kathryn gave detailed directions for how Cache would get to her place in Bel Air. She figured she had enough time to walk Duke, change into something more appropriate and then head out. From what she could find online, she estimated that her drive would be about thirty minutes with traffic if she took Interstate 405. That would give her a few hours to spend with Kathryn, and then she would have to dart back to the beach house and clean up for her dinner with Jake. The perfect set of distractions to keep her mind off of Jillian.

The drive out to Kathryn's place took a little longer than expected, as traffic was heavier at this time of day than Cache had expected. As she wound her way down Roscomare Road, she looked for the cross street Kathryn had advised her to take. Many of the homes had enormous gates, and several appeared high on a hill. Cache accidentally passed the entrance to Kathryn's place a few times, as the street entrance comprised a black iron gate, two glass coach lamps perched above the black iron pillars and thick foliage on either side blocking any sight of the home from the street. The numbers were barely visible, and a box out front with a keypad and intercom stood on the left-hand side.

Cache pulled up beside the intercom box, rolled down her window and pressed the button.

"Hello, Kathryn, it's Cache. I think I'm at the right place." There was silence for a few minutes, and she feared she had gone to the wrong location.

A young male voice came over the call box: "Hi, it's Freddy.
Kath is still at the office, but I'll buzz you in."

With that the gates opened in the middle, parting on each
side of the driveway. Cache drove through them and up the
winding road to the top of a hill. She could see the gates close
behind her through her rearview mirror. The path zigzagged its
way up the hill with small trees on either side of the driveway,
to the right a stunning green lawn cut low, until you came to
the top of the hill. Kathryn's home was a breathtaking turn-of-
the-century Spanish-style house. Composed of white plaster
walls and orange clay roof tiles, it featured two turrets, one on
each corner of the house. Cache could see arches on the walls
leading up to the turrets, providing various places to sit outside,
and the top of the main portion of the house was rectangular,
with what must have been a rooftop garden or something. In
the middle of the driveway stood a bronze fountain and a drive-
through section that appeared to lead to garages at the back of
the house.

Cache got out of her truck and walked to the main entrance,
wearing jeans and a white T-shirt and white leather running
shoes. She suddenly felt extremely underdressed for this location and wondered what cosmetic surgeons made these days.
The front entrance consisted of two large oak doors with glass
inserts with black wrought iron in front of the glass. There was
a brass doorbell to the right and a video camera above her to
the left; she rang the doorbell and within a few minutes, Freddy
opened the door and let her in. His hair was messed up,
looking like he might have just gotten out of bed. Freddy had
on a long pair of flannel pants with different-colored ice-cream
cones in the pattern. He had flip-flops on and no shirt, which
gave Cache an unobstructed view of his chiseled abs. Freddy
was muscular, in his early twenties, and given the look of the
property, had not a financial worry in sight.

"Did you find the place okay?"

"Yeah, I abs—I mean I drove by it a few times, but I found it."

Cache couldn't stop staring at his chest. Had Kathryn not been expected any minute, Cache could have thought of a few ways the two of them could spend the time. She walked into the main foyer, which had marble floors throughout. There was a large, circular oak table in the center, with a marble inlay. Fresh-cut flowers in the middle in a crystal vase gave off a citrus aroma. There were two large white marble staircases a short distance from the front doors, each one going up along one of the walls to the second floor.

"Kathryn had to go into the office this morning, but she called a little while ago and said she was on her way home and that you would be coming over."

"Yeah, I talked to her just before noon."

"Would you like anything to drink, water, soda, beer, wine?"

"A glass of white wine would be great."

Cache and Freddy made their way down to a lower level of the house. He shared with her that this was the basement of the house, though it didn't look like a traditional basement. There was a large entertainment room with a huge L-shaped couch and flat-panel television that had to be over sixty inches wide. A billiard table, pinball machine, formal bar and entrance to a private movie room filled the space. They even had a glass-enclosed wine room, with bottles of wine lining the walls and several wine fridges set to different temperatures. The room had white subway tile on the walls, black granite countertops and marble floors, with four stools under the counter. Freddy asked if Cache had a region preference and she suggested Italy. He stood back, pondered which fridge contained the Italian wines and pulled out a new bottle, uncorked it and pulled a wineglass down from a rack attached to the ceiling. He poured Cache a glass and asked if she wanted to see the rest of the house.

The two of them roamed through the house from room to room as Cache sipped on her glass of wine.

"Have you ever heard of Randolph Wright?" he asked.

"I have to confess, I haven't."

"Back in the early days of the motion picture industry, Randolph Wright came out to California from Indiana. He made a fortune providing supplies to the movie industry, and with the revenue he earned, he purchased large tracts of land throughout the Los Angeles area."

"Wow."

"This was originally his home. The house and estate are around one hundred and twenty years old. When he built the home, it was out in the middle of nowhere. The house has stood through the golden age of movies, prohibition, the wars. There are pictures of the original property in black and white, but it's in one of two rooms I am forbidden to show you. Kathryn wants to show that room to you, it's where her nun painting hangs."

"Not a fan of art?" Cache asked.

"It's okay. Just not my thing."

"You said there are two rooms you can't show me. Out of curiosity, what is the other?"

"That is Kathryn's office." He pointed down the hall. "She has patient files in it and prohibits anyone from going in there."

The main floor of the house consisted of Kathryn's office, the drawing room, a music room, a family room, a kitchen and a formal dining area. On the top floor of the house there were five bedrooms, three bathrooms and doors opening onto an upper garden and sitting area, from which you could see some other homes in the area. In the back of the house there was a large swimming pool, a four-car garage and a few other buildings dispersed among hedges, trees and several large flower beds.

All in all, it was a stunning home, and as they walked down

the stairs from the bedroom level, they ran into Kathryn coming in from the back of the house, where the garages were.

"I see you found the place and Freddy has been a dear and shown you around," Kathryn said.

"He has. You have a beautiful home, though he said I wasn't allowed into the drawing room until you got here, and he couldn't show me your study, which is understandable."

"Cache, I would love to show you my study, I think it is breathtaking but it has a lot of patient files in it which means I can't take you in there. I just have patient files to drop on my desk." She held up her briefcase. "The room is solid oak, with a big fireplace, though one doesn't need it in this weather. Let me drop this off, and I will be right back and I can show you what you came to see."

Kathryn departed toward her study; Cache could see she took her privacy seriously as she drew a key from her pocket to unlock the door. From her observations, it appeared to be the only room in the house that had a lock on it. Even Kathryn's bedroom door seemed to be void of one. After a few minutes she returned and led Cache to the far west side of the house.

The drawing room was a large room with several paintings, photographs and illustrations lining it. In the middle were three small love seats forming three sides of a square. A small tapestry rug lay underneath the love seats, sitting on a rich oil-stained oak floor. Kathryn led Cache to the center of the room, the so-called focal point; one of the love seats was positioned there. In all its brilliance, Barbosa's *Monja de Medianoche* stood, the heavy layers of oil depicting Barbosa's questions about what nuns did in their time off.

"It's beautiful," Cache said, "the textures, the tones, you almost want to reach out and touch it."

"Go ahead," Kathryn said. "We're not in a museum, no one is going to tackle you to the floor if you touch it." And then Kathryn extended her hand and flowed it over the painting.

She motioned with her head that Cache could do the same, and Cache lightly ran her fingers over the canvas. It felt brilliant. The surface felt smooth in places, chunky in others. Kathryn smiled, and Cache returned the smile. They stood for a while just taking in the painting, and when they were done, Kathryn took Cache around the room to show her the other pieces she had collected over the years. She had old photographs of the house from when nothing surrounded it but empty land. There were photographs of Kathryn at Windsor Castle in England, the Great Pyramids in Egypt and Ayers Rock in Australia. From the various photos that lined the walls or sat in silver and gold frames, she had spent a good part of her life traveling. Some pictures were of her alone and some of them with a young boy, who Cache presumed was Freddy, but never with a man beside her.

After the tour was over, she invited Cache to join her on the back terrace. A once gloomy day that had threatened rain now gave way to the warmth of the sun.

"I thought it was going to rain today," Cache said.

Kathryn said, "It might, and then it might be sunny again. California weather is so inconsistent. Back on the East Coast, when the forecast called for rain that day, that is what we got."

They walked over to a metal table flanked by metal chairs with soft white cushions; Freddy sat there smoking a cigarette.

"Did Mom let you see the painting?" Freddy asked.

"She did. Oh, you live in such a beautiful home, and that painting is breathtaking."

Freddy took a big drag of the cigarette, the embers glowing as he drew the tobacco smoke into his lungs. "Not my cup of tea, but Mom likes it and it's her money," he said, looking at Kathryn. "What?" Freddy said as Kathryn looked at him with a smile on her face. "Do you want one?" he asked, picking up the pack of cigarettes and putting it down in front of her.

Kathryn looked at Cache, picked up the pack and offered her one. "No, I don't smoke," Cache said.

"Neither do I," Kathryn said.

Freddy looked at Cache and said with air quotes, "Yes, Kathryn 'does not smoke.'"

Kathryn said, "Well, it's unhealthy, I'm a doctor and I know these things."

Freddy looked at her and retorted, "Then why do I always find them missing from the pack after I buy them?"

Kathryn had a playful annoyed look on her face and said, "Well, okay. Cache, are you okay if I have one?"

"It's your house, it's your choice."

Kathryn pulled out a cigarette and put it to her mouth. Freddy reached in with an old-fashioned gold-toned flip lighter and lit her cigarette. She took a drag in and blew it out into the air like she had done it many times before. They sat out on the back terrace for about an hour telling stories about their lives. They talked about Kathryn and Freddy's beautiful home, and Freddy told Cache it was considered a historical home. For that reason, it could never be torn down. The land was envied by every developer; all of them would have torn it down and put up a mega mansion if they could. Kathryn explained that the house about forty years ago had fallen into hard times. It had become just another beaten-down home from a forgotten age, but given its historic nature, no one had wanted to touch it until her stepbrother, Bill, and his wife, Laura, came along. Laura fell head over heels in love with the home, and Bill worked in Hollywood. He was an illustrator like his father and grandfather before him and had been very successful in real estate and the stock market. Laura spent countless months restoring the home to its full glory, and somewhere along the way, they had a baby boy. Kathryn ran her hand along the back of Freddy's head as she said that.

Kathryn went on to explain that the house was actually

Freddy's, but he wasn't allowed possession of it until he turned twenty.

"Lucky for me, on his twentieth birthday, he didn't tell me to get the heck out." She smiled at him as she said that.

Freddy said, "Well, I take it easy on her regarding rent; you know you can't live here for free." There seemed to be an inside joke there that the two of them shared. If someone were to walk in on the conversation not knowing the relationship, one might have assumed they were a couple, romantically linked to one another, as they playfully bantered back and forth, but maybe growing up with your aunt fostered that type of relationship.

Cache turned to Freddy. "I take it your parents are no longer with us?"

"Yeah, that was an unfortunate period in my life. They always had a date night in the middle of the week where they would get a sitter for me and go out on the town. One night as they drove home, a drunk driver who was well over the limit hit them, crossed the median and drove head-on into them."

Cache, in a sympathetic voice, said, "I'm so sorry to hear that."

Kathryn jumped in. "My stepbrother was killed instantly, and Laura passed away a few hours later in the hospital. Freddy didn't even get a chance to say goodbye." Kathryn went on to explain that they'd left her with a tough decision. They had appointed her guardian over Freddy. She could either bring Freddy back east, where she had an established practice, friends and her own life, or she could move back to Los Angeles. Kathryn couldn't think of creating any more misery in Freddy's life by taking him away from the place he had always called home. She closed her practice and moved back to Los Angeles. Between the financial resources her stepbrother and sister-in-law had and her earnings as a surgeon, she could keep them in this home that they both loved.

She shared with Cache that she had known Jonathan in

medical school and called him to tell him he would have some competition; he had suggested that instead of competing with one another, they should partner, and that was how their practice had come into being.

"I guess he also got a lot of questions about Jillian?"

"Yeah, they wouldn't let up this morning. They only had a few for me, as I told them she worked for him and I had very little time for her. What happened after we left?"

"Jillian stopped by our table on the back patio. We talked and then she left. She really seemed like a sweet girl."

"Jillian is that perky little nurse at your office?" Freddy asked.

"Yes, and I wouldn't refer to her as perky, at least not now. What did you talk about, if you don't mind me asking?"

"I think she has a thing for your partner but had concluded it wasn't going anywhere."

Freddy moved from being stretched out in his chair to sitting upright and leaning in toward Cache. "She said that?"

"Yeah, why?" Cache asked.

Kathryn looked at Freddy and back at Cache. "I think he had a thing for her, and she may have suggested in the past that she wasn't available to date, that's all."

"So, I was the person who found the body."

"What? You found the body? How did that happen?"

Cache shared the story about the shoes in the parking lot, the trip in the dark down into the ravine and the body lying on the ground. She decided not to say anything about the playing card. Both Freddy and Kathryn seemed eager to hear what Cache had seen, as if they were on the inside of a juicy story that would circulate among their social set.

"So, they found nothing on the body that pointed to who did this?" Kathryn asked.

"Nothing. From my viewpoint it looked like she was strangled, but beyond that I think the police are going to have a hard time figuring out who did it."

"And nothing was found?" Kathryn asked again as she looked over at Freddy.

"Nothing."

"That's too bad. I would have hoped they would have found something that would lead them to whoever hurt that poor girl."

"So, Cache, what are your plans while you're in Los Angeles?" asked Kathryn.

"Well, as I mentioned last night, my tour guide best friend had to go out of town on business last-minute, so I'm going to explore on my own."

"What places are you looking to see? Maybe I can suggest a couple for you," Freddy said.

"Going to the Bradley House was a dream. I want to go to the Getty and the Griffith Observatory, and I would love to go out to Catalina Island. Oh, and there is an art gallery in Beverly Hills that I would like to visit."

"Which one?" Kathryn asked.

"Mayhem," Cache said. "I visited their gallery in Paris when I was in Europe, and I know they have one in Brazil and in Beverly Hills."

"Interesting," Kathryn said.

Kathryn shared how much she loved Catalina Island and said Cache should go and plan to spend the day there. She asked if Cache would like company to go to the Griffith Observatory, and Cache thought it would be wonderful to go with someone who knew more about it. They decided that they would meet tomorrow at the Dream Design offices in Beverly Hills around two o'clock, and then they would go together.

Kathryn turned to Freddy to ask if he would drive her to work tomorrow and said that then, if Cache didn't mind, she could drive her home at the end of the evening since she had already been here once. They agreed that it was a date. Kathryn had some patient meetings in the morning and a meeting after lunch, though she asked if Cache could be there at two o'clock sharp. Cache told her she would try her best and Kathryn replied she had a specific reason for the request but was very cryptic and wouldn't explain further.

The afternoon rolled on, and Cache looked at her smartphone and realized she needed to get back to Duke and get ready to see Jake.

"Kathryn, I have to head out, I'm meeting an old friend from back home for dinner tonight."

Kathryn walked her to the front of the house and took her by the hand, which she thought was odd, though she'd taken Cache by the arm last night, so maybe that was just her thing. She asked about whether Cache thought she was going to "get lucky" that night, an odd question for two people who'd just met, but as Cache had felt last night, being in her presence was oddly comforting, as if they had known each other all of their lives.

Cache shared with her that it would not occur, as Jake had someone significant in his life already and this was just two old friends catching up. Cache thanked her for allowing her the chance to see the painting and to get a glimpse of one of these homes behind the big metal gates. She confirmed that she would see her tomorrow at two o'clock sharp. She could see that Kathryn's wheels were turning over something, but she had no clue about what.

Cache departed her beautiful home and found her way back to Vanny's place. She sat down with Duke after freshening up for her dinner date with Jake and opened up her laptop. She was curious about the story she had been told about the passing of Kathryn's stepbrother and did a search for William Jamieson. Sure enough, as they'd described, the press reported that a drunk driver had collided with the car after crossing the median at ten thirty at night. All three individuals involved in the crash had died, two on impact and the third later in the hospital. Other articles said that a small boy had been left without parents and was now in the custody of relatives. While Cache didn't doubt the authenticity of the story they'd told her, her investigative side always wanted to confirm a story from other sources. She then typed in *Jillian Douglas*, and a few fresh stories filed that day told of the discovery of a fourth victim of the Pinup Killer, this one found close to the Bradley House in a secluded ravine. There was no mention of Cache or any other details and nothing about the mysterious circular mark that Cache had observed above Jillian's heart. With that, she closed the lid, sat on the couch with Duke and waited for Jake's arrival at seven o'clock.

8

Jake was punctual as usual. Right at seven o'clock on the nose, the doorbell rang. Jake had once told her he had arrived at the ranch almost thirty minutes before their first date and parked on the side of the road, just to make sure he wasn't late. He walked in, his hair dark, sporting a beard and mustache. He had been clean shaven the entire time they'd dated, and while she had seen pictures of the new look online, it was something different to see it in person. They exchanged hugs at the door, and Duke seemed eager to get some attention and found himself in between them. Jake bent down to rub his face. He thought Duke had just been a puppy the last time he'd seen him, but his scent must have seemed familiar to Duke, as his tail wagged as if he too had been reunited with an old friend.

Jake had made reservations at a seafood place he knew in Santa Monica, and they made a quick drive over to the restaurant in his Jeep. Cache remarked how he had traded in his pickup truck, which was more familiar from their surroundings back home, with a vehicle suited for the beach lifestyle. The waiter showed them to their table and lit the candle in the center. Cache assumed he thought they were on a date as the restaurant gave off a very romantic vibe. She wondered why he had picked this setting to take her to as they had evolved more of a hamburger-and-shake type of relationship than something that might suggest other things would happen later that evening. After she asked him several questions, he confessed that he came here with his girlfriend Diana, that it was their favorite place in Santa Monica, and that he thought she would enjoy it. It explained the romantic vibe.

He looked at Cache and she looked at him, and they smiled at each other as if the years of distance had not occurred at all and they were just two kids back in high school in Montana. He looked down at her left wrist, took it in his hand and read Cache's tattoo on her arm.

"*Flectere si nequeo superos, Acheronta movebo,*" he said perfectly. Few could recite those words as elegantly.

"Do you remember what it means?"

He laughed at her and said, "I would never forget those words and could never think of anyone else if I were to hear them again. It means 'If I cannot move heaven, I will raise hell.'"

Cache looked at him. "Good. I'm glad you remember."

Jake said, "I remember because your father blamed me for you getting it. He had forgotten how stubborn you could be and that when you decided to do something, no one was going to stop you. Not me, not him, not Tommy or Cooper. Speaking of Tommy, how is he doing these days, still scaring your boyfriends off?"

Cache laughed; she sometimes had forgotten that her eldest brother, who had been her great protector growing up, had a tendency to scare most people. Tommy was built like a rancher, six foot three and broad. When he played football, he played on the offensive line; when he played hockey, no one wanted to come in contact with him. In the world of hockey, he was what people referred to as "an enforcer."

"He is happily married with two young daughters to look after."

Jake didn't know how to react to that. "Those poor, poor girls, they are going to die virgins or not be able to go near a guy until Tommy is well into his seventies."

"He is not that bad," Cache said, defending her brother's honor.

Jake was quick to point out that she'd never dated herself. He refreshed her memory of a date they'd had shortly after they had started going together. They had been out past her curfew, Jake's hands in places her mother would not have been too pleased to learn about, and then he'd brought her home. As they pulled into the driveway of the Iron and Sons ranch, she could see her daddy sitting on the porch waiting, rocking back and forth, drinking scotch or rye and not looking too happy.

Jake walked her up to the house and apologized to her daddy for the lateness of the hour. Cache's daddy simply referred to him as Jacob—no one called him Jacob—and told her to say good night and get in the house. After she had walked in and the door had closed, Jake turned to walk back to his truck. A few feet from his truck, standing in the darkness, was her brother Tommy. Tommy made it clear that he liked Jake, but if he brought her home late again, they would have to have a private conversation. Jake said now that he didn't scare easily, but that scared him, and for the next four years, Jake had ensured Cache never missed her curfew.

The wine was served, and then the appetizers, the main course and a dessert that they split because that had always been their thing. They talked and talked and remembered stories of their youth and friends she was still close with back home whom Jake had not seen in years. He shared what he liked about the FBI and living in Los Angeles, and he shared what he didn't like. They scrolled through their phones; Cache showed pictures of when she was overseas in the army and he shared pictures of Diana. Cache asked him how tall she was, as there was always something that caught her attention when she saw his pictures on social media. He confirmed her suspicions when he replied that she was about Cache's height. Cache asked whether she reminded him of anyone, with her straight brunette hair, athletic build and ample chest; he paused for a few seconds and admitted that he had a type, and when she suggested he call her Cache 2.0, he asked if they could not.

He asked if there was anyone significant in Cache's life and she told him there wasn't, and that seemed to please him. She assumed he figured he was an act that was tough to follow. Cache shared her adventures over the past few days with Angelo and then the gallery exhibit last night, capping it off with the discovery of Jillian's remains.

"Cache, what were you thinking going down into the woods by yourself?"

"That someone I met might have been in trouble."

"Did you at least have your gun with you?"

"I... I kind of left it in the truck."

"Are you insane? The killer may have been down there; you might have ended up his next victim."

"So, it's a him and not a her?"

"What are you talking about?"

"The killer. You said it was a him; is that what the bureau thinks?"

"It was just a casual reference. We are not involved; it's a local matter for the time being."

"Since it's a local matter, and you're in the local office of the FBI, can you ask questions?"

"What are you getting at?"

"Look, I saw the pinup card that Jillian had on her; I moved some fabric with a stick to get a better view."

"You contaminated evidence?"

"She was lying facedown in the dirt; don't you think she was going to have traces of dirt on her already?"

"Good point."

"There was a marking about the size of a quarter over her heart. It was black, almost looked like the marking left when we brand cattle back on the ranch."

"Okay, where are you going with this?"

"Can you find out if they learned anything more about the marking or if they found anything more about her death?"

"Why?"

"'Cause I think I want to help if I can. I met her, she was sweet, and the place last night was crawling with security; a random killer is not going to show up at a place like that, when they could grab someone going to the laundromat or grocery store."

"You're not an investigator anymore."

"But I was; I still have the same skills."

"If I promise to look into it unofficially and get you some answers, will you promise me you won't do anything reckless?"

"Have I ever done anything reckless?"

"Are you kidding? It could be your middle name."

The hours passed by as if they were minutes. There was a natural flow between them, and even though it had been years since they were this close to one another, it felt like it was just yesterday.

They paid the bill—Cache insisted they split the check—and he drove her back to the beach house. She invited him in for a drink. She knew Vanny had some beer in the fridge and Cache was confident that there was someone inside who would want to see him again. He took her up on the offer and they went inside.

They spent time playing with Duke and then sat down on

the couch with a couple of beers. Cache moved her neck and he could hear the crack.

"Ouch," he said.

"Just a reminder we are all getting old," Cache said.

"Here, let me see if I can fix that," he said, and he asked her to turn around so her back was to him. He rubbed her shoulders. She had forgotten how incredible his back rubs felt. As he moved, each hand dug into the knots in her back. It hurt, but it felt good to release the tension from the past few days. He rubbed her shoulders for about fifteen minutes and then swept her long hair to one side to reveal the base of her neck.

Cache wasn't prepared for what came next. She could feel the hot feeling from his mouth against her skin and he kissed the back of her neck. Cache's breathing grew heavier. Definitely something he was used to when he did that. As she thought back to their younger years, she thought this was how he'd always gotten her out of her clothes. He continued to rub her shoulder with his left hand while his mouth breathed hot air on the back of her neck. His right hand fell on her hip and she picked it up and brought it around her waist. He stopped rubbing her left shoulder and brought his other arm around her waist and continued to kiss the back of her neck.

A million thoughts ran through Cache's head in a split second. How she wanted to take him by the hand and lead him to her bed, telling him there were no limits to what they could do tonight. She thought about Diana and didn't want to become the other woman; she thought about how Diana was just a clone of her, and he wanted—no, he *deserved* to have the real thing. Their naked flesh rubbing against each other as they worked to excite one another. Her head was rolling backward as his hands slipped under her T-shirt and cradled her breasts. He whispered in her ear, "I want you." In that split second, she decided he could take her here on the couch. Getting to a bed would take too long.

"Ruff, ruff, ruff!" Duke barked as he stared out the window into the darkness.

"Duke!" Cache yelled, gritting her teeth, but Duke continued to bark for several minutes until she got off the couch and walked over to the window. She peered outside but could not see anything.

"Is there anything there?" Jake asked. "Do you want me to go outside and have a look?"

Cache said, "No, I can't see anything, he probably just saw a rabbit."

Jake looked at her and said, "So where were we?"

In that moment of clarity, with Duke flipping out, Cache realized she did not want this. She didn't know Diana, but she knew she existed, and she didn't want to come between them. If they weren't together, it would be a different story, but they were, and Cache knew that.

She looked at him. "You have a girlfriend and I can't be the thing to come between you two."

Jake rubbed the back of his neck; Cache knew how bad he wanted to take her to bed but he knew she was right.

"You're right, I'm sorry, I just got caught up in old times."

She looked at him and said, "Yeah, me too, but it's not right. You're more than welcome to spend the night, but I'm sleeping in my bed and you're sleeping on the couch."

The rest of the night remained uneventful. They slept in two separate areas of the house and at no time did Jake try to see if she had changed her mind.

Cache and Jake woke in the morning within an hour of each other and Cache whipped them up some breakfast with eggs in the fridge and some orange juice.

As they sat at the small kitchen table in Vanny's cramped galley kitchen, Cache asked, "Can I ask you something?"

He looked at her and with a straight face said, "I don't know if I want to have sex with you, if that's what you're going to ask me."

Cache gave him a smirk he knew too well, which in one subtle facial expression told him she thought he was being a dick. She also knew perfectly well that if she stood up and took her clothes off, the eggs wouldn't be the only thing cooking in the kitchen.

"What?" he asked.

Cache had thought about the murders she'd read about online, trying to tie them to Jillian and the location of her death.

"Do you think the pinup murderer is a guy?" Unknown to Angelo and Jake, her efforts to bring George Wilkes to justice had excited her and caused her to reflect on her time in the military police and how she missed that part of her past.

"Are you suggesting that it could be a woman?"

"Is there another gender I don't know about?"

They finished up breakfast and Jake and she exchanged goodbyes outside. Duke stood by her side. She didn't think he wanted to see Jake go, but she told him they couldn't keep him, he belonged to someone else. Jake had promised to talk to some forensics colleagues to see if the Los Angeles Police Department had reached out at all and see what he might be able to dig up and pass along in an unofficial capacity to Cache. He knew from experience she would not let it go, and any help he could provide might keep her safe.

As Jake pulled out of the driveway and Duke and Cache started for the front door, something caught her eye. Over by the edge of the garage were a few things on the ground that she hadn't noticed before. She walked over and crouched down and picked them up.

Cigarette butts, a couple of them. She held them up to her nose. The tobacco that remained seemed fresh, not weathered down as if they had been there for weeks. Cache looked back at the house. There was a direct line of sight to where Duke had been last night when he began his barking. Had someone been there in the darkness, smoking, last night as Jake and she almost ended the evening by taking an intimate trip down memory lane? It hadn't occurred to her last night that she had pulled up the blinds so that Duke could look out that window, unobstructed.

A shiver ran down her back. One thing she'd noticed in the photos that Jake had shared with her, one key difference between her and Diana, was that in several photos it looked like Diana had a cigarette in her hand.

Cache went back inside, disturbed at the thought, and lowered the blinds. She took one of the cigarette butts into the house and found a plastic bag in the kitchen to store it in. Cache looked at it under the light in the kitchen. A small gold crown was imprinted just above the filter tip, a portion of the edge burned down from whoever had been inhaling the tobacco. Along the filter there was a small mark of red. Could that be blood, she wondered, or could it be lipstick?

9

The events of the morning weighed on her mind as she got ready for the day. Kathryn had been adamant that Cache be at her office exactly at two o'clock in the afternoon. She made sure Duke had everything he would need after they had spent the morning together. Cache would have loved to have brought him with her, but some places are not dog friendly, and with her driving today, she didn't know if Kathryn would be keen on sharing the front seat with Duke.

Cache found Kathryn's offices in Beverly Hills, but parking in town cost a fortune and she had to park a few blocks away. The offices of Dream Design were in a four-story building. She walked into the small lobby and looked at the directory. There were entrances to two different shops on the main floor, one a clothing boutique and the other a jewelry store with some very expensive brand-name watches in the windows. The second floor listed the offices of Dream Design, the third floor a fashion design house and the top floor an investment firm.

She grabbed the elevator, which was a little smaller than the average size; it was covered in mirrors and had LED lights in the ceiling so you knew how you looked when you got on and off.

The elevator doors opened on the second floor to an office with frosted glass walls to either side of the elevator and glass doors with silver trim in the middle of each wall. Ahead of her in the middle of the room was a receptionist desk, made of gleaming metal and a white marble top, with two receptionists working side by side. Glowing in a soft blue neon, the front counter displayed the words *Dream Design* with a small waiting room behind the front reception. Cache walked to the receptionist desk, where there was a small sign that read *Ingrid*. The two redheads were both wearing white pantsuits, one with a blue top underneath the white jacket, the other with a pink top underneath the white jacket.

Cache cleared her throat, "Um, Ingrid?" she asked.

The two receptionists turned to her and said in unison, "Hello, how can we help you?"

"Are you both named Ingrid?" Cache asked.

The one on the left introduced herself as Ingrid A, the one on the right introduced herself as Ingrid C. Cache couldn't help but think this was creepy. As Cache stood at the reception desk, she glanced over her shoulder to the right glass door and could see Kathryn emerging from an office wearing a white medical coat, a stethoscope and what appeared to be surgical scrubs. She was with a patient, and as she saw Cache, she motioned with her hand for Cache to come to her.

"Okay if I go in?" she asked the Ingrids. "I can see Kathryn waving at me."

"If Dr. Jamieson is waving, then you should go in," Ingrid C said.

Cache proceeded through the glass doors and noticed another small waiting room to her right. This one didn't appear as sterile; it had black wooden-frame chairs with red fabric and several small tables with magazines and books stacked on them, with fresh-cut flowers throughout. There was another small receptionist desk to the left, with an older woman with dark hair working behind the desk. She smiled at Cache and looked down the hall.

"You must be Cache"—she glanced at her watch—"and you're right on time."

Cache smirked at the comment and proceeded down the hall, when she noticed an older woman emerging from behind Kathryn. Cache stopped, concerned that she was about to interrupt something important, but Kathryn motioned for her to come with a look of frustration that Cache was not obeying her command. The woman next to Kathryn had to be in her early sixties. Her silver hair hung just above her shoulders. She had a gorgeous figure and wore rich brown leather stiletto boots and tight black leather pants. Cache only wished she'd look that good when she got to that age. She had black leather gloves on, and her left hand held what looked like a very expensive Italian leather bag with the initials NM in gold. She wore red-framed glasses and turned to smile, dazzling Cache with blinding white teeth.

Kathryn said, "Cache, I want you to meet a very old friend of mine; this is Nina. Nina, I want you to meet a very new friend of mine. This is Cache."

Kathryn seemed to be beaming from ear to ear, though Cache had yet to realize the significance. Nina extended her hand and said, "It's very nice to meet you."

Cache shook her hand and told her that she loved her handbag. Nina shared how she had picked it up in Milan and had two others in different colors.

Kathryn, turning to Cache, said, "Nina owns three art galleries."

"That's wonderful. I studied art, would I know them?" Cache asked.

Nina said in the friendliest of tones, "Well, it depends. I've got three right now around the world, one here in Beverly Hills, one in Paris, and one in São Paulo, Brazil, and I'm thinking about adding a fourth in the United Kingdom."

"Wow," Cache replied. "Can I ask what the name of the galleries is?"

Nina flipped her hair out of the way of her glasses. "Well, I have to admit I was a little vain; I named them after myself. They're called Mayhem."

In that split second, Cache realized she was standing in front of Nina Mayhem herself.

Cache felt like someone meeting their favorite quarterback or favorite rock star when she realized she was talking to Nina Mayhem. Cache had been to her gallery in Paris when she was overseas and had hoped to go to her gallery in town. They took a few minutes to talk about art, then she told Cache to stop by for an espresso so they could talk more. Nina offered her a tour of her gallery, and with that she shook her hand goodbye, told Kathryn they needed to do lunch and stop being strangers, and proceeded down the hall, passing through the glass door.

"Thank you for that, that was incredible," Cache said.

"Now you understand why I was adamant that you be here at two o'clock sharp. Nina and I had an appointment at one o'clock, and I thought if I timed it just right the two of you might meet."

They had only just met, and for Kathryn to introduce her to someone Cache idealized was a kindhearted gesture.

"Nina and I go way back, to before I came to Dream Design, back when I had my practice in Boston."

"She seemed nice."

"She is; she is one of those rare people you find. If you are ever in trouble, Nina is the person you call, and she will have a solution. Never judges, always supports."

Kathryn told Cache that she needed to change into the clothes she'd brought with her this morning when Freddy dropped her off, so she would be a few moments, and then they could go about their day. She encouraged Cache to explore; she didn't have many patients today, which made it easy for her to take the afternoon off and go do something fun. Cache walked around the office and talked to Becky, the receptionist on this side of the office.

She extended her hand. "Hello, I'm Cache."

"Oh, I know who you are. Dr. J can't stop talking about the new friend she met."

Cache looked at Becky and thought that was odd. Becky was in her late fifties, a little heavier than one might think for a receptionist in a cosmetic surgeon's office. She had black hair with touches of gray running throughout, her face was round and she had a narrow nose that held a set of metal bifocal glasses.

"So, I hear you are from Montana. What do you think of LA?"

"There are a lot more people here than where I'm from."

"Any big plans while you're here?"

"Kathryn is going to show me the Griffith Observatory this afternoon, and I would like to go to the Getty and Mayhem, and then maybe take a trip out to Catalina Island sometime this week if the forecast isn't calling for rain."

"My husband, Ben, and I try to get out to Catalina Island a few times a year. It is amazing there. Make sure you check out the Avalon Theatre, and there is incredible artwork throughout the island, which sounds like what you're interested in."

"It's one of the reasons I came out to LA—that and to see an old college roommate."

"I heard you were out at the Bradley House the other night. It's horrible, what happened to Jillian."

"I'm the one who found her and called the police."

"Oh my, you poor child."

"Did you know Jillian well?"

"We passed each other a few times a day, made chitchat in the coffee room. They divide the offices into two sections. This side belongs to Dr. J, and Ingrid C looks after her; Dr. John is in the section to the left when you come into reception, and Ingrid A looks after him. Jillian spent most of her time over on that side of the office. The coffee room is on the other side."

"It's kind of strange setup you have here, in particular the two Ingrids."

"Honey, welcome to LA. Even though it's one big practice, Dr. J and Dr. John run their own sections independent of each other."

"Were Dr. John and Jillian close?"

Becky leaned over the desk and whispered, "I caught them holding hands on more than one occasion," and then sat back down.

"What do you think about Mrs. Armstrong?"

"Oh, that woman would try anyone's patience."

"So, where on Catalina Island should I go?"

"There are some great scenic areas, especially out at Lovers Cove, and look for a bistro there called Daphne's; they have incredible drinks and delicious seafood, and if you're missing the beef, my husband swears by their steaks."

"Well thank you for the information, I appreciate it."

"If you decide to stay on the island, there are some beautiful inns to check out."

Cache explained to her she had brought her dog with her on vacation and didn't want to leave him all day. She asked if she could bring her dog with her to the island. Becky said she'd seen several dogs on the island, walking with the owners, but didn't think they allowed them in a number of the venues or restaurants. Cache had felt that if she was going for a hike, the island would be a great place to bring Duke, but given that she wanted to explore several of the island's attractions it might be another day at the beach house for him. They were still gabbing about other things she should see while in town when Jonathan walked into Kathryn's side of the offices and handed some files to Becky.

"Cache, right? Jonathan; we met at the gala the other night."

"Hi," Cache said. "No, I remember."

"Are you here looking for a consult? I have a few minutes free if you want to talk."

"No, Kathryn and I are going out to the Griffith Observatory this afternoon, but she's changing out of her scrubs."

"If you want, you can come wait in my offices while she gets ready."

Cache followed him out the door, waving bye to Becky and thanking her for her help. The reception area was void of anyone not named Ingrid, and Cache followed Jonathan to the other side of Dream Design. Unlike Kathryn's area, the area on Jonathan's side remained cold, like the reception area. The walls were clinical white, with white marble countertops, and the small reception area had metal chairs with white leather upholstery. Another receptionist, with a name that looked like it would be too difficult to pronounce and get right on the first try, manned the desk on this side. A few staff were in hospital scrubs, standing around a computer and gossiping. Cache thought she heard Jillian's name in passing.

Jonathan's office was nothing like the rest of his side of the facility. With lots of vibrant colors, bold reds and greens, it was quite the contrast to his personal reception area. Jonathan had adorned his office with prestigious medical degrees and certifications from well-known institutes. There was also a reconditioned soda pop machine from the 1950s, and black-and-white photographs of Hollywood at the turn of the 1900s. Behind his desk was a large framed illustration of a young farm girl, wearing a very short skirt, chewing on what looked like wheat, wearing black silk stockings, and the top of her pantyhose was showing as her skirt blew in the wind.

Cache gazed at the illustration; she could never remember wearing black pantyhose out on the ranch.

"Not what you were expecting from my office?" Jonathan asked.

"It's nice; the illustration on the wall catches your attention."

"You know that is an original Logan Leger? It might not seem like much compared to the oil paintings you viewed the other night, but that illustration itself in today's market would fetch in the mid-thirty-thousand-dollar range at auction."

"Really?" Cache said, surprised by that number. "I'm not familiar with the artist."

Jonathan looked at her and pointed his finger at her. "Maybe not, but I'm quite sure you have seen his work before. You have to understand back in the 1940s a picture like that was considered racy, sexy, forbidden. Not like today, where I could search the internet for pancake recipes and get an assortment of naked people doing different things with pancakes."

"Huh, I never thought of it. We're so used to seeing sex in everything, you forget that there was a time where we were a little... little..."

Jonathan chimed in, "Prudish!"

"Not the word I would choose, but kind of."

Jonathan went on to explain that Logan Leger had not only produced large-scale original illustrations but illustrated a number of movie posters for some very big motion pictures and designed book covers. Some of his female profiles had even found their way onto the nose cone of World War II bombers and fighter planes. Cache listened as he recounted the days of old Hollywood and of some other collectibles he displayed in his office. Cache turned her attention back to the farm girl.

"Did you pick her up at a gallery or at an auction?"

"What many people don't know—I mean, collectors do, but

not the everyman on the street—is that Logan Leger was in fact the alter ego of Bill Jamieson Sr."

"You mean like Kathryn Jamieson, that Jamieson?" Cache asked.

"Yep, one and the same. I mean, they're related by marriage, not by blood; Kathryn's mother married Bill Jr. when Kathryn was about five and Bill the Third, Kathryn's stepbrother, was about seven. Logan Leger was Kathryn's stepgrandfather, if I have that right."

"Wow, and you got the picture right from him?"

"Oh no, he passed away years ago, before Kathryn's parents died. No, when Kathryn moved out here to take guardianship of Freddy after Bill and Laura were killed, she came across some of Logan's work in the attic of the house she was moving into. She gave it to me as a thank-you for joining my medical practice. At the time, it still would have been worth between ten and fifteen thousand, and Logan Leger's work has been climbing in price—even more so in the past few months."

Looking up at the picture, he said, "Yesterday morning, this little lady could have landed me in jail."

Cache said, "Why? If you got it as a gift from Kathryn, there shouldn't have been an issue, unless it had been stolen from a previous owner or the original artist."

"No, nothing like that. I don't know if you heard, but did you meet Jillian Douglas at the event the other night?"

"Yeah, I sat and talked to her at one point."

"She was murdered later that night at that location. Someone discovered her in the woods and called it in. I haven't been able to stop thinking about it. If I had only stayed and walked her out to her car, she would be bouncing around here today."

Cache decided not to tell him that she was the one who'd found the body. Kathryn and a few others at the clinic knew, and if they wanted to share that with him, that was their choice.

"So why did that picture almost get you arrested?"

"Have you heard about the Pinup Killer? He leaves vintage pinup cards on his victims. The police believe he killed Jillian; those cards are vintage Logan Leger cards."

"So, you think... ?"

"I think they see me, a Logan Leger fan, and Jillian worked for me—we were close, like really good friends... I mean, they didn't say it, but I would suspect me too. But we were just friends; you can't arrest someone for being someone's friend, right?"

"Right. You know, they just have to follow every lead. Besides, didn't I see you leave with your wife? She's your alibi."

"She would have been, but we got in kind of a fight waiting for our car; she ended up going home without me and I went and slept at the club."

Cache was curious what the fight had been about. Had it been about Jillian? She didn't want to come out and ask him and thought Kathryn might know something that she'd be willing to share while they went to explore some local attractions.

A voice came from behind her: "Has he bored you to death yet?" Kathryn asked.

"I'm not boring, I'm well informed," Jonathan said to the obvious dig.

Kathryn walked in and sat down beside Cache, looking up at the farm girl on the back of the wall. "She never ages, just gets better looking with each passing year."

Jonathan laughed. "But, Kathryn, that is what we do, that's what makes us rich—pardon the expression." He glanced at Cache. "Our job is to help people shave those years off and get back to their once-youthful look."

Kathryn smiled and said, "With that, I'm taking my date and leaving. See you, Jonny." It was evident that he didn't like being called Jonny.

They ambled down the streets of Beverly Hills toward the lot Cache had parked in. Cache and Kathryn looked in the windows of the various shops and shared their opinions of what they saw with one another, popping into the odd shop. The store managers may have questioned someone like Cache being in their store, but they all seemed to know Kathryn by name and usually had a question about something only someone who had a personal relationship with her would know or share.

They made their way to Cache's pickup truck. While Kathryn tried to seem enthusiastic, Cache kind of got the impression she would have preferred if they were in her SUV.

Cache drove along Melrose Avenue to the observatory as Kathryn pointed out different locations and offered trivia that only a local would know. Cache managed to get to the observatory in time to take in the early show at the planetarium. It was a wonderful experience as she and Kathryn roamed around the exhibit and looked through the telescopes they offered. As the sun started to set over LA they sat outside at the observatory's little café. Kathryn eyed the other couples that surrounded them, a few puffing on their cigarettes. It was hard for Cache not to notice what she was looking at.

"Go ahead, I don't mind," Cache said.

"Mind what?" she asked.

Cache wasn't sure if she was trying to play dumb or genuinely didn't know what she was talking about.

"You can have a cigarette, if you want one, don't let me stop you," she said.

She looked at Cache. "I don't have any." She put her hands up in the air in an almost defensive position. "I don't buy any, never have, never will, but I do steal them from time to time, and that is just in my home."

Cache looked around and leaned in to Kathryn to whisper in her ear, "Do you want me to ask someone for one for you?"

Kathryn laughed and said no to the idea. She asked if Cache had heard from Vanny, and Cache told her not since before the art exhibit, but she should call her and see how she is doing.

"So how did your date go?"

"It wasn't a date, just two old friends getting together; nothing happened."

"Did you want something to happen?"

"He has a girlfriend."

"That is not what I asked."

"No, and I kind of worried that she might be one of those stalker-type girlfriends."

"Oh, you want to stay clear of that. Last thing you want to deal with is someone with emotional problems."

A waitress came over and asked if they wanted anything from the bar. Kathryn ordered a gin martini and Cache a glass of wine and a ginger ale because she was driving.

"Why, please share, are you seeing someone?" Cache said.

"I was for a while. It got complicated, and they were so needy and filled with drama, I just didn't need that in my life. I've got someone that I occasionally see when I need to scratch an itch." She said with a rather devilish smirk and finished the martini the waitress had dropped off, then looked around the café for their waitress. "Do you want another one?"

"No, I'm driving, I need you to get home safe."

Kathryn caught sight of the waitress, held up her martini glass and made the peace sign, telling her she wanted two more.

"He wouldn't be a doctor, would he?"

Kathryn thought for a moment. "Oh, no, no, no, we thought about that back in med school—I think we even tried it out one drunken night after exams—but no, we decided long ago that we were just friends."

"So why are you not seeing anyone serious? You're beautiful, you're intelligent, you're rich, from what I can tell, and funny—why is there no Mr. Kathryn?"

"As I said, there was someone, but they were married. Everything clicked and they were going to leave their spouse; it would have been messy, but we would have made it work. In the end they decided to stay, and left me as damaged goods on the side of the road. I mean, the things I did for that person, things that no one should have to do to prove their love, but they kept demanding more until I said enough was enough and ended it."

Cache put her hand over Kathryn's. "You are not damaged goods. The right guy is out there, and I hope you find him."

The waitress dropped off two gin martinis at their table and asked Cache if she wanted something. Cache asked for another ginger ale whenever she had a moment.

Cache wanted to talk to her about Jillian and Jonathan but did not want to spoil this moment the two of them were having, so she decided to approach from a different direction.

"You know, Rachel seemed nice."

"Rachel is a piece of work."

Cache wanted to follow that up with more questions, but she had learned over the years that if you remain silent, sometimes people will offer up more than if you asked them a direct question. The martini might also prove to bring Kathryn's guard down when it came to Jonathan, so the fact that Cache was the designated driver might work out well that evening.

"You know, Rachel doesn't care who she hurts as long as she gets her way. It's never enough; she is just one of those people who take and take. She's come to me on more than one occasion because she wanted me to make her boobs bigger or her waist smaller, and when I said not without talking to Jonathan first—after all, there is some conflict between them—she would get into a rage and not talk to me for weeks."

"Why did she want her boobs bigger?"

"I think she thought it would keep Jonathan from looking at other women. Sometimes I don't think she has figured out boobs are one of the things we do."

Cache laughed as Kathryn went off on a tirade about boobs. She was happy with what she had; in fact she never thought about changing anything about herself. She was fine with what God had given her.

"Here's proof, in case you think I'm being a bitch."

"I don't think you're a bitch."

"Well, some would disagree with you. Anyway, Rachel is really into the whole Roman/Egyptian era—you know, Cleopatra, Julius Caesar."

"Okay."

"Watches all the specials on television that talk about that era, goes to the museums for special events. So, there was an auction in New York about a year or two ago. They were selling off artifacts from that time period. Jonathan paid about ten thousand dollars for a set of Roman sex coins for her. When she got them, she was elated, until he told her about some of the items at auction that had gone for more than he could spend. She threw the coins at him and stomped off."

"What are sex coins?"

"He showed them to me; they're not worth ten thousand dollars in my opinion. They were little coins with sex acts on them. He must have thought they were funny; I didn't think so."

"I heard her and Jonathan got into a tiff when they left, at least according to him."

"You know, it wasn't smart on his part to invite Jillian to an event his wife was involved in hosting, but he was leaving with her. If he'd left with Jillian, she would still be alive. Jonathan should have walked the two of them out, but he is too much of a coward sometimes."

"He told me she went home alone, and he went to the club. What's the club?"

"From what he told me, I think he is going to be staying there a lot. It's a private club that has various facilities—men only—and offers accommodations to its members."

"You mean like an athletic club or a pub?"

"I mean where you go when you can't take your mistress home because your wife is there."

"Oh..." Cache thought about it for a few seconds. "Oh, that type of club. Was Jillian his..."

"I don't know. Jonathan prefers things to not be complicated; he prefers to order his company, if you get my drift. It's a transaction. The girl shows up and then she leaves. Jillian would have been complicated."

"But what if he loved her?"

"It's a romantic notion, but he loves his money more. The only reason he asked me to be his partner is he thought otherwise I would be actual competition for him. It wasn't out of friendship or what could have been. It scared him to compete with me."

As Kathryn polished off her third martini, she seemed to be more open to sharing things. Cache kept trying to circle back to Rachel as a nonthreatening entry point to talk about Jonathan and Jillian. After the kiss she'd witnessed and what Jillian had shared with her, she was convinced there was more to their relationship than professional colleagues.

"So, if he's afraid of losing his money, why would he do something that could send his wife in that direction?

"He likes to have fun. Rachel is jealous and insecure, and Jonathan is around attractive women all day; he likes to drop little comments and see what happens. It's not rational, I have told him it's stupid, but he has a mind of his own."

"So, Rachel is the jealous type?"

"Oh... extremely. If she feels she has a connection with anyone—her husband, friends, colleagues—and she sees them interacting with someone else, her insecurities go through the roof, her jealousy meter breaks the dial."

"That's sad."

"Tell me about it. When she gets into one of her rages, everybody better run to the storm cellar. Should we order another around? What time is it?"

Cache looked at her watch. "It's nine o'clock."

"You know, we probably should get going, let's get the check instead."

Kathryn flagged down their waitress and pulled out her credit card, and told her to close out the tab and charge the card.

"What are your plans tomorrow?" she asked.

"I don't know, I may get up and see how the weather is. I do want to get out to Catalina Island this week. Would you like to come?"

"I would love to, but Catalina is going to be an all-day thing and I do have to spend some time in the offices this week."

"Your assistant recommend I check out a bistro called Daphne's and said they have amazing seafood."

"No, no, you do not want to go there. Man, I don't know what she is thinking sometimes. You would hate it. The food is overpriced to snag the tourists, and the quality is subpar in my opinion. Where you want to go is Hemingway's in Descanso Bay. You will love it. Promise me you will check that out."

"If you say so, I will check out Hemingway's."

"Good girl, now let's get the hell out of here."

10

C ache and Kathryn walked from the café to her truck. Kathryn seem to have a slight issue with gravity and swayed back and forth. Cache was happy that she'd driven that night. In hindsight, they should have gone for dinner somewhere, and Cache could hear her stomach tell her it needed something. They arrived back at Kathryn's home just after nine thirty. There was a warm breeze in the air rustling the trees. The exterior lights were on and they bathed the Spanish mansion in white floodlights, with only a few lights on in the home.

"Is Freddy home tonight?" Cache asked.

Kathryn had to think about it for a second. "No, I think he said something about some errands he had to run, or maybe he had a hot date. He hardly tells me anything anymore. Would you like to come in for a glass of wine?"

Cache looked at her watch. "You know, I should get home to Duke, plus I'm hungry."

"Do you have a lot of food at the beach house?"

"Dog food; people food, not as much."

"Then come inside. I'm sure he will be fine; we'll throw a

frozen pizza in the oven, have a glass of wine, and you will be on your way."

A pizza sounded good to Cache. She knew she would either have to find a place on the way home or try to get delivery once she got there. This seemed like the best solution to her hunger pains.

They entered the home; the air-conditioning was on in the house and a cool breeze glided over Cache's skin. A loud clank could be heard, then quiet.

"Did you hear that?"

"That sound like trucks crashing into one another?"

"Yeah."

"It's the AC unit. I've had someone out to look at it. I think I'm going to need to replace it; every cycle or two it makes a weird noise. The technician couldn't diagnose the issue, other than he thought we should update the system." Kathryn told Cache to go down to the wine cellar and grab a bottle of Italian red for her and a bottle of white from the fridge for herself. She was going to go upstairs and change, and would then throw the pizza in the oven.

Cache wandered downstairs past Freddy's elaborate gaming setup and turned the light on in the wine cellar. She perused the labels, looking for a red wine that she was familiar with, and then grabbed a white from out of the fridge. She walked back past the gaming area and noticed Freddy had left a pack of cigarettes on the table. Cache grabbed the smokes, figuring Kathryn had wanted one back in the café. She glanced at the pack and saw kangaroos and the name Kangas on it. Cache tucked the smokes into her jean pocket and, grabbing the two bottles of wine, made her way upstairs. She poked around the different rooms, not sure where the kitchen was, but managed to find it and set the bottles down on one of the two islands in the kitchen.

Kathryn was hovering over the oven, a pizza box on the

counter. She had changed from her more formal attire to a tiny pair of satin shorts and a short-sleeve red blouse that matched her hair color.

"Should be about fifteen minutes according to the box."

"I'm surprised you have frozen pizza."

"I have a twentysomething-year-old living here; sometimes it's the only thing he eats. I mean, I can think of a few other things, but I would have to go with pizza as my number one answer."

Kathryn moved around the kitchen looking for where she put the wineglasses last. Cache offered to go back downstairs and get two, but Kathryn assured her they were in one of the cabinets. She found the stemware, and the two sat down at a small bistro-type table and filled their glasses. Cache reached into her pocket and slid the pack of cigarettes over to her.

"I think I love you," she said, looking at Cache.

"If I can get your love for a pack of smokes, it must come pretty easily."

Kathryn threw her a devilish smirk and grabbed a bowl from the cupboard to use as an ashtray. She glanced around, looking for something else.

"What are you looking for?" Cache asked.

"Matches. You didn't happen to see any, did you?"

Cache reached into her pocket and pulled out a gunmetal-plated flip lighter that she carried with the mark of the military police engraved in the side. She flipped it open and sparked the flame. Leaning in, she lit the cigarette.

"Why do you carry a lighter if you don't smoke?"

"Comes in handy sometimes, plus I'm always around someone who does."

Kathryn took a deep drag and held it in her lungs for a few seconds before exhaling. "It's almost as good as sex."

"I will take your word for it."

After several minutes, the timer on the oven went ding.

They pulled a large all-meat pizza from the oven, divided it into quarters and brought it over to the table. Pizza always tastes better when you are starving; it's as if the cheese gets better according to the degree that you ache for it. The two of them continued to chat for the next half hour, finishing their wine and pizza. Cache could hear that her stomach had stopped growling.

"I love this home and everything the two of you have done to the place," she said.

"I kept it up; Freddy's mother, Laura, did most of the work, bringing the home back to the present state it's in. Over the years the old home has presented some challenges that we had to come up with creative solutions for."

"Like what, if you don't mind me asking."

"When Freddy was taking you around the house, did you notice two buildings out by the pool that might have looked like they were metal blocks?"

"Yeah, I did. What are they?"

"They are shipping containers. The first one closest to the house is a workout facility. I'll show it to you sometime. It's got gym equipment, punching bags, yoga mats. The second building we use for storage."

"So why are those a challenge?"

"They were the solution. I wanted to build those rooms into this house, plus I would have liked to add a few more, but given the home's foundation, the age of it and the fact that the historical society considers it historic, getting a permit to drill down below the house was impossible. So we had to look at temporary structures."

"So does Freddy spend a lot of time on the punching bag? It always gives me a great workout."

"Excuse me, the bag is mine. I spend about thirty minutes on it a day doing a little kickboxing."

"Look at you, you badass."

Kathryn reached over for the wine and started to fill up Cache's glass before Cache waved her off.

"I'm driving and I have to think about heading out."

Kathryn filled her glass anyway. "Okay, well, here's to a fun day," she said as she clinked Cache's glass.

"You know, I wouldn't mind checking out that painting one more time before I go."

Kathryn motioned with her hand. "Well, then the painting awaits you," she said, and led Cache into the drawing room, flipping on the lights as they walked into the room. They sat their wineglasses down on two tables as Cache continued to explore, looking at various photos of Kathryn's travels around the world.

"You know, you look beautiful in these."

"Thank you, but many of those were a number of years ago."

Cache looked over her shoulder. "Kathryn, you're still beautiful." She continued to wander around the room, stopping in front of *Monja de Medianoche* to take in the beauty of Barbosa's work. She stood there and followed the lines throughout the painting, some layers heavier than others, the bold, rich colors blending together. Cache was so absorbed in the stunning work in front of her, she didn't feel her long brunette hair being swept to one side and a pair of wet lips being placed firmly at the base of her neck.

She closed her eyes and rolled her head from side to side. Cache felt a set of hands coming across her waist, and she reached for them and pulled them farther across her body. She thought about Jake. How did he always know? Why couldn't he just tell her what he wanted? Cache felt a hot breath on her earlobe, the base of it slowly being bitten. She felt her body quiver, a slight tremor going off, as if she were experiencing her own private earthquake. Cache smelled the scent of roses in the air, flowers in full bloom. I don't think I care about his girl-friend, she thought, and then she realized that Jake was not there. She turned and found herself staring into Kathryn's deep blue eyes, her hot, wet breath cascading over Cache's lips.

She put her hands up against Kathryn's breasts and pushed back.

"I'm, I'm not—I'm sorry, if I gave you the wrong impression..."

"Well... well, I have to say I'm a little embarrassed." Kathryn lowered her head. "I don't know what I was thinking, an old broad like me and someone like you."

Cache swept the hair from Kathryn's face. "Don't talk like that, you're gorgeous." Staring into her blue eyes, Cache could feel the energy pulling them closer together. She reached her hand around Kathryn's head and pulled her lips in closer to her, their flesh smashing together a theirs tongues started dancing like two kids and a disco ball. They would pull back from one another, feeling each other's fiery breath being pushed out onto each other as their two faces stood inches apart, and then would come another wave of tongues dancing in the night.

Cache nervously unbuttoned Kathryn's blouse, fumbling with the buttons, having to pull one through the loop with her teeth. She ran her tongue up along Kathryn's chest, the salt from her skin tasting good in her mouth as her tongue glided over the lace pattern of Kathryn's bra, the grooves flicking over her tongue as Kathryn's nipples hardened and pushed up against the fabric. Kathryn reached down and pulled Cache's T-shirt from her frame. Since Cache opted not to wear a bra, it meant one less obstacle for Kathryn to deal with. The two of them fell back onto one of the love seats, running their hands over each other's bodies.

"I have never done this before," Cache said.

"Had sex?"

She laughed; it helped to break the tension she was feeling. What if I'm not any good at this? she thought. "I've had sex, just not with a woman."

Kathryn maneuvered herself so that Cache fell below her.

"Then maybe I should drive."

She reached down and unbuttoned Cache's jeans.

Cache swallowed, almost holding her breath like she was about to jump into the deep end of the pool from a high diving board.

Kathryn's hands found their way inside, and Cache responded with a variety of sounds, from whimpers to outright screams. Kathryn knew what to do and how to touch her, where and when, until Cache's honey pot began to fill.

Kathryn pulled her jeans off and dropped her shorts and panties to the floor. There was a honey pot that need tending to, and Kathryn was hungry. Cache's honey pot broke, spilling its contents over Kathryn. The intensity was too much; Cache just couldn't stop herself from screaming out, "Don't stop, whatever you do, don't stop!"

The women continued touching and caressing each other into the early morning hours. Kathryn guided Cache through the ride, the enthusiastic teacher and the student interested in learning as much as possible.

Cache had always been a quick learner, and after a while she took control of the situation, making Kathryn feel everything she did to her. The heat coming from the two of them was enough to set the house on fire.

They woke in the morning in the drawing room on one of the love seats, their bodies tangled up with one another as a soft blanket hid them from view.

Cache leaned over, grabbed Kathryn's long red hair and pulled her in close to kiss her good morning. "Hey, good morning."

"Good morning to you. How do you feel?"

She smiled and kissed her again. "I feel good," she said as she looked around the room. "Where did the blanket come from?"

"I have no idea," Kathryn said.

11

C ache and Kathryn eventually got up from the love seat that they'd dented the cushions on. Kathryn went up to shower and invited Cache to join her, but Cache declined, saying that she needed to be getting back to Duke before he did something that would need some cleanup. She sat down on a small blue chair over by the wall and pulled on her jeans and top.

"Do you have to take off?"

"I do. I never thought... didn't occur to me I might end up sleeping over."

"So, I'm just a one-night stand, your booty call, is that what they call it?"

Cache walked over and kissed her. "No, you're not my one-night stand. I will call you later today."

"It's okay, I'm just messing with you."

Kathryn left to head upstairs, covered in her mysterious blanket. "Grab some coffee before you go if you want."

Cache sauntered into the kitchen. Freddy was there eating waffles, smoking a cigarette with the newspaper open, drinking coffee.

"Hey."

"Hey," he said without looking up.

Cache went to the cupboard to look for a coffee mug and found what she was looking for. She reached for a pod in the coffee pod rack, a light roast, and put it into the coffee machine.

"Did you have fun?" he asked.

Cache didn't know how to respond and just looked at him as he continued to read the paper.

He turned the page. "I threw the blanket over the top of the two of you, you looked cold." Cache could not think of anything to say other than "Thank you." She collected her coffee and walked over to the kitchen table to grab the cream and sugar. Cache didn't know where the silverware was and didn't want to ask Freddy, just as she didn't want to answer any questions about last night. She went to the kitchen sink, washed her hands and then stuck her finger in her coffee and swirled it around. The coffee burned her finger, but it was better than playing twenty questions with someone reading the paper with a big grin on his face.

Cache walked out to the backyard and sat down by the pool. She pulled her phone out of her pocket. Sometime last night she had received two calls with voice messages, yet she didn't remember the ringer going off; her mind had been elsewhere. The first phone call was from her mom, checking in to see how her vacation was going. She'd left a ten-minute message telling Cache everything that was happening back home in the week she had been gone. Definitely someone she didn't want to talk to at the moment. The second voice message was from Jake. His message indicated that he knew what the black mark was on Jillian's chest and asked her to call him so they could talk about it. She thought about calling him right there but felt uncomfortable about her surroundings. As she scanned the backyard, she looked to the higher levels of the house, where she could have sworn she saw the drapes move in one of the upstairs rooms.

She drank her coffee and left it on the table beside one of the lounge chairs. She had no reason to go back inside and walked around to the front of the house, passing the garages in back and then going under an arch that led to the front of the driveway, where she had parked last night when they got home. Cache drove back to the beach house, with the windows rolled down and the music from a local rock station turned up high. She wasn't ready to process the events from the prior evening and locked them away in a mental box inside her head. She had done this in the past, as if there were a walnut chest of drawers in her mind where she could tuck things away and take them out when she was ready to deal with them. Cache pulled into the driveway. Her faithful companion had heard the truck and she immediately took him for a walk so that he could do any business he might have been holding off. They walked for a few miles up the boardwalk and then turned around and went back. The sky was a bright blue today, with very few clouds in sight. People were scattered along the beach, couples playing volleyball as men with chiseled abs, dark shades and surfer pants roller-skated along with blond-haired girls in bright neon bikinis, admiring the sights as they passed. She reflected on whether it had been fair to bring Duke on this trip if he was going to be locked in a house most days. She looked down at him, he seemed happy.

Cache got back to the beach house, grabbed a bottle of white wine from the fridge and went with Duke up onto the balcony. The woman next door was out watering her plants in a floral sundress, and they exchanged waves. She sat down and pulled out her phone; the last person she wanted to talk to was her mother, so she thought she might just phone her brother Cooper and ask him to tell her that everything was going great. Cooper was not one for long speeches, so she knew the call would be brief and to the point. But she opted to call Jake instead.

The phone rang, and he picked up on the third ring.

"Hey, Cache, thanks for getting back to me."

"So, what did you find out?"

"I spoke to someone in our forensics group, just part of a casual conversation. Some of the team have been brought in on the Pinup Killer investigation, only in a consulting capacity."

"Okay, so don't keep me in suspense."

"The mark that you found above her heart came from a spintria, and before you ask, because I didn't know what it was either, they were brothel coins in the days of the Roman empire."

"Interesting. So how do you know it was this spintria?"

"The guys had the image under a microscope. It showed a woman having sex with a man who looked rather large, if you know what I mean. These coins have a different image depending on the sex act, and the other side has a number that used to correspond to the room where the sex worker would be to perform those services."

"And the killer burned this into her chest?"

"Just like cattle being branded back home," he said. "However, they believe it may have been done postmortem."

"Were the other victims branded?"

"Afraid so, all around the heart area of the chest."

"How common are these coins?"

"The real ones, not so common; the fakes, there are tons of them for sale on the web."

"Did they find anything else out?"

"Why? I told you I would let you know what the black mark is, and I did that. Leave it alone."

"How long have you known me?"

There was silence for a minute. "Well, promise me you're not going to be reckless like you usually are."

"I promise to be less reckless."

"The pinup card you knew about; I've told you about the mark; the police found cigarette butts at the edge of the parking lot close to the path, but those could have been there for months."

"What was the brand?"

"Let me check my notes, um... they were California Crowns, but that is a popular local company, so they could have been there for a while. The only other thing to note was they found footprints leading away from the body, down the hill to the street below.

"So how was your night, did you do anything interesting?" Jake asked.

"It was fine."

"What did you do?"

She thought for a moment. Did he just ask her who she did? Did he know? How would he know? Was he spying on her? "What did you say?"

"I asked you what you did. Did you go anywhere?"

"Yeah, some friends I met out here took me to the Griffith Observatory. Hey, I wanted to ask you, does your girlfriend smoke?"

"She used to, she gave it up about four months ago. I'm proud of her. Why do you ask?"

"No particular reason. I thought I had seen her in some of your photos with a cigarette in her hand, and since she is a clone of me and I don't smoke, I just thought it was odd."

"She is not a clone of you. I have to go, stay out of trouble."

Cache hung up and reflected on the idea that Jillian and the others had been branded. The reason cattle were branded was to show ownership. Was the killer trying to show that they owned these women somehow? Brands were usually done on live creatures, not in death. What message was the killer trying to send? She ran through different ideas in her head as she sipped her wine and scratched Duke's ears. As hard as she tried, the drawer in her mind kept sliding open and she would have to think about her night with Kathryn. What did that mean? Was she gay? Had she always been gay? She liked guys —she liked guys a lot. Women always talked about that time in college when they hooked up with another girl; was this just a story for her to remember down the road, that time when she was on vacation in California? She hadn't hated the experience. It was nice to be with someone who knew how to touch all the right buttons. She smiled and leaned her head back. Cache looked at Duke. "I'm overthinking this. We're heading home soon."

She went inside and grabbed Detective Murphy's business card and called him. The phone rang and rang, and she was about to hang up when she heard from the other end, "Detective Murphy here. How can I help you?"

"Detective Murphy, it's Cache Iron calling. I wanted to follow up with you about Jillian Douglas."

"Ms. Iron, you know I can't discuss the facts of an ongoing case with you."

"I just want to help. I feel sorry for her."

"Well, you helped get one rapist off the street; the saddlebag you brought us helped with other cases in the past that had gone unsolved. Your friend Mr. Wilkes will probably spend a lot of time in jail, thanks to you."

"Appreciate you saying that, thanks. I just wanted to check in."

"While I got you on the phone, let me ask you something. Was Jillian wearing a solid gold hair clip that night?"

"No, I don't think she could afford a solid gold hair clip. Why? I didn't see one."

"We found one, not too far from where you discovered her body. Not likely something someone would just lose. We thought it might have been lost during whatever went down."

"What about hairs in the comb? Wouldn't that tell you?"

"We found one or two of hers and several that didn't belong to her, but we weren't able to trace them to anybody."

They said their goodbyes and Cache hung up the phone. She knew she had seen someone that night with a gold hair clip, but she couldn't remember who.

———

Cache spent the first half of the afternoon relaxing with Duke out on the balcony of Vanny's beach house. She kept thinking about the sex image branded into Jillian's chest and wondering to what purpose. The Pinup Killer already had left his calling card tucked down inside her underwear. The coins sounded similar to the ones purchased by Jonathan at auction a few years ago, and she thought he might have some information on them, as Cache was only learning about what they were. She knew she had to call Kathryn but didn't know what to say. Cache didn't want to lead her on when she didn't know if this actually was anything. She bit the bullet and called Kathryn to let her know that she was just planning on staying in tonight and hoped they could see each other tomorrow. Kathryn was gracious not to read too much into it; she understood that this had been Cache's first time and she would need to process the events of last night. She told Cache it was for the best, as Jonathan had taken the day off and work that he needed to address had fallen onto her desk, so she might be at her office late into the evening.

Cache got off the phone and thought that maybe she could visit Jonathan at his club away from Kathryn and others in the office to ask him a few questions that she had. Her options were limited; Kathryn hadn't disclosed the name of the club to her, and if she called back to ask, Kathryn would want to know the reason. She could call Rachel but first she would need to get the number from Kathryn or the Ingrid's which could raise questions why she wanted it. If she did get a hold of Rachel, Rachel might get the wrong idea and fly into a jealous rage. No, Cache had to be clever about this. She called the main reception at Dream Design to talk with Ingrid A.

"You have reached the offices of Dream Design. To speak with Dr. Armstrong's reception, please press one; to speak with Dr. Jamieson's reception, please press two."

Cache pressed one. "Dr. Armstrong's office, Ingrid here. How can I help you?"

"Is Dr. Armstrong there?" Cache scrambled for a fake name. "It's Peggy Perdue, I'm having an issue with something he left in me."

"Oh, dear, he is not in, but I will transfer you to Dr. Jamieson. She's here in the office today."

"No, you don't understand, I want to speak with Dr. Armstrong."

"He is not in. Are you in pain?"

"I'm pregnant, you fucking moron, and it's his, and if I don't talk to him today, I will call every newspaper in town, after I call his wife," Cache rattled off from the top of her head.

"He's staying at the Meyers Club."

Cache hung up. She felt bad yelling at the poor girl, having met her yesterday, but now she knew where he was without having to involve Kathryn. Cache grabbed her laptop and looked up the Meyers Club.

The club had been founded in 1920 as a gentlemen's club in Burbank, California. It boasted brownstone architecture similar to that found in its sister club in Manhattan. The club offered distinguished gentlemen workout facilities, dining, social functions and limited accommodations for those who preferred not to stay in a hotel while traveling. Cache browsed the pictures. Everything looked opulent, as management seemed to have spared no expense in the interior design. There was nothing on the site about fees. Cache felt it was one of those situations where if you had to ask, you couldn't afford it. She got up and walked inside, putting her laptop down on the table, and glanced at herself in the hall mirror. This did not look like a jeans–and–T-shirt establishment and she wasn't sure how far inside it she would get, but some women were allowed, based on Kathryn's comments.

Cache popped into the shower and cleaned herself up. She shaved her legs and put the right amount of makeup on. Cache found an extremely short black dress of Vanny's, one that caused her boobs to push upward, and a pair of black stiletto boots that came up past her knees. She called for a cab, as she didn't want to deal with parking wearing these boots, and she parted company with Duke, promising him she would be back soon.

It took more than an hour with LA traffic to go from Santa Monica to Burbank. The dress caused her underwear to ride up on her, and the older gentleman with dark tanned skin spent most of his drive watching her from his rearview mirror. He continued to engage her in small talk, trying to be charming, hoping she might take a personal interest in him. The cab was an older-model sedan, and the smell of sweat from the warmth of the day filled the small compartment. Cache desperately wanted to roll down the window for fresh air but didn't want to mess up her hair, something she normally couldn't have cared less about.

They arrived at the front of the Meyers Club. The building had four stories and ran the distance of a city block. The main entrance had a small set of stairs leading up to a set of large glass doors with the building numbers in gold above the entrance. An assortment of men were coming and going, most in suits, shiny patent leather shoes and colorful ties with pocket squares. The odd gentleman, usually a bit older than the others, was dressed casually but still looked expensive. Cache paid the driver, and the doorman, wearing a red coat and hat, opened up her car door and welcomed her to the Meyers Club. Cache proceeded to the entrance. A handsome man with a shaved head and dark skin, wearing an expensive Italian suit, held the door open for her as she smiled and winked at him as she walked in.

The lobby had marble running throughout. There were several pockets of chairs and tables with men sitting reading the paper, talking on the phone or chatting with one another. Cache could see two large staircases beyond the reception desk as tall gentlemen in black suits with noticeable earpieces stood on either side ensuring that no unwanted guests made it up the stairs. A large grandfather clock along one wall chimed seven bells and only added to the ambience of her surroundings. She walked to the main reception area, her hips swinging with each step, which caused more than one gentleman to put down his paper, even for just a moment, and take in the landscape.

"Hello, miss. Can I help you?"

The man behind the counter was in his late fifties, with gray hair around the temples, his skin showing signs of wrinkles, and of average build, wearing a set of black-plastic-rimmed glasses. He had on a pressed white French dress shirt with cufflinks and a plaid vest with a brass name tag that said "Walt."

"Walt, I'm here to see Mr. Armstrong."

"I see. Is he expecting you?"

"I hope so. He requested the pleasure of my company this evening."

As she was talking, another woman approached her from behind. She was tall, around five foot eight, and slender, wearing high heels that added two inches to her height. It looked like she was of Asian descent; Cache thought Japanese, based on her time living in Tokyo. The woman looked at Walt and smiled.

She passed a card to Walt, black with gold leaf on it, that

simply read, "The Chevalier Firm," with nothing else on the card.

"I'm Jasmine, here to see Mr. Beckett."

Walt looked at the card, smiled and told her the elevators were behind the main desk and that she would find Mr. Beckett in room 304. She looked at Cache and walked around the lobby desk and up the stairs to a brass set of elevator doors.

"Sorry to interrupt you, miss."

Cache tried to play the new girl with him. "Man, I forgot to bring my card. I'm new with the agency."

He eyed her up and down. "Don't forget in the future; these cards are how I get paid. You owe me, and I plan on collecting."

Cache pondered what he had in mind, but he told her Jonathan was in room 405 and allowed her to make her way up to the elevators.

She got off the elevator and walked to the end of the hall. There were few doors on this floor, so she understood why the club had indicated the accommodations were limited. She stood outside his door, still wondering what she was going to say to him. Maybe this was a bad idea, she thought. These things always sounded good when she was planning, but this was when that reckless streak of hers came and bit her in the ass.

She rang the doorbell and waited a minute, until Jonathan came to the door wearing his bathrobe and opened it up.

"Cache, what are you doing here?" he said as he looked around her to see if someone else was in the hall.

"I was hoping I could talk to you."

"Now? I'm kind of expecting friends to drop by. How did you get up here?"

"Walt was nice enough to let me in. Can I come in?"

He stood back as she walked into his room, her hips swinging in each direction, the fabric of her dress barely covering the cheeks of her ass. The black leather boots tied up with laces in the back. He thought this might work out great.

The accommodations at the Meyers were more than your average hotel room. There was a small living area with a fireplace, and Cache could spot a galley kitchen to the side. Two doors led to who knew where, and a set of double doors that Jonathan had left open revealed a large private bedroom with a king-sized bed and a bottle of champagne chilling in a silver bucket filled with ice. Cache walked over to the seating area and sat down, crossing her legs so that Jonathan, who parked himself on the couch, couldn't see what was happening up between her legs.

"Wouldn't you be more comfortable over here?" he asked as he patted the seat next to him.

"Oh, I'm fine here. I'm on my way to a club, but I had a quick question for you."

Jonathan looked like a little boy who had just realized someone had popped his balloon. "What can I do for you?"

"The spintrias that you bought at auction, do you still have them?"

He paused for a few moments. "Not with me, why?"

"I would like to see them, if you still have them. I hear they are real?"

"Why, have you heard they're not? Tell me if they're fake; I was assured they were real. Paid a fortune for them, and I've already lost two grand."

"What do you mean by that?"

"One is missing. There were originally five that I purchased as part of a set. It must be somewhere under a couch or in a vent somewhere; hopefully the housekeepers didn't vacuum it up."

"So, if I wanted to check them out, do you have them in the office?"

"No, Rachel has them."

The doorbell rang, and Jonathan continued to stare at Cache.

"Are you going to get that? Maybe it's your friends."

"Probably not. I don't think they're due here for a while; whoever it is will probably just go away."

Cache got up, proceeded to the door and opened it up to see a gorgeous, tall black woman, midtwenties, with a bronze Afro and bronze eye makeup. She was busting out of her tight little dress, and her heels tied up in a crisscross pattern reaching up to just below her knees.

"I'm Sabra from the Chevalier Firm for Mr. Armstrong."

Cache motioned for her to come inside.

"Will it be the three of us all night?" she asked.

Cache looked at Jonathan. "If I wanted to see those coins...?"

"This stays between us."

"I don't see why not."

"I'll call Rachel, tell her you might pop by tomorrow. That work for you?"

"Can you give me your home number, that way I can touch base with her before I go over."

Jonathan walked over to a table and scribbled something down on a pad of paper and pulled a sheet from it. He walked back to Cache and handed the paper to her, "Here you go."

Cache smiled and looked at Sabra. "Enjoy yourself." She left the room, closing the door behind her. As she stood out in the hall, she couldn't get out of her head how stunning Sabra was. What does that mean? she thought. I can admire a beautiful woman and still be attracted to guys, right?

12

C ache woke up in the morning and pulled the sheets off of her. She rubbed Duke's ears and speculated about how Jonathan's evening had progressed after she left. She got up and walked around the house, opened the windows and the balcony doors to let the fresh air in. At about ten thirty a.m. the phone rang.

"Hey, how you are doing?"

"Good, we just got up and are rummaging through your house. I think we drank all your milk."

"It's no problem, I just wanted to quickly call and tell you I will be back in two days. You'll still be there, right?"

"I will be here."

"Good, I will see you then and we are going to have so much fun."

"Love ya."

"I love you too."

Cache leashed Duke up and then ran for two miles up the boardwalk and came back. Cache hadn't done her yoga routine since Arizona, so she laid a mat out on the deck and proceeded to move through her routine. The stretching felt good. As she had lain awake this morning, she'd remembered where she had seen the gold comb but didn't feel appropriate calling Detective Murphy right away. She now had an excuse to go see Rachel today, to look at her coins, and would ask to see the hair comb she'd had on the other night. If she couldn't produce it, Cache would thank her for allowing her to come see her coins and call Detective Murphy to let him know what she'd found out, and they could take it from there.

Cache called Rachel and they exchanged pleasantries. Jonathan, true to his word, had called Rachel that morning and asked her to show Cache the coins. She came across as if Cache were making her put out a lot of effort. Cache had suggested the afternoon, but Rachel provided her with countless reasons why that would not be possible. Only when Cache mentioned she might have plans with Kathryn later that evening and was hoping to stop by did Rachel react like a starved plant that was receiving water. She seemed keen, even too eager, to know what was going on with Kathryn, and they agreed that six p.m. would work for the two of them. Cache then called Kathryn and got her voicemail; she told her that she had errands to run today but maybe they could hook up later. As soon as she got off the phone, she regretted using the phrase "hook up," but as she had realized their first night together, she wasn't eager to toss out the possibility that there was something between them because it didn't fit into her life plan.

Cache spent the day cleaning Vanny's place. They had made a mess, and Cache, normally a very tidy person, felt guilty that Vanny would return home to chaos. After spending a few hours dusting and vacuuming, Cache grabbed her laptop and opened up the search engine to find out more about the Chevalier Firm.

Their website suggested that they provided premium companionship for gentlemen who needed company for business functions and private events. Need a companion that speaks multiple languages? They had that. A companion with a PhD or master's? They had that as well. Cache surfed the website and looked at some of the companions they offered. Most were very attractive young women; there were a few guys mixed into the selection and a few older women for men who either wanted a woman the same age or were into someone older. The bios provided their educational background and areas of expertise, such as marketing, medicine and law, presumably for conversation purposes. They listed their height, weight, hair color, eye color, whether they had tattoos. Nothing on the site mentioned sex. It was all geared to the single business guy who needed a pretty girl on his arm for the staff Christmas party or a similar type of function. As she scanned the various women of different ethnicities, she spotted a face that looked familiar. In her twenties, with short frizzy hair and dark skin, she looked like another person that Cache had spotted a few days ago surfing a different website. She flipped back to an article in the local newspaper about the Pinup Killer's victims and went to the profile picture they had for Emily Peeters.

Cache flipped back to the site and looked at the name next to the photo. It read Uma James. She clicked on the bio and read that her height was five foot six inches. She went back to other sites querying Emily's height until one showed it as five foot six. The resemblance could have been a coincidence, but Cache didn't like unexplained coincidences. Cache scanned the bio; Uma was a lover of education, loved children. Cache pressed her tongue against the inside of her cheek. She tended to do that when she was deeply mulling over something. She next went to the search engines, typed in *Gabriela Perez* and found a photo of her, but as she scanned the website looking at Latin women, she found none who looked like Gabriela. Cache went to the kitchen and grabbed a notepad and pen that Vanny had by the phone on the wall and came back to where she was sitting. She clicked on the contact information for the Chevalier Firm and jotted down the phone number.

Did the police know about this? she wondered. Was Emily also a paid companion? Could that be the connection to the killer? Was she also a frequent guest of men at the Meyers Club? Cache went to the liquor cabinet and found the tequila. It was noon, and for what she planned to do next, she needed to find some of the reckless courage that she counted on too often. She poured herself a shot and fired it back. "Better make that two," she said, and poured another one, toasted Duke and sent it flying down her throat. She hated tequila; it always made her do things she regretted in the morning.

She grabbed her cell phone and called the number she'd written down.

"Hello, the Chevalier Firm, how may I direct your call?"

"Hi, this is Ingrid. My boss Dr. Armstrong would like to arrange another meeting with a companion that he had a little while ago. He told me her name was Uma."

"Just one moment while I look that up."

Cache sat there and tapped the end of the pen into the table. She was surprised she hadn't gotten any questions and that there wasn't a special code word; however if a firm required special code words, it could alert the authorities that they might be more than they were representing themselves to be.

"Hello, yes, I see Dr. Armstrong had Uma James as a companion on a few occasions, but according to my records she is no longer with the agency."

"Oh. Do you know how I might reach her?"

"I'm afraid not, my notes show that we have a left a few messages for her but have not heard back. I can make a note on Dr. Armstrong's account if you like."

"No, that's not necessary." On a hunch Cache pulled up the website that described the physical attributes of Gabriela Perez and asked the contact person if they had someone fitting that profile in the doctor's history, as he'd enjoyed his time with her.

A few seconds passed, and the receptionist returned to the phone.

"According to our history, that would likely have been Maya Garcia, but she is also no longer with the agency. You know, between me and you, some girls try the companionship thing out for some extra money on the side, decide it's not for them and we don't hear from them again. I am really sorry."

"It's okay."

"I can recommend a few names the doctor might want to try. Perhaps his last companion?"

"You know something, it's not my decision, let me talk to him and I will call you back."

Cache hung up the phone. While without a picture she couldn't be certain that Maya Garcia and Gabriela Perez were the same person, the police should have no problems connecting the dots. Cache called Kathryn and suggested that she come out to the beach house that night. She didn't feel like she could leave Duke alone another night but wanted to see her, and they agreed that she would drop by after nine. Cache shared that she had an errand to run before then but failed to provide her with any specifics.

———

At five o'clock Cache headed out to Holmby Hills, which the Armstrong's called home. With traffic, she figured she would be at Rachel's place just before six. She'd ask her some questions and skedaddle back to Santa Monica for her date. Anything she learned, she would pass on to Detective Murphy tomorrow, and she could feel good that she'd done what she could to help solve Jillian's case.

She traveled out to Holmby Hills via Sunset Boulevard.

Rachel had said that they lived on Monroe Boulevard, a small street off of Sunset. Cache tried to pay attention to the road. As she passed large mansions with pristine green manicured lawns, it was hard not to glance at them. Her GPS on her phone suggested that she was close to the Armstrong residence, when she heard sirens coming from behind her. She looked in her rearview mirror and pulled to the side of the road as two blue Ford Fusions with silver shields marked on the doors and blue flashing lights whizzed by her. Cache signaled and merged back onto the road and noticed the two sedans turning right on what appeared to be Monroe Boulevard, according to the GPS. She had a weird feeling in her stomach and put her foot down on the accelerator. As she approached the Armstrong residence, a large white-and-brown Tudor-style home, she saw the two sedans that had passed her were now parked in the driveway.

Cache pulled to the side as neighbors gathered around the entrance to try to understand what was going on. Cache could hear the sound of an alarm bellowing from the house. Cache walked up to the house and a uniformed officer from what looked like a private security company stepped in front of her path.

"I'm sorry, I can't let you go in there."

"Rachel Armstrong lives there, we're meeting at six p.m., what is going on?"

"I can't say, I just need you to stay here. The police are on their way."

Cache returned to her truck, pulled down the gate on the back and sat down, watching as private security officers scoured the grounds looking for something. During this time, there was no sign of Rachel; she wasn't with the officers, so Cache could only assume that she was inside, and she hoped she was all right.

After ten minutes passed, the sound of sirens grew louder

and came from more than one vehicle as uniformed patrol officers arrived on the scene from multiple directions. Cache just sat and waited. Several attempts to talk to the uniformed officers only resulted in their asking her not to leave, as they might have questions for her later. She continued to sit outside.

After about forty minutes, a black unmarked sedan arrived on the scene with red lights flashing from the front window. Cache recognized Detective Johnston emerging from the driver's seat but didn't recognize the other officer with her. She waved at Detective Johnston to say hello. The detective motioned to her partner that she would be back in one minute and walked over to Cache's truck.

"Ms. Iron, why is it that every time we get called to a scene you're there?"

"If you figure it out, can you let me know? My life is not this eventful back home."

"Can you tell me what you are doing here?"

"Ms. Armstrong, who lives here, had invited me to meet with her at six p.m."

"Any special reason why?"

"She had some Roman artifacts she was going to show me. Can I ask you what is going on?"

She grinned. "This is against my better judgment, but you have been helpful in the past, so follow me and touch nothing."

"I know the drill, I was a police officer once."

As they approached the home, a uniformed officer was running yellow tape around the entrances into the house. Cache feared the worst as they approached the back door of the house. The backyard contained a three-car garage, a shed and a swimming pool and was surrounded by fifteen-foot cedar hedges to ensure privacy. A large white-framed door with glass inserts that led into the house was open, broken glass was on the ground around the door frame and someone had punched a windowpane in. The kitchen looked like a tornado had gone through it: chairs were overturned, and a wineglass and bottle were smashed on the floor near the sink. Police officers were putting down little markers to show items of interest as others photographed the area. The detective and Cache walked into the hallway that opened onto the living room. A few chairs were overturned, a path of destruction that seemed to stop about twenty feet from the front door. Cache spied traces of blood on the cream-colored plush carpeting.

"Where is Rachel?" Cache asked.

"Your guess is as a good as mine. We have started a search of the property, but there is no sign of her."

"The blood?"

"Don't know yet; we'll check against her medical records. Maybe it belongs to whoever broke in."

They continued to walk up the front staircase and made their way to the master bedroom. The police were photographing the bedcover. On it there was a vintage pinup card depicting a woman in a negligee, red garters and stockings holding a champagne flute.

"Doesn't look good, does it?" Cache asked.

"First time he's broken into someone's house."

Cache looked around the room and noticed a dressing stand in a large walk-in closet. There appeared to be a set of drawers with jewelry on it. Cache walked over and looked at the jewelry, touching nothing.

"That has me a little stumped," Detective Johnston said. "I am assuming some of that is real, and it's been left untouched; it could be worth thousands."

"Detective, could you do me a favor?"

"What?"

"Can you open some of these drawers? I just want to have a look."

"Are you looking for something in particular?"

"I don't know, but if I see it, I will let you know."

The detective obliged the request and opened the six drawers one at a time. There were expensive watches, diamond earrings, an emerald brooch, a ruby pendant and tons of gold bracelets, but Cache could see no gold hair comb there with Egyptian markings.

"Do you see what you're looking for?"

"No."

"Mind telling me what it was that you were hoping to see?"

"I will tell you, but not today. I need to figure something out first. Is there a safe? There has to be a safe somewhere."

"If there is, we haven't come across it. We're trying to find Dr. Armstrong to let him know what has happened."

"He said he was staying at the Meyers Club in Burbank when I talked to him last."

The detective escorted Cache out of the house and down the driveway to the other side of the yellow tape. Cache thanked her for allowing her to see what was going on, but now she was puzzled more than before. Why would someone take Rachel? In the past the killer had always left their victims with their calling card; they had never left the calling card without a body.

———

Cache looked at her watch. It was nearing nine o'clock, and she knew she wouldn't make it back to the house before Kathryn. She grabbed her cell phone but Kathryn's phone went straight to voicemail.

"Hey, Kath—sorry, Kathryn, I don't know why I just said that. If you get to the house before me, I'm on my way. I got unexpectedly delayed, I'll tell you about it when I get there. Love ya."

As soon as she hung up, she whacked her forehead with the phone. Why did I just say that? she asked herself.

She drove to the beach house, trying to keep her mind on the road. She received a few honks and waved her hand in the air to apologize. Cache just couldn't get out of her head what had happened to Rachel. She had gone over there to clear up a few loose ends that she would drop on Detective Murphy's desk tomorrow and let him determine if he was coming to the same conclusions as her. Cache had thought she had it all figured out, yet she hadn't expected Rachel to be the next victim. Cache pulled into the driveway; an expensive white SUV was already there with its taillights shining. She hadn't put any outside lights on, figuring she would be back before it started to get dark.

The SUV's lights turned off and Kathryn emerged from the driver's seat as Cache put her car in park.

"Got your message, we could have rescheduled."

"I went somewhere earlier and got unexpectedly detained. I'll tell you about it; let's get inside."

They went into the house, and Duke jumped up on Kathryn.

"Well hello there, you must be Duke."

"Get off of her, Duke." Cache grabbed for his collar to pull him down. "I had hoped to be home hours ago and figured I would get him out for a walk before you got here. Interested in a short walk?"

"Sure, why not?"

Kathryn's phone rang, and she looked down at the screen. She motioned with her hand to Cache that she would be only a minute and said it was a call from Freddy that she was expecting.

"Hey, I was expecting your call earlier. Well, I tried to reach you and it went straight to voicemail. Okay, okay... well, were you able to pick up that package for me? Great. No, don't do anything with it, just make sure you put it in a safe place, and I can figure out what to do with it when I get home tomorrow.

Yes, I said tomorrow, you're a big boy, use your imagination. Bye."

Cache looked at Kathryn with a bit of confusion on her face, holding the leash to a dog itching to go outside.

"I ordered a porcelain sculpture a few months ago from Nina's gallery in Paris and it showed up today. I didn't have time to go retrieve it myself, so I sent Freddy. If he damages it at all, I will kill him."

"Oh, I would love to see it,"

"Once I get it unwrapped and know where it's going to go, I will show you. Does someone want to go for a walk? Do ya? Do ya?" Kathryn said.

Cache could never understand why adults always went to baby talk when talking to a dog. She never did; she always had adult conversations with Duke. The three headed for the beach to walk along the boardwalk. It was a half-moon that evening; the light reflected off of the ocean waves as they crashed into the shore. The lights along the boardwalk were on, and couples were sitting on the various benches scattered along the walk, taking in the evening breeze. Few people could still be spotted on the sand, and the lifeguard stations looked closed for the evening.

"Hey, I have to tell you something," Cache said.

"From the tone in your voice, I'm guessing I will not like this. Is this where you let me down gently?"

Cache looked at her, puzzled, thinking about her comments, and then realized the relevance of her words. She had never been in this situation before, and it hadn't occurred to her that Kathryn might perceive the way she started the conversation in that light.

"No, no, nothing like that. What I am about to tell you could impact you, but it's not about us."

"Okay, now you've got me curious."

"I went to see Rachel tonight; that was my appointment."

"Can I ask why?"

"She had some Roman artifacts I was curious about, and I called and set up a time to go over."

"Was she her bitchy self or was she down a half a bottle of wine when you got there?"

"No, she wasn't there at all."

"That bitch stood you up after setting up a meeting time? I told you she is a piece of work."

"No, when I got there, there were security company cars all over the place and then afterward the police arrived."

They stopped on the boardwalk, Kathryn turning to Cache and putting her hand down on Cache's wrist and gripping it.

"Oh my God, did she kill Jonathan? Tell me she didn't kill Jonathan."

"I don't think so. He wasn't there, but it looked like someone may have broken in and taken her."

"Taken her where?"

"I don't know, but I should tell you this, and can you keep it between us?"

"Of course."

"There was a pinup card there, like the one left on Jillian's body when I found her dead in the woods."

"Poor Jonathan, this will devastate him."

"And what about Rachel?"

"And of course, poor Rachel. Hopefully she will be okay. I should call him, see if there is anything he needs."

"Do you want to head back to the house? You can use the landline."

Kathryn linked her arm through Cache's and pulled her in close. "Let's walk a little farther before we head back."

13

They woke in the morning entwined in each other's arms. Cache let the sun from the windows drown her face in the morning rays. A cascade of red hair covered her neck and the top part of her chest as the duvet covered them both. Cache rose from the bed and went down to make breakfast for the two of them. Not long after she left the room, she heard the shower go on overhead. They had gotten back to the beach house last night just after ten o'clock and Kathryn had immediately called Jonathan to see how he was doing. She repeatedly tried to get in touch with him, but her calls went straight to voicemail. They retired for the evening and Kathryn made it very clear that she was feeling frisky, but Cache found that kidnappings had a tendency to kill the libido and they lay there in each other's arms until two o'clock a.m., when Jonathan called.

Kathryn and Jonathan had spent more than an hour talking. Cache could only hear bits of the conversation but spent most of the rest of the night reflecting on the events that had led her to visit Rachel Armstrong's home.

"Those for me?" Kathryn said as she walked into the

kitchen, hair wet and fully dressed, sitting down to a plate of eggs and bacon.

"That will get you going," Cache said as she set down the coffeepot in the middle of the table.

Kathryn ran her hand up Cache's leg. "I can think of something else that could get me going."

Cache walked away. "Sorry, just not in the mood."

"It's not me, is it?"

"Just what happened yesterday is weighing on my mind."

Kathryn poured herself a cup of coffee and then filled up the mug closest to Cache. The two ate their breakfast in silence for a few moments.

"So, you have to go into work today?" Cache asked.

"Yeah, I told Jonathan I would look after his stuff while he sorts everything else out. The police questioned him for a bit last night before his attorney arrived, and he agreed to meet them at headquarters this morning to go over some additional items."

"Sounds like you will have a busy day."

"Want to come over tonight? We can play house at my place," Kathryn said with a grin on her face.

"How about I meet you there around ten? That way I can spend some time with Duke before heading out."

"Then we have a plan."

Cache finished her breakfast and took her plate over to the sink. She walked behind Kathryn and leaned in around her, feeling her still-damp hair on her face. "Try not to wear something tonight that'll be too hard to get you out of."

Kathryn smiled and appeared content with the idea. "So, what are you going to do today?"

"I think I might go down to Mayhem and check it out."

"Do you want me to call Nina for you? I don't mind."

"No, don't bother her, if she's there then I'll see her, if not, then another time. I just want to check out the gallery."

Cache gathered up Kathryn's stuff when she was done and saw her to the door. Kathryn kept a spare pair of scrubs at the office and would change there for the day ahead of her. The two parted around eleven thirty a.m., giving Cache the opportunity to do some morning yoga, shower and change for the day and then get Duke out for a long walk.

———

Her drive to downtown Beverly Hills was uneventful, the way she liked it. She lowered the windows to feel the warm breeze blow into the cab. The radio was turned down so she could ponder Rachel's disappearance, and she only increased the volume when a news story covering the disappearance came across the airwaves. The reporters talked about the facts that the police had shared but lacked some details Cache had seen firsthand at the crime scene. A body had yet to be discovered; Cache was uncertain what that meant. Was there a body in a section of woods that would someday be found and tell Rachel's loved ones for certain what her fate had been, or was she off somewhere being put through the torture of someone's sick game, praying for death to end it? Cache found parking a few blocks away from the gallery and walked down the street, browsing the windows full of products she could never afford—purses, jewelry, clothes with prices that might require her to take out a bank loan just to purchase one of the things.

The Mayhem Gallery of Beverly Hills looked the spitting image of the gallery in Paris. Two large picture windows stood on either side of the main door, featuring various paintings sitting on brass-plated easels. The building itself was all brick, painted with a slightly off shade of black that someone might get if they combined midnight black with a deep purple. Above the black door, which had a frosted glass insert and red awning, were thick gold letters spelling the word *Mayhem*. Cache entered the gallery. The air-conditioning was on full blast; it felt like she'd just entered a refrigerator. Paintings lined the walls; the gallery was deeper than it was wide, and a dark oak staircase against the left wall led to the upstairs. Marble sculptures were scattered throughout the area, usually in spaces that would help deter them from being accidentally knocked over. Short walls jutted out toward the middle of the room to provide additional space to showcase paintings, and little ottomans in a dark shade of green were dispersed throughout, allowing patrons to sit back and look at a piece they might consider purchasing.

The main reception area was on the left side, about fifteen feet from the staircase leading to the upstairs. A woman with black hair and very tan skin stood behind the counter. She was thin in an almost unhealthy sort of way. She wore a gray knit top without sleeves, which supported a small chest, and a short black skirt. Her eyes were brown and lips a bold shade of red. A brass name tag indicated that her name was Claudette. There was a large brass antique coffeemaker on the counter; apparently she worked as both the gallery's assistant and its own private barista.

"Welcome to Mayhem. Can I offer you coffee, cappuccino, or espresso?" she asked.

"Coffee would be great, thanks."

She pulled out a short white porcelain mug and saucer from behind the counter and poured a cup of coffee. "Would you care for cream or sugar?"

"Two of each, please," Cache said.

She reached `over to a set of silver dispensers, one to pour the cream from and the other to collect two sugar cubes. She handed the completed product to Cache and asked, "Is there anything in particular you were looking for?"

"I was wondering if Nina was here."

"Madame Mayhem only sees people by appointment. Did you have an appointment?"

"No, but she said I could stop by at any time. Could you let her know that Cache Iron is here?"

"*Oui*, I will let her know you are here."

Cache wandered around the gallery. There were traditional marble sculptures of people and then abstract pieces in a variety of shapes. A few patrons were roaming among the art. An older gentleman in khaki slacks, a bright pink jacket and a white pressed shirt stood admiring a piece by Salvador Dalí as two women in their late twenties with long blond hair and tight black leather pants that looked like they had been painted on stood admiring a painting by Lucas Barbosa. The gallery had several pieces by Cache's favorite artists, Sergio du Jant, Pablo Picasso and Claude Monet, at prices that would have required her to mortgage the family ranch.

"I was wondering if I would see you again," a voice came from the stairs as Nina descended them like a screen goddess from the silent era of motion pictures. In her midsixties, she wore a tight black miniskirt, showing off her well-toned legs and a pair of black leather heels. "Come up this way."

Cache followed Nina upstairs and to the back of the gallery, where she had her private office. The furniture was dark cherry oak and heavily polished. A laptop and desktop sat on her desk, which also had stacks of art books and albums resting on it. She motioned for Cache to sit down in one of two leather upholstered chairs with brass buttons.

"It is nice to see you, how are you?" she asked with a warm, inviting smile.

"I'm doing good. I wanted to see your gallery before I head home."

"Are you leaving soon?"

"Probably within the next week. I have a friend that I was supposed to visit who had to go out of town on work. She's due back in the next day or so, and then I need to think about heading home."

"Where is home?"

"Hart, Montana."

"You know, she is going to miss you when you leave."

"Kathryn? What is it I don't get?"

"I am not following you."

"She's gorgeous, talented, rich, funny, smart—I'm surprised she's not in a serious relationship with someone, surrounded by tons of friends, but she isn't. What am I missing?"

"You see all that, and so do I, but she keeps herself walled up. When she told me she had a new friend I was floored, not because I was jealous or anything but because she doesn't put herself out there."

"What is she afraid of?"

"Being hurt. I've known her twenty years, since her time back east. She doesn't tell people much about her upbringing; they see all the Hollywood stuff and figure she grew up privileged. She grew up with a few advantages that others didn't have, like a roof over her head and food on the table, but she clawed her way to get where she is."

"I don't understand."

"Please don't repeat this to her, she might be mortified if she found out I told you, but I think it's important that you understand where she is coming from, and then you will realize, despite how short a time you've known each other, how fond of you she is."

"You have my word; I won't say anything."

"Her father—her biological father—died when she was five; cancer took him. Then it was just her and her mother living out in Kansas. Her dad's father lived out here, and he encouraged her and her mother to move out this way, so he could help look after them. Her mother met William Jamieson and remarried. He too was a widower and had a young son,

Bill, Kathryn's stepbrother, who was a few years older than her. Bill had everything handed to him, while Kathryn had to beg; her childhood was a meeting of the haves and have-nots, and she was one of the have-nots."

Cache's right eye started to tear up, and she wiped it away with her hand.

"I can't say for certain, Kathryn has only ever alluded to it in passing comments, but I suspect her mother was abused, if not physically then mentally, by Will. Kathryn worked hard in school, earned scholarships to university and moved as far away as she could to start a new life. She has fought hard for what she has, she's always scared that someone is going to take it away from her, and because of that she is extremely guarded and won't let anyone in."

Cache picked up her coffee and didn't say a word.

"How you broke through, I would love to know. Cache, when you go home, don't forget about her. Call, write, let her know you're thinking about her."

"I plan to. I care about her. Unfortunately, there isn't a life for me out here, and I don't think we need a cosmetic surgeon in Hart; I don't think she would be happy there."

Nina motioned to her and took her on a private tour of her gallery. They stopped and talked about the different artists that she featured and how she went about locating new artists. The tour took about half an hour, after which they hugged and smiled, and Cache thanked her for sharing what she had with her. Cache got back into her truck, reflected on what Nina had told her about Kathryn and began to cry. To anyone passing by she would have looked like a terrible sight, especially if they knew Cache and realized that she rarely cried for many things. She wiped away her tears and returned home to spend some quality time with Duke before heading out to see Kathryn.

———

At about nine forty-five p.m. she arrived at the gates of
Kathryn's home and was buzzed in. Cache had hoped this
holiday from the ranch would be lighthearted and fun, and yet
it had turned into heaviness, filled with emotions. Kathryn
opened the door wearing a short little pink satin robe with an
embroidered flower that fell to her thighs, barely covering her
ass and cinched around her waist. Cache walked in, grabbed
her face with her hand, ran her other hand through Kathryn's
long red hair, and pressed her mouth tightly against hers and
kissed her deeply. She could smell the rose-scented perfume on
her neck, feel the softness of her skin as she reached down and
underneath her robe to grab hold of her tush. Cache thought,
Tonight I'm going to be the guy. She pulled back from Kathryn,
her lips still somewhat puckered and her eyes open.

"I was going to ask how your day was, but given that kiss, I
don't think I care."

"We can make small talk, or we can get down to business.
Which do you want?"

Kathryn bit her lip. "I'm all yours," she said. Cache grabbed
her hand and led her up the stairs to the top, and then needed a
refresher as to what set of doors led to her bedroom. The two of
them crawled over each other for the rest of the evening. If they
felt they had lacked enough cardiovascular activity that day,
they made up for it. Cache made it very clear in no uncertain
terms that she wanted her, and she was going to enjoy every
moment they had with each other. The first time they were
together there had been a certain shock element for her.
Tonight was about knowing what she wanted and ensuring she
got it. Kathryn responded as Cache took charge of the moment,
receiving the intensity of the heat that Cache was putting out.
After a while they tired, and like steeds who had grown tired of
bucking their riders off their backs, they fell asleep in each
other's arms.

Cache woke at about five o'clock in the morning as the

result of a bad dream. She had dreamed Kathryn was in trouble and was calling out for help, but Cache could not get to her. Cache glanced down at a mop of red hair falling over her breasts. She looked up to the ceiling. Kathryn was asleep on top of her; she could hear her breathing.

The house would creak when the air-conditioning was running, with periodic clanks. This was probably to be expected in a house over a hundred years old, and Cache thought she too would creak at that age. She looked around the room. The sun had begun to rise, and the room wasn't completely dark. Cache could make out the silhouettes of certain pieces of furniture in the room that she hadn't stopped to take notice of last night. She closed her eyes and pulled Kathryn's arm to bring her in tight against her.

"Help me."

Wait, what was that? Cache stopped and listened but only heard the sound of the air-conditioning. She looked around the room but saw nothing. Cache gazed down at Kathryn and leaned closer to her to see if she was muttering in her sleep, but she just breathed quietly as she rested. Cache closed her eyes and lay there as the room gathered more light as time went by.

"Help me."

Her eyes popped open. That wasn't in her head, she was convinced of it, but again the house was quiet. Cache squeezed out from under Kathryn and tucked the covers around her. She hunted for her panties and T-shirt, which had been thrown on the floor, and pulled them on. Freddy had already seen her naked once. She would not give him a second showing. Cache eased herself out of the bedroom, walked into the hall and looked down the corridor toward Freddy's room. The door was closed. She tiptoed down the hall toward his room and pressed her ear to it. She could hear someone snoring inside, though there was no proof it was Freddy. Cache decided she didn't want to open it to find out. She walked back to the top of the stairs closest to his room and listened. The house was silent. Cache wandered down to the first floor and walked through the large home, starting at the drawing room. She stood in the middle of the room and listened and heard nothing. Cache made her way to the bottom floor, where Freddy's entertainment room was, and wondered as she descended the stairs whether maybe he'd left a video game on. Cache stood there in the darkness and listened and heard nothing.

Maybe it was her imagination, brought on by the dream she'd had, she thought. She climbed up the stairs, walked into the kitchen and listened, and thought she heard a faint voice; then it was gone. Was her brain playing tricks on her? Cache walked out into the main hall and looked to her left. The only things in that part of the house that she could recall were the doorway to the garages in the back of the house, a door that led to the back patio and pool, and Kathryn's study. Cache walked closer to the study and listened, and could have sworn she was hearing whispers. Cache walked to the study door and grabbed the door handle. She moved it in either direction, but the door was locked. Cache pressed her ear to the door but heard nothing. No movement, no one talking, nothing. Standing in the hall, listening, there was only the sound of the air-conditioning. Cache thought maybe she was losing it. She walked to the front of the hallway and glanced around in all directions, when in the still of the darkness, she felt something grab her.

"What!" she yelled out, jumping two feet ahead.

"What are you doing in the dark, with those back on?" Kathryn asked, standing naked in the doorway into the kitchen.

"You scared me half to death, don't do that."

"What are you doing down here?"

"I heard something, listen."

The air conditioner made a clanking sound.

"I told you, it's old, it needs to be updated. Why, what did you think you heard?"

Cache said, "I thought I heard voices."

"I don't hear anything."

"It's not there now, but I could have sworn there was something."

"It's an old house, dear, it creaks. Come back to bed," she said, extending her hand to Cache.

Cache grabbed her hand, and they walked upstairs together, Kathryn glancing over her shoulder down the stairs once.

"Aren't you afraid of Freddy seeing you like that?" Cache asked.

"That boy has been trying to see me naked ever since he hit puberty. Don't forget I'm his aunt, not his mother, and the two of us gave him an eyeful the other night."

The bedroom was now starting to be lit up as the sun rose. The two of them slipped beneath the covers and wrapped themselves in each other's embrace. Cache continued to listen but heard nothing.

t nine o'clock the alarm on the end table closest to Kathryn chimed. She reached over and turned it off and leaned in to kiss Cache on the lips.

"Did you hear any more voices?"

"I know you think I'm crazy, but I could have sworn I heard something."

"Well, you know, many people think ghosts haunt these homes. I don't personally subscribe to it, but I'm pretty sure Freddy thinks there is something roaming these halls at night."

"Really?"

"Yeah. I used to catch him late at night when he was thirteen with a flashlight sneaking through the halls, looking for ghosts."

"Maybe he was looking for his hot aunt?"

"No, that didn't start until he was between fourteen and fifteen."

Cache pulled back to look at her. "You're kidding, right?"

"No. At first I didn't pick up on it. I would bend down to get something and then realize he was taking a real long look down my top, or I might turn around and catch him looking at my tush."

"Did you say anything?"

"What was I going to say? I would find porn under his bed or in his browser history. What boy going through changes probably wouldn't take a good look at his aunt if she was hot?"

"And apparently modest."

She pushed Cache's head away with her hand. "You brought it up. So what are your plans today?"

"I have to go back to the beach house and let Duke out for a walk. You?"

"I'm going to get some sun down at the pool and then head into work later this afternoon. Stay for a bit; I've got some extra swimsuits lying around here you could borrow, or you can strip down naked; Freddy and I won't mind."

Cache and Kathryn got out of bed. Cache got dressed and walked downstairs to the kitchen, where Freddy was enjoying a cup of coffee and smoking a cigarette. After a few minutes, Kathryn joined them, wearing a dark blue one-piece with three gold buttons in the middle, carrying a bottle of suntan lotion, sunglasses and a paperback book. She walked over to Cache, reached down to take the cigarette from Freddy's hand and took a couple of deep puffs and handed it back to him. Cache glanced down at the pack and noticed a crown on the cover with a surfer riding a wave in the middle of the crown.

"Ran out of Kangas?" Cache asked.

Freddy looked down at the pack of cigarettes. "No, they're still in the house somewhere. This is my normal brand, California Crowns, but they were sold out at the store I go to, so I picked up the Kangas instead."

"May I?" Cache reached down and took the cigarette from his hand.

"You can have one, if you like," he said as he held the pack up to Cache.

"No, I'll just take a drag of yours." She sucked the smoke in and then blew it out, rotating the filter in between her fingers so she could eye the gold crown logo on the filter tip. She handed it back to him. "Thanks."

"You don't want to change into a swimsuit?" Kathryn asked.

Cache looked out at the pool; the blue shimmering water looked so inviting.

"Oh, all right."

"Upstairs, my bedroom, second drawer on the left." Kathryn then rubbed Freddy's head, walked out the double French doors in the kitchen that led to the pool, and sat herself down and put on her shades.

Cache left the kitchen and made her way back to the bedroom. This provided her with the perfect opportunity to snoop without someone looking over her shoulder. People always hid things in their bedroom they didn't want others to find. Most rooms in the home could be considered public rooms to be shared by all occupants of the house. Bedrooms were private sanctuaries to keep your secrets in. Kathryn had two sanctuaries in this house: her bedroom, and her study, which was kept secure. Cache poked through Kathryn's bedroom. To the right of the foot of the bed, a door led to a large walk-in closet, neatly organized. Formal dresses hung on one rack, casual dresses on another. Slacks hung in the middle, and an entire wall was devoted to shoes. In the middle of her closet she had a small table, with drawers dedicated to jewelry and others for various undergarments. Cache emerged from the walk-in closet, walked over to the door at the far end of the room and entered the bathroom. Cache poked through the medicine cabinets and bathroom drawers. She found a hair dryer, various curling irons, toothpaste, makeup and a few bottles of non-prescription medicine, but nothing out of the ordinary.

She walked over to the nightstand that was to the left of the bed and pulled it open. A small flashlight, some change, and a couple of paperbacks were tucked away inside. Cache went to the nightstand closest to where she had slept the night before and pulled it open to discover an array of sex toys, including two vibrators, nipple clamps, fur-lined handcuffs and a red silicone ball gag. She took a step back and held up one of the vibrators.

"I guess this comes next at some point," she said, and put the vibrator away and closed the drawer.

To the right, an enormous set of double doors led to a balcony that had a single folding chair and a few plants. Next to the doorway was a small table with a silver-plated table lamp with a white linen lampshade and a selection of photographs in gold and silver frames. All the photos seemed to be of family members, one of whom was clearly her mother from the resemblance. Another Cache picked up was a black-and-white photograph of a small girl holding up a fish with an older gentleman hugging her with a small dock in the background. Cache put the picture down and walked over to the chest against the wall.

In the chest's bottom were drawers dedicated to socks, nylons, garters and an assortment of undergarments. The top drawer on the right included a collection of nightgowns, mostly see-through. The last drawer on the left was the one that had the bathing suits in it. Cache pulled a couple out that consisted of the smallest pieces of thread imaginable, which would hardly cover anything. To a horny teenage boy, this might be like waving a red flag in front of a bull. Down at the bottom there were two one-piece bathing suits, the first in white and the other in bright neon green. She pulled her clothes off and pushed herself into the neon suit. She had spotted a drawer of sunglasses in the closet and grabbed a pair of black plastic shades and made her way down to the pool.

"Thought you got lost. Fifteen more minutes and I was going to call the police."

"Sorry, was hunting for shades," she said as she pointed to the sunglasses on top of her head.

"Did you find anything interesting while you were snooping?"

"I wasn't snooping. I resent you saying that."

"Oh, please, I would be if I were you." She grabbed Cache underneath her chin and held it in her hand. "I have a something red for that mouth if you're interested."

"Not likely any time soon, but maybe I can put it on you."

Cache stretched out in the lounge chair. The sun was overhead and would provide a great opportunity to catch some rays. She turned her head toward Kathryn, who was lathering on the suntan lotion. She looked in Cache's direction. "Do you want any? I'll put it on for you."

"Nah, I'm good."

"Don't complain to me if you end up red like a lobster."

"What do you think Jonathan is doing right now?" Cache asked.

"If I know Jonathan, he is worried like hell that they are going to think he had something to do with it."

"Why do you think that?"

"Isn't it always the husband, at least in the movies? And where do they make the movies? Here."

"Doesn't mean he did it."

"Oh, I don't think he did it at all, but your question was what do I think Jonathan is doing. Rachel was a constant for him, an annoying constant, but someone that served as a rock that would always be there for him. Without that I suspect he might be feeling a little lost at the moment."

"What do you think her chances are?"

"Knowing Rachel, not good."

"No optimism there?"

"None. The woman doesn't know when to keep her mouth shut."

Cache lay back on the lounge and closed her eyes. She hoped that the police would find Rachel and that she wouldn't end up like the others. She opened her eyes and looked at the pool. Mostly it was clean, but there were streaks of green algae along the pool liner. "Does Freddy clean the pool?"

Kathryn chuckled. "That would require manual labor. No, I have Bruce from Perfect Pools clean it."

"When is he due out next?"

Kathryn, lying back on her lounge chair with big plastic sunglasses on, turned to her. "He was here the other day, why?"

"Looks like he missed a few spots," Cache said, pointing to different areas throughout the pool that had not been vacuumed properly.

"I must call him and let him know, thanks."

"Is your pool boy cute?"

"I'll have to work harder, if you're thinking about the pool boy."

Cache continued to lie out in the sun for the next few hours. When Kathryn got ready to go to work, Cache walked around the house until she found herself outside of Kathryn's study. She grabbed the handle and tried to open it, but the door was locked.

"What are you hiding in here?" she muttered to herself.

A search of the bedroom had only shown that Kathryn had a healthy appetite for sex, no different from her own, but it gave her no private insight into who Kathryn was. Smart money was on leaving it alone. This was her private area and Cache should respect that, but the urge to discover what hidden secrets lay within was far too tempting. Cache kept a lock pick set in the back of her truck. What harm could there be, to just sneak down here in the middle of the night while all were asleep and poke around a bit? she thought. She could scratch the itch; no one would would be the wiser, after all, and if she was even remotely thinking about something more serious with Kathryn, she ought to know what she was getting into.

Cache returned to the beach house a little sorer than she was prepared to admit. They agreed to reunite at Kathryn's place around seven o'clock that evening, providing Cache plenty of time to spend with Duke, and giving Kathryn ample time to deal with whatever messes were going on at the office.

15

A t eleven forty-five a.m. Detective Frank Murphy and Detective Marjory Johnston had stopped at a Mexican food truck parked on South Broadway, close to their offices at the headquarters for the Los Angeles Police Department. With the Pinup Killer on the loose and the latest victim taken a wealthy socialite, it was all hands on deck to find and capture the killer and bring Rachel Armstrong back to her family unharmed. The public had been demanding an arrest, and the mayor's office wanted updates so they could reassure the public that the matter was being looked after. Beyond the pinup murderer, they were dealing with a domestic violence case in which the husband killed the wife, suspecting her of cheating on him, and attending to the murder of a young man suspected to have been killed because of a gang drive-by shooting. Work never seemed to cease when you were a homicide detective.

The two of them parked in their dark-colored sedan at the side of the road, red flashing light positioned on the dash. Today it was tacos for the two of them, with water for Detective Murphy, who was trying to shed a few pounds, and a diet soda for Detective Johnston. Frank Murphy had been on the job for almost twenty-five years; he was white and had wrinkles around the eyes, a receding hairline and a bushy brown mustache with touches of gray in the spots he missed when trying to erase them with dye. He had gained some weight since his days as a patrol officer. Detective Johnston had been a police officer for fifteen years. She had dark skin and short, frizzy hair. She tried to keep herself in good shape and could outrun her partner when the demands of the job called for it.

"Don't give me that look," Detective Johnston said.

"I just think it's a waste of time. This happens every time we set up a tip line."

"Well, we have to explore at least the ones that are credible."

"You think she's the first socialite to do a little recreational blow?" said Detective Murphy.

"No."

"And after this, do we have to meet with the air force on the off chance that aliens abducted her?"

Detective Johnston's phone rang.

"Hello, Detective Johnston, here... Okay, thanks, we will be there within the hour." She hung up the phone and turned to her partner. "Judge McKay signed off on the search warrant, so we are good to go."

"So, who did we get assigned?"

"Dickens and Bandit."

"I like Bandit; Dickens, not too much."

"Well, look at it this way, we go into the house, Bandit will sniff around to see if he finds anything, if he doesn't turn up anything, we have struck that tip off the list. How long do you think it's going to take a dog to run through the house?"

"Hopefully not long. We have other things to do. Besides, I don't buy the idea that someone kidnapped her to settle a drug debt."

They finished lunch and drove out to the Armstrong residence in Holmby Hills. Police had the area secure and as they arrived, they spotted Sergeant Dickens holding Bandit's leash next to a police SUV with *K9* printed on the side.

"Hey, Dickens, did you bring the search warrant?"

"I have it right here," he said as he handed the warrant over to Detective Murphy.

"How is Bandit doing?"

"Ready to go to work."

The police officers walked up to the front of the house. Sergeant Dickens took the lead, holding Bandit's collar, as they entered the house and proceeded downstairs. Detectives Murphy and Johnston remained on the first floor. After about twenty minutes of going through the lower level, Dickens came up the stairs.

"Nothing down there, it's clean."

He walked Bandit through the main floor, starting with the living room and checking the dining room, the kitchen, Dr. Armstrong's study, the family room and the workout facilities. They then entered the garage from a door inside the house and after fifteen minutes returned to the front hall, where Detective Murphy and Detective Johnston stood.

"Everything is clean on this floor."

"What did I tell you, complete waste of time."

Sergeant Dickens then took Bandit upstairs as the detectives followed. Bandit sniffed the spare bedrooms and bathrooms upstairs before proceeding into the master bedroom. Bandit sniffed through the master bathroom.

"Nothing there."

"The only thing left is the walk-in closets and then we are done." Bandit proceeded into Dr. Armstrong's walk-in closet but found nothing of interest. He then proceeded into Mrs. Armstrong's walk-in closet. He barked, which aroused the interest of Detective Murphy, who had been lost in thought on a different matter.

"Hey, you guys may want to come in here."

The two detectives made their way into the closet. Sergeant Dickens had removed a bottom shoe rack and four pairs of high heels from a shoe organizer. Bandit kept sniffing at the carpet and barking. The sergeant pointed out that someone had made three cuts in the carpet and it looked like it could fold back.

"Hey, thanks, Dickens, we will take it from here. Good boy, Bandit."

Dickens and Bandit left the area as Detective Murphy kneeled down on the carpet and pulled it back to reveal a wooden floor with cut marks in a rectangular shape. He reached into his jacket pocket, pulled on a pair of gloves and used a ballpoint pen to pry up the cover and see what was inside.

"Do you have your small flashlight?"

Detective Johnston handed him a small black metal flashlight, and he shined it into the cavity. He moved a few things around with his pen.

"We got something interesting here." He stood up. "Better call the forensics team down here. There are some unusual things in that cubbyhole." They returned to their car and called for a forensics team, which arrived on the scene within the hour. During their examination of the wooden tomb that had been unearthed, they photographed and collected evidence that consisted of a small brown glass bottle with a white screw-on lid and a substance inside believed to be cocaine. They located a deck of vintage pinup-girl cards containing illustrations of women in various professional capacities showing themselves in many states of undress, and the last piece of evidence pulled from the tomb was a twisted metal shaft approximately a foot long with a metal coin welded to the top depicting a sexual act.

Once the detectives were briefed on what they'd discovered, they transported the evidence back to the crime lab for further analysis and comparison to fingerprints found on the scene belonging to Dr. Armstrong and his wife.

Detective Murphy called into headquarters to advise them what they had found, and they returned to the detectives' room to await the findings from the crime lab.

————

As they sat in the detectives' room talking with other officers, Detective Johnston's phone rang.

"Hello, Detective Johnston... Are you sure?... Okay, I will advise the lieutenant and he will tell the chief."

She hung up the phone and looked at her partner.

"What did they say?"

"We're no longer looking for the killer's next victim; we are looking for the killer."

16

It was seven fifteen p.m. when Cache arrived back at Kathryn's. Cache pulled her truck through the archway and parked near the four-car garage behind the main house. She looked down at her smart watch and set her alarm to vibrate at three o'clock in the morning. By that point, she hoped that Kathryn would be tuckered out and fast asleep, and Freddy would hopefully be asleep as well. Cache's plan was simple, and simple plans were the easiest to execute: slip out of Kathryn's bed without making a sound.

She'd brought an overnight bag with her this evening; Cache had brought one of Vanny's see-through pink nightgowns to wear to bed, her toothbrush and toothpaste, a change of underwear, a T-shirt and jeans. She'd also included a small flashlight and lock pick set that she kept in the back of the truck.

Cache grabbed her bag and walked around to the front entrance of the house and rang the doorbell.

Kathryn opened the door and turned to her right to pick up a glass of red wine in her left hand and a glass of white wine in her right, handing the white to Cache.

"What have you got there?" she asked.

"Just something to wear to bed."

"Am I going to like it?"

"Probably."

"Maybe we should go to bed now."

"I'm hungry, can we deal with dinner first?"

Cache went upstairs and dropped her overnight bag beside the table that was home to the sex toys. Maybe she could use the handcuffs tonight to restrain her partner while she went and explored her secrets. She grabbed the small flashlight and lock pick set and tucked them into her pockets. She didn't want Kathryn to come across them if she got curious as to what she'd brought. Two oriental vases stood close to the front of Kathryn's study with large green palms planted inside and would provide an ideal hiding spot, keeping them out of sight and yet handy when needed. Cache made her way there before joining Kathryn and Freddy in the kitchen, and put the small flashlight in one vase and the lock pick set in its black nylon pouch in the other.

They decided that they would attempt to make a home-made spaghetti dinner and spent the next hour boiling water, cutting up a variety of vegetables for the sauce and arguing back and forth on the proper way to cook pasta. Freddy sat at the kitchen table and laughed, watching the two women bicker, rubbing tomato sauce on each other's cheeks. They filled the night with wine and laughter as the three of them sat down to an enjoyable meal. Cache watched how much wine she consumed, otherwise she would not satisfy her curiosity that evening. When dinner was complete, Kathryn pulled three tubs of ice cream from the freezer and a variety of toppings, and sundaes were made as the women retired to the drawing room to eat ice cream under the scrutiny of a watchful nun and Freddy went to join his friends online to kill off some zombie invaders and save the world.

As the evening grew later, Cache walked over to Kathryn, bent down and kissed her cheek, and informed her it was time to go to bed but told her to give Cache fifteen minutes first, and then ran up the stairs toward the bedroom. As Kathryn entered the room, Cache knelt at the top of the bed by the pillows, wearing a very short and see-through pink nightgown, holding a pair of fur-lined handcuffs in one hand and a vibrator, chattering away, in the other. Kathryn undressed in the doorway, turned off the lights and made her way to the bed. The smell of a sweet outdoorsy perfume came from Cache's neck, a fragrance that Kathryn knew well, as the source was likely a small bottle in her closet. The smell of damp cedar and flowers flowed from Cache's earlobes to between her breasts, and Kathryn followed the scent until the two of them were actively engaged. They ran their hands up along each other's thighs and down each other's shoulders. Even in the darkness they could still see each other's faces with vivid clarity and engaged in a night of passionate sex. While a few of Kathryn's toys saw use that night, the red silicone ball stayed in the nightstand.

At three o'clock sharp, Cache's smart watch vibrated, and she lifted her arm to look at the time and silence it. Cache lay still, observing Kathryn. She whispered her name but received no response as Kathryn slept, one arm draped over Cache's naked body. She slithered her way loose and braced her fall to the floor so as not to create any noise. Cache looked to her overnight bag, which she had laid her clothes on top of. It was hard to feel clandestine in any surroundings if you were running around in the buff. She pulled her panties and tank top on opting not to put on her jeans, as it might look more suspicious if she was caught roaming the halls in the middle of the night fully dressed with a flashlight. Cache crawled out of Kathryn's bedroom into the darkness of the early morning. She listened for Freddy but heard nothing. Periodically she could hear the air conditioner go on and off, but unlike the other night, there were no voices coming from the darkness. Cache walked down the stairs on the right-hand side of the house until she reached the main floor.

To her right, she could see light shimmering against the wall. Blues, reds and other colors were coming from the downstairs entertainment room. Cache, crouching, walked down the stairs to investigate. The light intensity grew as she crept into the entertainment room and saw the back of Freddy's head where he was sitting on the sofa. His voice was loud: "Go to the right, no, my right, shoot him, oh, come on, I can't do anything." The television was on and Cache could see that Freddy appeared to be still online gaming with friends, as his character was running through dark tunnels shooting the zombies that emerged. From the glow around his head and the sight of red LED lights on either side of his ears, it was evident that he was wearing a gaming headset, talking with his friends as they worked to save the universe.

Cache returned to the main-floor hall. Ahead of her was Kathryn's study. She walked barefoot across the marble floor, the outside lights creating window patterns on the floor as she walked across them. Cache made her way to the oriental vases, retrieving her tools for tonight's mission. She crawled to the study door, gripped the doorknob and twisted it. The door was locked.

Cache hesitated and muttered to herself, "Do I really want to be doing this?" She looked up the stairs; she had changed her mind. After all what right did she have to invade Kathryn's privacy. As she turned to walk away, from the other side of the door she heard a voice cry out, "Why won't someone help me." She went back to the door and put her ear against it but heard nothing. Was this all in her head? Was her mind playing tricks on her? Were there ghosts walking the halls at night? She looked back at the locked door. Cache felt conflicted and needed to know if there was someone in need of help or was it her imagination.

It would have saved her time had the door just been open. She reached for the small black nylon pouch that she had placed on the floor and inserted the flashlight between her teeth. Cache pulled two picks from the pouch. She pulled the tension wrench and a small metal pick with a bend in it toward the end. Cache inserted it into the lock. She inserted the other pick in above the tension pick. As she fiddled with the lock, she used the tension wrench to further her position with the lock as the pins fell into place. She then twisted the tension pick, and when she pulled on the doorknob, the door to the study swung open. Cache put the picks back into the pouch and tucked them away in the back of her underwear.

Cache looked around behind her and didn't see any movement from upstairs or down. She crept into the room, closing the door softly behind her and securing the lock. The last thing she needed was someone walking in while she was exploring a room that they had not invited her into and that she had no logical reason for being in. She turned the flashlight on and panned it across the room, starting from left to right. The room had dark, solid oak panels on the wall, rectangular in shape. The far left of the room had a large stone fireplace with a large oil painting hanging over the mantel. Cache could not determine the artist, but the image was of the back of a woman, half-dressed, holding what looked like a red towel or the bottom part of her dress covering her buttocks. Just in front of the fireplace was a small table with a brass light and white linen lampshade flanked by two leather high-backed chairs. As the light moved across the room, Cache saw a large stained-glass window that rose to the ceiling behind Kathryn's desk. On the right-hand side of the room was a series of built-in bookcases filled with a variety of books on medicine and art, among the many subjects. Two leather chairs faced the front of the desk, and a big leather chair sat behind the desk. The room reminded Cache of what the office of a railroad magnate or oil baron may have looked like at the start of the 1900s during the industrial boom.

As she scanned the room, she saw it was beautifully designed. Yet there was no indication of where the voice had come from, if it came from the room at all. Cache stood there in silence. The furniture was old but made when craftsmanship was considered to be important to the customer. She walked around the room to position herself behind Kathryn's desk. Numerous files sat in piles, one on top of the other. As Cache flipped through the files, she noted that they all seemed to be for patients. Notes of visits, X-rays, previous conditions, lab results—all the things one might expect to find in a room that was barred from one's eyes because of client confidentiality.

Cache now just felt stupid.

Maybe her previous experiences made her overreact to new situations and see shadows where none existed. She glanced down at the bottom of the door. She could see the light shimmering from the outside floodlights bouncing off of the white marble floors, and then Cache noticed that something had interrupted the light. Someone was now standing on the other side of the door, blocking most of the light from getting in underneath the door. She turned off her flashlight and walked slowly to hide behind one of the tall leather-backed chairs near the fireplace. Cache could see that someone was trying to turn the doorknob but the dead bolt prevented access to the room. The doorknob turned in the opposite direction; the figure moved away from the door and light now shined unobstructed underneath it. Cache exhaled the breath she'd been holding to ensure no sound was coming from the room. She felt as if she'd broken Kathryn's trust by being there. She hoped she could exit the room, that the figure had been Freddy and she could slip back into bed without Kathryn's being the wiser and put her suspicions to rest, embrace what could be the start of a new relationship.

Cache walked back to the desk and noted another copy of the black-and-white photograph that Kathryn had upstairs of a little girl catching a fish. Cache picked up another black-and-white photo next to it in a silver frame. The photo was of a cabin in the middle of a clearing flanked by groups of trees. A pond or lake of some sort seemed to be in the distance.

Cache thought she would wait a few minutes before leaving and walked toward the door past the built-in bookcases. With only a cotton tank top on, she noticed a temperature change as she walked past the far bookcase. She aimed her flashlight at the bookcase. Like the other three that stood beside it, it was tall, maybe ten feet high, in solid oak with a rich cherry stain applied to the wood. There were hand-carved symbols in all the corners, and a set of grooves ran vertically along the edges. The top and bottom had crown molding that was flush with the wall.

Each bookcase contained four shelves for books, mainly hardcovers on a variety of topics. One bookcase seemed to be dedicated to the world of art, another to tourism and far-off countries. The bookcase Cache felt a slight breeze coming from was filled top to bottom with medical textbooks. Cache pointed her flashlight all around the bookcases but could not see a vent anywhere that would explain the difference in temperature and the clammy feeling she had on her skin. She looked back at Kathryn's desk to see if there was any blank paper. Kathryn had a white notepad with the logo of her practice, Dream Design, in the upper middle of the paper. Cache pulled a sheet off and walked to the bookcase closest to the door, where the edge of one bookcase met the edge of the other. She started at the doorway, holding the paper in front of the edge of the bookcase. The paper hung still. She continued to walk to the far bookcase, holding the limp piece of paper in her hand, until she reached the fourth bookcase, where the paper fluttered in her hand.

She stood back to look at the bookcases and thought about the position of the room as it related to the exterior of the house. The stained-glass window on the opposite wall faced the garages in the back of the house and the archway that would protect people from the elements if they were to park under the arch and enter the house that way. The bookcases should have been flush with the exterior wall of the front of the house. As Kathryn had told her, it was an old house in need of some repairs; it was possible that the insulation in the wall had failed in this one corner. On the other hand, after touring several older houses, castles and even monasteries, she knew a secret passage could also exist, leading to some unknown destination. She remembered reading an article a few months back saying that many wealthier homes during the days of prohibition had special entrances to allow people to come and go with liquor so as not to arouse the attention of the authorities.

Cache looked at her watch. She had been gone for over thirty minutes and needed to return to the bedroom to ensure that she wasn't caught doing what she was doing.

She folded the paper up and placed it in the wastebasket next to Kathryn's desk. Cache then proceeded to the door, placed her ear up against it and listened for any sounds coming from the outside hallway. She heard nothing. She pulled the dead bolt back, slowly opened the door and peered through the crack for any noticeable figures. The hallway seemed void of people. She crept out of the study and closed the door behind her. Cache went to work returning the dead bolt to its original position and securing the door, and hopefully her secret intrusion. She looked around the hallway. No sign of anyone. She wondered who had come to the door to see if it was secure. The last thing she wanted to get caught with was her lock pick set, so she returned it and the flashlight to the original vases that she had stored them in.

She proceeded to go up the stairs quietly and then froze. Cache knew someone had been walking around; if it was Kathryn she could have been sitting in the dark upstairs, waiting for Cache to return, waiting to pounce on her, demanding that she explain what she had been doing for over thirty minutes in the house. Cache glanced down at the hallway and saw the flicker of light continuing to bounce off the white marble. Freddy was still up playing his game. Cache wondered if he wanted company; after all, who could resist a female with perky tits wearing very little clothing? If she went upstairs after a while and Kathryn was awake, she could say that she couldn't sleep and had ended up playing video games with Freddy. This would provide her with an alibi that was easy to confirm, and Freddy probably wouldn't be aware of the time. If Freddy was the one roaming the hall, chances were he hadn't gone upstairs to Kathryn's bedroom.

She moved downstairs and walked up behind Freddy, touching him on the shoulder. The poor boy almost jumped through the ceiling. "Hey, what do you think you're doing?" he said while taking a long hard gaze at Cache's partially naked body.

"Couldn't sleep, came downstairs, saw the flicker and wanted to know if I could join you." Freddy agreed and sat back down with Cache on the couch. He grabbed an extra controller and a headset that glowed blue once he plugged her in and logged her on. He explained the game and the two of them spent the next couple of hours running through a postapocalyptic Chicago, killing zombies with Wendy from Newfoundland, Tommy from Miami and Constance from Detroit. Her thought of creating a plausible alibi left her after a short while as she became more engaged in the game. They continued to play until the sun began to rise. There were screams and high fives as they continued to rack up points and raise their levels in this online environment.

As she leaned forward on the couch, her fingers moving furiously on the game controller like a master pianist's, the feeling of something grabbing at her waist caught her attention and she shrieked, standing up as if she had seen a mouse. Freddy looked back at Kathryn, who wore a cotton bathrobe and had her hand over her mouth to contain her laughter and not make Cache feel too bad.

"I wondered where you had gotten off to."

Cache looked at her watch. It was now six thirty a.m. "Sorry, I couldn't sleep and saw Freddy was playing down here, so I thought I would come join."

"Hey, mister, get your own teammate."

Freddy looked at her, bewildered, then waved her off and continued to play his game, apologizing to his online friends, who had no idea what had just happened. Kathryn reached for her hand and they walked up to the bedroom to spend a few more hours together before Kathryn would rise to go to work and Cache would go spend some time with Duke before venturing off to Catalina Island for the day. As they went into the bedroom, Cache walked over to the picture of the little girl holding up a fish on a fishing line with both hands and picked it up. The rubber boots she was wearing were swallowing up most of her tiny legs. There was an older man crouched down behind her with a big grin on his face and what looked like a small cabin in the distance.

"Who's the little girl? She's cute," Cache said.

"That's me when I was little."

"Can I ask who the man is?"

"That was my grandfather," she said, "on my dad's side of the family."

"Well, that's what Logan Leger looked like in his later years."

Kathryn said, "Oh no, that's not Logan. That is my actual dad's father, my birth father; his name was Chet."

Cache knew some details already from Nina but pretended this was new information to her.

"So, your mother remarried at some point."

"Yeah, my dad, my birth dad, died when I was young from cancer. My mom and I were out east alone, on our own. She wasn't sure how we were going to survive; I mean, we had nothing. My grandfather on the other hand was widowed, had lost his only son and wanted to have a relationship with me, to hold on to the memories of my dad, and convinced my mom to move out here to California, where he could help the two of us."

"You look happy."

Kathryn sat on the edge of the bed and looked at the photo that Cache was holding. "We didn't have much and missed my dad terribly, but I think we were happy."

"Then she met William Jamieson?"

"Yes, Will was also a widower with a young son, Bill, older than me, trying to cope."

"And they fell in love?"

"I've never been that sure on that," she said in a puzzled tone. "My mom once told me you have to do everything in your power to survive, you can't let people take things away from you."

"So, you think she married for money?"

"It's possible. We only ever talked about it once and her responses were cryptic, and I could tell she didn't want to go into much detail about it."

"So, your relationship with Freddy is by marriage and not blood."

"That is true, but I have had him so long, I think of him as mine."

Cache returned the photo to its original location and quizzed Kathryn about the remaining photographs on the table. One old black-and-white photograph was of her parents on their wedding day; another photograph, in color, was of her mother and stepfather, Will. There were photographs of her stepbrother and his wife at a few selected family events. As Cache surveyed all the photographs, she thought it was odd that there were none of Freddy when he was younger.

Kathryn decided that there were more interesting things to do than take a trip down memory lane. She held up the covers, and Cache slipped beneath into her warm embrace. It wouldn't be long before the day summoned them to their respective tasks.

17

It was one thirty when the ferry dropped Cache off on Catalina Island. It was a warm, sunny day and there were plenty of people walking around the island taking in the scenery. Boats were docked in the harbor as seagulls flew around looking for fish that came to the surface. Cache had seen most of the sights she had come to see in the first few hours of her visit and had just found herself walking aimlessly along one of the many paths on the island. Cache had come upon a beautiful scenic overlook. There were a mother with a stroller and an older couple holding hands, all looking at the beautiful scenery from this vantage point. Cache pulled out her smartphone and took some pictures to show everyone back home. As she continued to walk along the path, she came across a little bistro. It had various nautical-type items adorning the outside, including a wooden statue of a captain at the wheel of a ship, one or two brass diving bell helmets, and various nets and other gear likely used by local fisherman. She looked above the entranceway and saw large wooden letters painted in blue with a white outline that read *Daphne's*.

Cache remembered she'd promised Kathryn she would

try Hemingway's; she looked on a map the restaurant had outside that showed where she was and where other places of interest were on the island. Hemingway's would be a good thirty-minute walk in the opposite direction, and she was hungry, and this looked like a nice place. She could always tell a little lie to her, she thought as she scanned the menu. After all, she was her friend, she was her lover, but she wasn't her mother.

Cache walked into Daphne's and was greeted at the front door by a stunning young blonde who called herself Austin. Austin had a thin body with a deep bronze tan. She wore cut-off shorts, a light blue polo shirt that emphasized her large breasts with the word *Daphne's* stitched on the upper left-hand side, no bra—a girl after her own heart—and white canvas deck shoes. What was most striking about her to Cache was the long mane of blond hair that stretched down her back and stopped just above her butt.

She smiled with beautiful white teeth and said, "Welcome to Daphne's. We have seating out on the patio, in the main dining room and at the bar."

Cache surveyed the restaurant. While it was not too busy, it was evident that it catered to couples, as several sat out on the patio, toasting one another, holding hands, or cuddling in each other's arms as they enjoyed the view looking onto the ocean.

"I think the bar sounds good to me."

Austin smiled and gathered up a menu. "Will you follow me?"

Cache sat at the bar as Austin handed her the menu and told her the specials for the day. The chef had done a beautiful glazed salmon, lobster bisque and fried calamari. The specials all sounded good, but Cache couldn't take her eyes off Austin. She thanked her for the menu, feeling as if a new door had opened for her in her life. It was as if she had been told that she had to use the door on the right to go somewhere, but by chance she had taken the door on the left and nothing bad had happened to her.

The bar was nearly fifteen feet long with roughly a dozen stools with red leather backs and foot railings. Behind the bar they'd covered the walls in mirrors, making the room look larger than it was, with three shelves of premium spirits going from one end to the other. The bar had a glazed mahogany top fitted with brass rails and two sets of beer taps sat at either end. At Cache's end, there stood a large wooden cupboard, which likely housed barware, supplies or the coats of the staff. On top of it was a small television broadcasting the local weather.

Today only a lone bartender was manning the post and was down at the other end pouring drafts for a waitress when he spotted Cache sitting down.

The bartender came over and introduced himself as Kane and asked Cache what she wanted to drink. Kane was about five foot eight, with a slender build, long dark hair tied in a ponytail and a little facial scruff. He wore a pressed white dress shirt with the word *Daphne's* stitched on the right-hand side, rolled up to his elbows, and black slacks, from what Cache could observe. His arms were covered in tattoos that stopped at his wrists. If his shirtsleeves hadn't been rolled up, you would never have known he had any ink from outside appearances.

Kane mentioned several beers on tap, all local craft breweries, and one name stuck with her: Dillinger's Desire. Cache decided she would try a pint of Dillinger's and Kane filled a glass from the tap.

Cache said, "From what I've heard, I'm surprised you're this busy."

Kane said, "Right now you're seeing more of the lunch crowd, but dinners are by reservation only. Sometimes it can take a week's wait to get a table. As far as I know we're booked solid for this evening's dinner crowd."

"I noticed a lot of couples here, especially out on the patio."

"You have the ocean views out there—very romantic, hence the name Lovers Cove. There are a couple inns on the island close by, so we get visitors who are staying over for breakfast as well."

Cache glanced over the menu. "So what's good here?"

"I'm partial to the glazed salmon myself, but we also have a seafood pasta that is very popular with the regulars."

Cache looked over the menu. Everything looked so good, including several beef dishes. She flipped over the menu to read reviews by various food critics throughout the United States. Everyone seemed to like Daphne's, and yet Kathryn had insisted she eat at Hemingway's. Perhaps she'd thought she wouldn't get a table and didn't want her to be disappointed. As Kane made small talk with her, asking her where she was from and what she was doing on her holiday, Cache noticed a news report on the television that had a picture of Rachel in the top corner.

"Hey, would you mind turning that up? I know her, I wonder if they found her."

Kane looked at Cache. "I caught it during the briefing this morning. Hopefully they find her before she hurts anyone else." He raised the volume on the television.

Cache looked at him, bewildered, as the news anchor spoke.

"In today's top stories, police are searching for socialite Rachel Armstrong, wanted for questioning in relation to the pinup murders. People are advised not to approach her if they see her, but to call police immediately. She is possibly armed and dangerous. Turning to lighter news..." Kane turned the volume back down.

"What the fuck?"

Kane raised his eyebrows. "Problem?"

"No, just very confused. I know her—I mean, not well, but there is no way she is anything but a victim here."

"The story is on all the channels; I don't know what the police have but they aren't making her out to be a victim. She always seemed like a nice woman. A little high-strung, but you never know what people are capable of."

"Wait, you know her too?"

"She used to come in here a lot, hung out on the patio for hours."

"Probably with her husband. Tall guy, thin, clean shaven, graying around the temples?"

"Hmm, I... don't think so."

Kane waved to Austin, who walked over to them, her hips swinging from side to side as she moved like a hula dancer's. Cache went to her smartphone and called up a picture of the team at Dream Design. She pointed at Jonathan. "This guy."

Kane looked at it. "No, not him. I don't think I've ever seen him in here before, but we get tons of people, so you never know."

"What do you need?" Austin asked as she leaned on Cache's shoulder. Cache couldn't help but glance down along the lines of her cleavage.

"Hey, you remember us talking about that woman who was on the news, who used to come in the restaurant a lot?"

"Yeah, what about her?"

Cache showed her the image of the Dream Design team and pointed at Jonathan. "Did she come in with him?"

Austin took her smartphone and looked at all the members of the team. "No, she came in with her." She pointed at Kathryn in the photo. "I remember her long red hair. They used to always sit out on the patio, especially for breakfast."

Cache looked at her with an odd expression on her face. "Are you sure it was with that woman?"

"Yeah, I'm pretty sure." She looked around the room and spotted a slender waitress of medium height, with dark skin and dark hair, and waved her over. "This is Vivian, she works on the patio when we're slammed." Cache shook her hand as Austin showed the picture of Kathryn to her.

"That woman that was on the news, this was the woman she used to come in with, right?"

Vivian looked at the picture for a few moments. "Oh yeah, she was the nice one."

"You're sure it was her?" Cache asked.

"Positive. I remember they were in several months ago. The one on the news was just beaming and showing me this beautiful gold hair comb with Egyptian markings on it that she had gotten from the other one. In fact, the woman with red hair had one exactly like it. I remember it was beautiful and asked if she would mind telling me where she got it. The woman on the news seemed offended by the idea and told me I couldn't afford it. After I left them, I could see the redheaded woman scolding her, and then later she came by to apologize. She told me she picked them up in a little bazaar near Cairo, when she visited Egypt, and gave me a two-hundred-dollar tip to apologize for her friend. I don't get too many two-hundred-dollar tips from the breakfast crowd."

"Hey, thanks for sharing that with me. I know the redhead, she's a nice person, I think."

Vivian left to return to her customers as Austin made her way to the front door to attend to the needs of two older men waiting to be seated. Kane wiped the top of the bar with a rag. "I didn't want to say anything because I couldn't be certain, but I'm pretty sure I've spotted them all over each other, when they thought no one was looking."

Kane brought out her glazed salmon with green beans and put it down in front of her. He sensed the news had been a bit of a blow and left her to eat her meal in peace as he went about filling drink orders for other customers.

Cache poked at her salmon, drank her pint of Dillinger's and stewed on the fact that Rachel and Kathryn had had some type of relationship more intimate than Kathryn had suggested. She considered checking out some nearby inns but was convinced the management wouldn't say anything to her about the lives of its guests, and she had no way to compel them to share that information with her. The salmon was delicious and the Dillinger's helped wash the meal down so well that she ordered a second. As she weighed everything in her mind, she concluded that Kathryn owed her no information about her prior relationships, just as Cache didn't have to talk about Jake. She wondered whether Kathryn could be in any danger. If Rachel was indeed not the victim, as Cache had imagined, but was wanted in relation to the murders, it could mean that either she was directly involved or perhaps her husband was.

She grabbed her phone and called Kathryn. "Hey, have you seen the news?"

"Yeah, one of the nurses filled me in. Why, did you see it?"

"It was on in the restaurant."

"So what did you think of Hemingway's? What did you have?"

Cache panicked and covered the mouthpiece of the phone with her hand and waved Kane over.

"What are Hemingway's specialties, anything they are known for?"

"Probably their most popular dish is the swordfish. Why?"

"No reason," she said, flashing her bright white smile at him and uncovering the mouthpiece.

"Sorry, I needed to take a drink. I had the swordfish."

"Oh, I was hoping you would have the swordfish. I didn't want to be pushy, but I'm glad you tried it. Are you home now?"

"No, still on the island. I'll head out in the next hour or so. Is Jonathan in the office with you?"

"No, why?"

"Look, I am just going to say this straight out, no bullshitting here. If they want Rachel for questioning, is it possible that Jonathan is mixed up in this and could you be in... danger?"

There was silence from the other end.

"Kathryn, are you there?"

"I'm not sure how I am supposed to react to that. Should I be furious because you think I'm that gullible or smitten because you're worried about my safety?"

"Let's go with smitten, and I'm serious. You might be too close to the situation to see it for what it really is."

"I have nothing to fear from either one of them."

"Still, it might not be a bad idea for Freddy to come out and pick you up."

"Cache, you worry too much. I will be fine. If you want you can come over tonight and tuck me in."

Cache thought about it for a few seconds. "I want to. I need to go home and look after Duke; can I meet you there around eight thirty?"

She got off the phone with Kathryn and wished she had taken her concerns more seriously. Cache had this instinct to look after people, but she also had to care for Duke, who had spent most of the past week alone in a beach house. The thought of something hidden behind the bookcase had been in the back of her mind all day. She rationalized now that she owed it to Kathryn to check it out. What if it provided a means into the house bypassing the security? If Rachel knew about it, she could easily get to Kathryn in her sleep.

Cache left the restaurant, thanking Kane, Vivian and Austin for their help. She ran back to the ferry dock as fast as she could. Cache got there just after five thirty, and she spotted the ferry out on the water heading away from the island. It would be another few hours before she would be back in her truck, and she knew she needed to go see Duke first or he might end up tearing up Vanny's beach house.

It was nine o'clock when she pulled into the beach house.

She had called Kathryn to tell her she was delayed and would be there as soon as she could. The lights were on in the house, and she couldn't recall if she had left a light or two on or whether they were on timers. She hopped into the back of her truck, grabbed her M9 from storage and walked slowly up to the front door. She peered inside but could see no sign of Duke. Cache punched in the door code and made her way quietly into the front hallway. Everything was still except for the sound of the ocean crashing on the shore. She walked through the front of the house and then, as quietly as she could, she made her way to the second floor. No sign of Duke; she was growing concerned. She heard a noise coming from the master bedroom. As she turned the doorknob and entered, she spotted a single black suitcase with air travel tags on it and looked up to see Vanny sitting in her lounge chair looking over her shoulder, holding a glass of wine in one hand and rubbing Duke's ear with the other.

"You going to shoot me or join me?" she asked.

"I thought you were a burglar."

Vanny said, "I told you I was coming home in a few days, so why don't you get cleaned up, and then you and I will go out on the town."

"I need to get him out for a walk."

"Already taken care of. I've been home for a few hours. We went for a long walk; now he's just mellow."

Cache tucked her M9 in the back of her pants and walked over, sat on the lounge chair next to Vanny, grabbed her wine-glass and emptied the contents into her mouth.

"Thirsty?"

"I've got a lot to tell you, you might want to get another glass."

Cache shared everything that had happened to her in detail, from the time that she'd dropped Vanny off at the airport to what she'd learned while sitting in Daphne's bistro. She told her about George Wilkes, Rachel, Jonathan, Detective Murphy, Jake, Freddy and of course Kathryn. As Cache detailed everything for her, Vanny was glued to the story like she was watching her favorite soap opera, and she was on her third glass of wine when Cache finished filling her in.

"Well?" Cache asked.

"I'm speechless. You had sex with a woman! An older woman!"

"That's what you got from what I just told you?"

"I got the other stuff. You and I have serious differences of opinion about how to have a relaxing vacation."

"So, what should I do?"

"Why are you asking me? Are you in love with her?"

"My head's a mess right now, I have no idea, but I'm afraid she could be in danger and I don't think she thinks it's that serious."

"Are you planning on moving here to look out for her?"

Cache didn't respond. Vanny had hit on one truth of the situation. She would go home shortly, and Kathryn would need to look out for herself.

Vanny said, "Look, I don't know Kate—"

"Kathryn."

"Okay, Kathryn, but maybe this is just a fling, no different from when we hooked up with those guys at that frat party; it wasn't serious, it was just fun. And then when you throw in a killer... seriously, if I were you, I would get in my truck and head back to Hart."

"I don't think I could live with myself if I did that and something happened."

"So, what is your plan?"

"If you can look after Duke, I want to go back to her place tonight. I need to figure out that thing with the bookcase. That way, if it is an entrance into the house, at least I can warn her."

"I don't know if I like your plan. How about you try something else?"

"Vanny..."

"I think you are putting yourself too much at risk."

"I will check in with you tomorrow morning and let you know everything is okay. If, for some reason, you don't hear from me, I want you to call Jake and tell him everything. If I know him, he'll be there with a SWAT team in no time flat.

"Hey, Duke, come over here."

Duke got up and walked over to where Cache was seated.

"Hey, boy, I'm sorry, but I have to leave you again. I want you to know it's not because of you. Vanny will be here to keep you company." She looked up at Vanny. "Thanks for keeping an eye on him. I have felt so guilty the past few days, leaving him here by himself." She reached over and grabbed Vanny by the hand and squeezed it tight.

"You be safe, and if I don't hear from you by noon tomorrow, I'm calling the cavalry."

18

At ten forty-five p.m., Cache rolled into Kathryn's driveway. The weather had shifted since that afternoon; a combination of cold fronts and warm fronts over the area was producing fog in patches. The white floodlights on the house and the mist moving around Cache created a scene out of a horror film where a naive young woman with only a few lines gets hers when she ventures into the basement. She had put her pistol back in the lockbox, fully loaded, in the event she needed to get to it. Cache had contemplated bringing it into the house with her, but she didn't know how Kathryn would react and whether it would be safe to have it in there.

Cache rang the doorbell and Freddy answered it. "Looks like the fog has set in. How was your drive?"

"Visibility was poor in some spots, others it was okay. Where's Kathryn?"

"Kitchen. We had a late dinner. She thought you would be over earlier, but we couldn't wait; sorry."

The two talked as they walked toward the kitchen, Cache glancing over at the two vases, hoping that no one had discovered her lock pick set.

"Sorry I'm late, Vanny got home from her trip and we had some catching up to do."

"No need to apologize, you didn't have to come over. We could have connected tomorrow," Kathryn said.

"I wanted to come, today was just swamped. I missed the ferry I wanted to catch, so that delayed me; luckily Vanny got home and got Duke out, so here I am."

Kathryn walked over and touched the inside of her wrist and kissed her on the cheek. "Well, I am glad you came."

Cache walked over to the kitchen table and sat herself down. Freddy had hopped up on one of the kitchen islands; he had shorts on, and his bare legs and feet hung off the side. Kathryn stood behind the sink, a red wineglass in her hand.

"How was work?"

"Not good. People have been watching the news and then calling to cancel appointments."

"Have they found her yet?"

"Not going to," Freddy said with a smug look on his face.

"Why do you say that?"

"Yeah, Freddy, why do you say that?" Kathryn said in a somewhat irritated tone.

"She's a smart woman. She will lie low until the heat dies down and then get out of town. At least, that's what I would do."

"Well, I have known her for a while, and she is not that clever, so I suspect they will find her sooner or later. Cache, why don't we turn in, it's getting late. Freddy, would you be a dear and make sure you lock everything up securely and put the alarm on? We don't want uninvited intruders in the middle of the night."

"Aye aye, Captain," he said, saluting her.

Cache and Kathryn retired upstairs as Freddy walked to the front of the house, looked at the security panel to see that nothing was amiss and put the alarm on. The two women got ready for bed. While Kathryn was in the bathroom brushing her teeth, Cache set her smartwatch to give her a vibration in the morning. She laid out her shorts and T-shirt on a small gold chair with a puffy cushion close to the table so she would be able to locate them in the dark. Cache peered through the drapes to the balcony, looking down at the backyard. The fog was creeping over the pool and only a few of the garden lights shone through. Kathryn emerged from the washroom and said, "It's all yours if you want it." Cache grabbed the toothbrush and toothpaste that she had brought along as Kathryn climbed into bed and pulled out a book from her nightstand to read. Cache took care of everything that needed to be done, turned off the lights and tucked herself under the covers. It looked like they were a married couple. Kathryn continued to read for a while, and Cache was concerned that she might still be awake when Cache hoped to go and explore the study. Kathryn sensed Cache's desire to turn off the lights after a busy day, and the women snuggled together until they drifted off.

Buzz, buzz, buzz. Cache woke to her wrist vibrating. She lifted her arm to see the time was now three o'clock a.m. She gazed over at Kathryn, who had rolled to her other side. Cache tried to move out of the bed quietly and hoped that Kathryn wasn't lying there with her eyes wide open, alert for any sudden movement. She grabbed her shorts and T-shirt and threw them on and walked to the other side of the bed. Kathryn looked like she was in a deep state of slumber, which worked well for what Cache had to do. She walked into the hallway, closing the door behind her, and stared down the hall to Freddy's room but saw no sign of any light coming from it. She maneuvered herself down the stairs in a crouched position until she was certain that no lights were flickering from the gaming room below. Freddy was more than likely out for the night. Cache crawled to the vases and reached inside. At first, she couldn't feel her lock pick pouch and feared it had been discovered, but as she moved her hand around inside, she touched the edge of it and grabbed it. Her flashlight was easier to find, and she should have retrieved it first, as it would have made finding the black nylon pouch a lot easier.

She kept low and moved over to the study door. She pressed her ear against the door but heard nothing from the other side and went to work with her lock pick, getting the door open in only a few minutes. Not bad, Iron, she thought.

Once inside, she closed the door and secured the dead bolt. Cache panned the flashlight around the room. Everything looked the same as it had last night. She walked over to the far bookcase and ran her hand along the seam. There was still a slight breeze, and as she placed her nose against the bookcase, she could pick up a musty smell that she didn't notice anywhere else in the room.

Cache removed the medical textbooks on the first shelf and then touched all sides of the bookcase, waiting for something to happen, but nothing did. She did the same for the remaining three shelves of books, pulling them out, touching all around the bookcase, but the wall remained still. She was convinced that the removal of one of the books would open the door—after all, it worked in the movies.

Cache stood back after removing all the contents and then put them back in the exact same order so that her work wouldn't be discovered. She moved the flashlight over the exterior face of the bookcase, noting the hand-carved flowers in each of the corners. Cache had a hunch and went to the far corner and pressed in the flower with her thumb, leaving her thumb feeling sore and the bookcase still fixed to the wall. She moved to the corner on the top right and pressed in with her thumb. This time, she heard a click.

The bookcase popped out about three inches from the surrounding wooden face, and she pulled it forward. She was hit in the face with a damp, musty smell that made her bare arms feel clammy. She shone the flashlight into the darkness behind the bookcase. A set of stairs made of gray stone led down into the darkness. The walls and the arched ceiling were composed of gray stone blocks. From the position of the staircase, Cache determined that it led somewhere under the front lawn of the house. The beam of her flashlight caught cobwebs moving from a breeze coming up from the blackness and then reflected off of some glass near the ceiling on the left-hand side. Cache scanned the walls with her flashlight, spotted a brown circular switch and flipped it on.

Twelve old-fashioned lightbulbs lit up the descending staircase, which ended about a dozen steps down. Cache looked back at the bookcase, noted a brass lever on the back of it and pulled it closed behind her. She made her way down the staircase. The stones were moist, and her bare feet felt damp as she moved along them to arrive at a steel cage door at the bottom. There was rust wherever she looked and darkness beyond it. She listened to see if she could hear something, and her light caught a mouse running across the stone floor. From the angle she was at, it looked like a storage area of sorts. Several wooden crates were stacked in one corner, a table in the middle, and a series of brass rings were drilled into the opposite wall about ten feet apart. Cache grabbed the metal cage door to swing it aside, but it would not budge. Cache examined the lock, pulled out her lock pick set and went to work. The lock was tougher than most and it took her about twenty minutes before she could get the door open.

Cache walked into the room and moved her flashlight beam from wall to wall. There were a few metal tables scattered throughout the space. Bookshelves lined one far wall, and a large steel cage could be seen at the other end of the room. Cache noted similar glass fixtures in the ceiling and believed there was likely a light switch somewhere in the room, or that a wire was disconnected from the main line in the stairs. Near one bookshelf, Cache found a similar brown switch to that which appeared at the top of the stairs, and the lights came on in the room. A few mice ran to the corner of the room, and dust and cobwebs could be seen everywhere. She looked around; there was no other door, no other entry points. Several of the wooden crates had the names of distillers painted on the side, now faded from the damp air. This must have been where they stored their liquor during prohibition, she thought. When a voice came from the area at the back of the room surrounded by a metal cage, Cache moved in the voice's direction and pushed the flashlight through the metal bars. There were a metal cot, some plates on the ground and, in the corner, dirty, hair a mess, clothes torn in a few spots, curled up in a ball and muttering to herself, was Rachel Armstrong.

"Rachel," Cache called out to her, but all she got in return was verbal dribble. Cache scanned the room she was being held in and noted a couple of bottles of water closest to the door. She picked one up to examine it. The seal had been broken, and while the water was close to the fill line, there was a noxious smell coming from it; someone had mixed something in with it, likely to keep Rachel in a comatose state. "Rachel, who brought you here?" Rachel was not forthcoming with any answers. She thought about Freddy's odd comment about her being found earlier in the evening. "Did Freddy bring you here?" She grunted. Cache was certain that meant "yes". She needed to get Rachel out of here, get to Kathryn and call the police.

The door to Rachel's prison was locked with a thick steel chain and padlock. Cache made quick work of the lock and it sprang open. She moved inside the cage and hoisted Rachel up over her shoulder. At this point, she didn't care about the lights and made her way up the stairs, opening the bookcase and moving out into the study. She burst into the room, uncertain whether Freddy could be waiting there; she hadn't thought this through. The room was deserted. She lowered Rachel down into one of the high-backed chairs and went over to the desk. In leaving the bedroom upstairs, she had forgotten to bring her smartphone with her. Cache spotted a cordless phone sitting on the desk and picked it up. "Please have a dial tone, please have a dial tone."

Cache punched in 911 and hoped that her using the phone would not be detected elsewhere in the household.

"What's your emergency?"

"I need the police."

"Can you tell me what the issue is?"

"I've got Rachel Armstrong in my possession, the killer they're looking for. Can you get ahold of Detective Murphy and let him know? My name is Cache Iron."

"Can I have your address?" Cache gave her the details and advised her that Rachel had been held captive and that she believed Freddy Jamieson was who the police really wanted.

The dispatcher asked Cache to wait on the line until the police arrived, but Cache told her that the safest plan was to get Rachel out of there and that she would take her down to the gates.

Cache looked around the room. There was no button to open the front gates, and the only one she had ever spied in the house was in the kitchen, beside a screen connected to a camera that was positioned on one gatepost. She moved over to where Rachel was and picked her back up. She would have to be quick to avoid getting caught. Cache opened the study door and made a beeline for the front door of the house. She threw open the dead bolt and glanced at the red light on the security system. This will wake up a few people, she thought.

She grabbed hold of the doorknob and threw open the door. The alarm screamed, and she ran as fast as she could with a woman over her shoulder down the driveway to the front gates. She imagined the security company would also be en route soon and she should have enough backup to deal with the situation. Cache found an area next to the front wall that had a couple of shrubs and pulled Rachel in against the wall, sitting her up so she would remain concealed until help arrived.

She waited for a few minutes but saw no sign of the security company. Cache ran up toward the house. Most of the lights were on in the rooms, but the front door was now closed. Cache moved to where she had parked her truck, crawled into the bed and retrieved her gun and a pair of handcuffs. Tucking the gun into the back of her shorts and the handcuffs into her pocket, she hopped down and looked around. The fog had lifted a bit, but there was still some fuzziness in the air. Cache made her way to the door to the kitchen but did not hear any alarm going off. It all sounded quiet. She pulled out her lock pick set and played with the lock. She had used the set more that night than any other night. As she pulled the door open, the alarm screamed again, and she ran to the area of the kitchen where the button for the front gate was positioned. She slammed her hand against the button and could see from the monitor that the gates were opening up. The alarm stopped, the phone rang and then there was silence.

She pulled her gun from the back of her shorts and moved out into the front hall of the home. Cache passed the door to the study, but it was now closed. She drifted from room to room, monitoring all the corners, as she returned to the front hall. Cache spotted Freddy coming down the stairs with some object in his hand.

"Stop there," she said.

"What the fuck are you doing?" he asked. "This is my home."

"I want you to get down here on your knees, the police are on their way."

"Good, I'm going to have your ass arrested."

As Cache moved closer, he could see the handgun she was holding. She had him kneel on the ground with his legs crossed in the back and fingers behind his head, enabling her to get the handcuffs on him and leave him facedown in the hallway.

"Where is she?"

"Where's who?"

"Kathryn, what have you done with her?"

Cache raced up the stairs, taking two at a time, until she reached the top. Placing both hands around the grip of her gun, she went from room to room, checking closets, bathrooms, screaming out Kathryn's name, but she couldn't locate her. Cache went back to the master bedroom; someone had pulled the covers back from the bed, and in the closet a small cabinet drawer was open in the center island. She ran downstairs and kicked Freddy in the side.

"Where did you put her, you piece of shit?"

"I did nothing with her."

Cache ran down the stairs to the entertainment room and scoured the rest of the rooms, looking for Kathryn, to no avail. She made her way back up to the main floor; Freddy had rolled over on his back and was looking up at her. "Lose something?" he said, and laughed. Cache continued on the main floor going from room to room, but she could not locate Kathryn. Could she be in one of the outside buildings or in the garage? Cache looked back at the study. She ran to it, grabbed the doorknob and pushed the door in. It was unlocked.

"Kathryn, are you in here?"

The room was empty as Cache surveyed all the areas, but the bookcase was back locked against the wall. She went over to it and pushed the upper right-hand flower in, and the door sprang open. The lights were still on as she made her way down the stairs, but the metal cage door was shut. She spotted something at the bottom and turned on her flashlight, focusing a beam of light into the corner. A large stone block had been put up against the steel cage door and the room beyond was dark again. Cache pushed her face through the bars, looking into the darkness, until she noticed a small red burning ember about twenty feet away from her. She aimed her flashlight in that direction and saw Kathryn sitting on one of the metal tables smoking a cigarette in the dark.

"What are you doing in here? I captured Freddy. Come, let's get you to safety."

Kathryn hopped down off the table, walked over to the light switch and flicked on the lights. She tossed the cigarette to the stone floor and ran her fingers through her long red hair. She was dressed, wearing blue jeans, white tennis shoes and a blouse. A small white duffel bag sat on one table. She walked within ten feet of Cache.

"I see you let my pet out. Now, why would you do that?"

"What are you talking about? I got Freddy upstairs handcuffed, the police are on their way, you don't have to cover for him."

Kathryn stood back and put her hand over her mouth. "You don't get it. Man, I love you."

"Get what?" Cache said.

"This. Do you think Freddy is smart enough to pull this off?"

Cache, in that moment, realized that it wasn't Freddy but her. "Why?"

"Doesn't matter."

"How?"

"If you get Freddy in police custody, I'm sure he will share some details with you. I never saw that boy lasting long in an interrogation."

"Listen, give yourself up, you can get a lawyer."

"And do what? At my age they will lock me up for life and what are you going to do? Are you going to move here from Montana to visit me on the weekends? No, you would visit every week or so, then every few months, then maybe once a year, and then I'd be a forgotten memory. I will be in a concrete box smaller than this room for the rest of my life. No, I like my freedom."

"Kathryn, where are you going to go? The only exit is up these stairs, and I'm sure the police will not stand by and let you leave."

"Cache, if I can impart one piece of wisdom to you: always have a backup plan."

Kathryn walked over to the table. Cache looked at the cage door. It might take her another twenty minutes to pick the lock, but removing the stone would take more time. Kathryn picked up her bag.

"Cache, a few years from now you might get a postcard from some far-off land. If you're interested, come visit."

Kathryn walked over to one of the brass rings embedded in the far wall and gave it a tug. A portion of the wall opened up to reveal a tunnel. She clicked a switch on the wall and Cache could see lights from where she stood. Kathryn blew her a kiss and pulled the stone door shut behind her.

"How many passageways does this house have?" Cache asked.

She turned and ran up the stairs and intercepted Detectives Murphy and Johnston in the main hallway with four uniformed police officers.

"Mind telling us what is going on here?"

"You got it all wrong. Rachel wasn't the killer, she was just another victim."

"Where is she?"

"She is sitting up against a wall at the main gate behind some shrubs. She's pretty heavily sedated, I think he had something to do with that" she said as she kicked Freddy's foot.

"So, he is the killer?"

"No, I think Kathryn Jamieson is behind the killings."

"Where is she?"

"I don't know, she just went down a tunnel that must run out somewhere on the property. The entrance is blocked."

"You there, go find Ms. Armstrong and call an ambulance," he said as he pointed to one uniformed officer. To another he said, "You take care of him"—he pointed to Freddy—"and the rest of us will fan out, see if we can figure where the rabbit hole Ms. Jamieson might pop out of is."

19

In the time since the police had arrived and assessed the situation, Kathryn had realized she needed to leave Los Angeles as quickly as possible. The tunnel that led from the storage area to the edge of the property had been used to smuggle liquor into the house during prohibition. It ran underneath the property and came up where a large twelve-foot cedar hedge surrounded the grounds, allowing her to exit beyond the property line to a small side street used by city workers to collect garbage from some nearby homes. It was now nearing six o'clock a.m. The sun was rising and the advantage the darkness would have provided her had all but disappeared. She walked down the alleyway, putting as much distance as she could between herself and her home, and rounded the corner onto a small street with some funky little shops and a dry cleaner that she had used on several occasions.

One of her few friends had always told her to have a "go bag" handy in case she ever needed to flee a situation in a hurry. Filled with certain essentials, it helped to prevent you from losing valuable time looking for items at the last minute. Kathryn ducked down an alleyway and put her duffel bag on top of a large green metal dumpster with dents in the sides and patches of rust that had yet to be emptied, as yesterday's deposits reeked in the air. She opened up her bag, which held a few useful items. Kathryn had ten thousand dollars in cash, in separate stacks in a variety of denominations. With credit card usage, the authorities could track your whereabouts; with cash, not so much. She grabbed for a Glock 43 that rested in the bag's bottom. Kathryn had spent many days at the local gun club becoming one with this device, and now she pulled it out and tucked it down in her jeans, flipping her blouse over it. She had a couple of burner phones, hair dye, and a small medical kit with sutures, a scalpel, a syringe and two vials filled with a street drug called Wild Monkey, which knocked a person out immediately.

Taped to the inside of the bag was a phone number in pencil. She pulled it off the inside of the bag and grabbed a burner phone and dialed the number. She had been given the number to use only in extreme emergencies, and the predicament that she found herself in would count.

The number rang and rang for a few minutes before a voice answered.

"Welcome to Lunar Tradicity. At the sound of the beep, please enter your consultant's code."

Kathryn typed in the numbers 29734, handwritten below the telephone number, and pressed the pound sign.

"One moment, we are attempting to connect you with your consultant, thank you for using Lunar Tradicity, your business is our business."

The extension rang three or four times before a female voice answered.

"This better be good, Kathryn."

"How did you know it was me?"

"You're the only one with that code," Nina Mayhem said in

her slight British accent, diluted from years of living in the United States.

"Nina, I'm in trouble."

"Well, what type of trouble are you in?" Nina asked.

"Murder, conspiracy to commit murder, kidnapping—I think those are the highlights."

There was a pause; Kathryn worried she would just hang up.

"I take it this wasn't a surgical procedure gone wrong?"

"No," Kathryn said.

"Well, darling, everybody murders someone at some point in their life; not that big a deal." Kathryn was a little taken aback by her statement, as if Nina didn't appreciate the gravity of the situation. "So, darling, the first thing we need to do is to get you out of Los Angeles. I would come get you myself, but I'm in Idaho."

"What are you doing in Idaho?"

"New and up-and-coming artist, you wouldn't believe what he paints with, but that is for another day. No, you need to be away from Los Angeles as soon as possible. It won't be long before every police officer is keeping an eye out for you. Did you create a go bag, like I told you?"

"Yep, I have it here. Once Cache figured out my secret, I knew she would call the cops. I grabbed it and got out of there."

"Cache ratted you out? You two do have an interesting relationship. Do you have a place you can go and lie low until we can get you out of the country?"

"Yes, it's a ways from here."

"Do you have a car stashed somewhere?"

"No."

"No! Someone wasn't paying attention. Do you know how to hot-wire a car?"

"I'm a surgeon, not a car thief."

"Well, one could kind of see the similarities there, messing around in the inside of things. Okay, in a nutshell we need to find someone to give you a car; you can't rent one without a credit card and the police will be watching your cards."

Kathryn could hear her humming for a few minutes as she contemplated the situation.

"Okay, I have an idea. You need to get laid."

"I think that is what got me into this predicament."

"Well, that's not what I'm thinking. You see, dear, there is an area of the city where men like to pull up in their cars, hoping a pretty girl will climb in and then do all sorts of things to them for cash."

"You want me to be a hooker?"

"I want you to get in someone's car and shove a gun in their ribs. You have a gun, right?"

"Yeah."

"Good. Then I want you to have him take you somewhere dark and out of the way and then dispose of him."

"You want me to kill him?"

"I want you to get his car; you can screw him for all I care. Look, this is what you do: if you don't want to hurt him, take all of his clothes, cell phone, wallet, etc. It will be some time before he reports what happened to him. Try to look for an older model; newer ones have GPS and the internet, which will make tracking you easier. Then drive halfway to your destination, until you can find an area like a truck stop, where you may be able to steal something else, and then make it to your destination."

"Okay, I think I can do that."

"Kathryn, you have to do that. The longer you're in Los Angeles, the greater your risk of being caught. Did you set up an offshore bank account?"

"Yep, I did that a few years ago."

"All right, I need you to hang up, take a deep breath and destroy the phone you are on, but don't lose my number. When you get to your destination, I want you to call me with your coordinates. I will need to find a small airfield somewhere where I can get you a plane and a pilot to fly you out of US airspace and take you down to São Paulo, where my people will get you to where you want to go."

"Nina, thank you for doing this for me."

"Sistas got to stick together. I will wait for your call."

Nina hung up.

———

Kathryn got off the phone and threw it to the ground, watching it smash. She kicked the remains underneath the green metal dumpster, hearing them skid along the ground. Kathryn poked around inside of her duffel bag and found an elastic band to tie her hair into a ponytail, a baseball cap and a pair of sunglasses. She took Nina's phone number and taped it back on the inside of her bag and pulled out enough cash to cover her cab rides for the day. While Nina's plan had merit, it meant she had to wait until dark, when hungry men would leave their wives to go buy milk and instead cruise the city blocks looking for a good time. Kathryn figured she would go hang out down at the beach, take in the sun until it got dark and then grab a cab into the downtown core to an area frequented by streetwalkers.

After a day of avoiding eye contact with every stranger that came near her, she hailed a cab and had them take her to an area of the city that was crawling with sex. Whenever they came in the line of sight of a police cruiser, she looked the other way, and she never looked at the cab's mirror, where it was standard to have a camera filming passengers in the back-seat to protect the driver. As they approached the area where she stood the best chance of catching her ride, she had the driver drop her off and provided a generous enough tip that he would forget he'd even seen her. Kathryn slipped into an alleyway, pulled a few hundred in cash from one stack in the bag and tucked her gun in the back of her jeans, down far enough so the edge of the grip could not be seen by a passerby. She pulled off her bra and tied her blouse into a halter top, frizzed out her hair and made her way down the street. After a few blocks she noticed girls in three-inch stiletto boots, short shirts and see-through tops with frizzed-out hair. Every ethnicity was there, no one was excluded; there were even men pretending to be women. The street was dirty based on the standards that Kathryn was used to, with alleyways where behind-the-scenes deals were going down and hookers could take their clients. This area of the city attracted all types, the homeless, the pick-pockets, the tourists. There were older, run-down stores and cheap hotels where a room could be rented for the evening for the price of a burger and a drink. Kathryn could see neon signs in hot pink and blue in windows and on rooftops. Hustlers stood in the archways of doors giving their women directions, while others sat in their cars in darkened alleyways, taking their cut from the girls for their managerial services.

Cars traveled up the street honking, their passengers screaming from their windows as they passed by.

"Show us your tits!" came from a late-model sedan with a bunch of horny teenage boys protruding from the windows. The city had turned this street into one-way years ago to limit the number of cars that it would see at night. Uniformed police could be spotted every now and again, roaming up and down the sidewalks, there to ensure everyone kept the peace.

Kathryn knew the vice squad frequented this area, and the last thing she needed to do was get picked up on a soliciting charge, only for them to learn she was wanted for much more serious crimes. As she walked down the street, she noticed a late-model black SUV pulled to the side with its blinkers going and a tall black girl in white go-go boots, a tiny pair of white shorts and a fluorescent green tube top with large boobs and long blond frizzy hair leaning in on the passenger-side window. Kathryn just wanted to get this done and over with and be on her way to where she would feel safe and could plan out the next phase of her life.

She pushed up alongside her and could feel her skin on hers and looked at the man sitting behind the wheel. He was older, maybe in his late forties. Black curly hair and a black mustache, tanned skin that made his gold wedding ring stand out. He appeared to have a bit of gut as it tucked itself under the steering wheel. The woman next to her smelled like a mix of body odor and cheap perfume.

Kathryn flashed him a smile.

"Hi, I'm Kate and I'm super horny, can you help me?" The words sickened her as they came out of her mouth.

"Skank, what do you think you are doing? Get your old dried-up skin away from here."

Kathryn ignored the competition. "What do you want, sweetheart? I'll give you anything you want for twenty bucks."

"Did you say twenty bucks?" he asked.

"Yeah, I'm super horny and you're super cute."

"Bitch, get out of my face. I'm warning you, this is my turf. If you don't leave now, I'm going to tell Boney Tony about you, and he will mess up that charming little face of yours. You won't be working this street corner ever again."

"Well, sugar, your decision." Kathryn looked back and pretended to see a police car coming. "Looks like the fuzz is coming. What do you want to do?" The girl next to her, at the mention of police approaching, decided she didn't need to be charged that night and walked away from the vehicle, giving Kathryn her best angry face.

The man started checking his driver's-side mirror, beads of sweat forming on his forehead, and Kathryn feared he might just pull away from the curb. She would have to try again with someone else and possibly contend with someone named

Boney Tony. This was like being on the one-yard line and going for it. She couldn't lose. She reached into the door, opened it up and hopped in, throwing her bag to her feet.

"What are you doing?" he asked.

Kathryn pulled up her top to reveal her tits. "These need your attention"—she reached over and patted his crotch with her hand—"and I need this big guy inside of me."

The thought of oncoming police left the driver's mind, and he pulled out from his parked position. Kathryn leaned out the window and looked at the tall black girl, extended her arm and gave her the finger. If all worked out right, she would never see this street corner again.

―――――

As they drove along, Kathryn tried to make small talk with the driver. He told her his name was Hank; not really imaginative. If you are going to cheat on your wife, why not call yourself Valentino? She suggested they find a dark alleyway, away from everything, so she could give him what he was looking for. He eventually came across a shadowy lane, the wet road reflecting two lights attached to the exterior of the building on the left. To the right was a large concrete retaining wall with a fence up on top and graffiti painted everywhere. As the vehicle ambled down the alley, the headlights caught sight of rats and cats running from its path. He found a spot behind some office or restaurant that lacked any light, pulled into the blackness and turned off his lights, put the vehicle in park and let it idle. Kathryn reached over and turned off the radio. She could hear his breathing becoming heavier and wasn't certain whether this might be the first time he had done something like this. Kathryn reached over with her left hand and rubbed his crotch. She could feel something squirm underneath his khaki pants. As he stared down, watching her hand, she slipped her right hand down into the back of her pants and pulled out her gun and rested it under her leg with the grip facing the door.

"I noticed the ring on your finger. What's her name?"

"Why?"

"You might just want to call me that, so, you know, you don't say the wrong name when you get home."

"Donna, you can be Donna."

"What do you want Donna to do to you?" Kathryn started to have fun playing Donna.

"You said twenty bucks, right?" His voice sounded dry and high-pitched as he got the last word out.

"I'm going to do this for free. Donna wants you to fuck her hard, can you do that?"

He didn't make a sound, just nodded his head up and down like a bobblehead on a salesman's desk.

Kathryn reached over and pushed the interior lights on.

"What are you doing? People can see us."

Kathryn looked around and asked, "Who? How is Donna going to get that fly down with her teeth if she can't see it?"

As he adjusted himself, taking off his jacket and unbuttoning his shirt, Kathryn pulled out her Glock and pressed it into his ribs.

"I think you're going to get screwed tonight, just not how you had hoped."

He looked down at the gun and looked at her.

"Please don't kill me, you can have whatever you want, just please don't hurt me. Kathryn reached over with her left hand, turned off the ignition and removed the car keys.

"Hank, this is what I want you to do: I want you to take out your wallet slowly and put it on the dash, then I want you to step out of the vehicle. Can you do that?"

Hank complied with her request, got out of the vehicle and moved about fifteen feet back from it. Kathryn slid herself into the driver's seat, turned on the vehicle, locked the doors and rolled down the driver's-side window.

"Now, Hank, Donna has to run an errand, but I want to be able to fantasize about your body, so how about doing a little show for Donna? Take your pants off and throw them over by the front tire."

"Please don't do this."

"Donna doesn't want to get mad; do you want Donna to get angry?" she said, raising her handgun in the event he had forgotten its presence in the situation. Hank kicked off his shoes to get his pants off. She ordered him to remove everything he had left on him until he stood there, a middle-aged guy with a potbelly in a pair of stained boxer shorts with little smiling faces on them.

Kathryn instructed him to back up even further, stepped out of the vehicle, retrieved his clothes and threw them into the backseat. She ordered him to run in the opposite direction and waited until he was out of sight. Kathryn rolled up the window, locked her doors and continued down the alleyway in the opposite direction, hanging a left when she came to a cross street, and drove up a few blocks before pulling over to the side into an empty street-parking space. She grabbed a paper map of Los Angles from her duffel bag and identified the street she was on. Kathryn needed to find Interstate 5 to start her on the right path to her destination.

Kathryn grabbed the wallet from the dash and looked at the driver's license. The owner's actual name was Charles; he belonged to a couple of social organizations, from the membership cards she spotted, and had a wife and two kids. Bastard, she thought. He had one hundred and twenty dollars in cash, all in twenties, and a couple of credit cards. She kept his driver's license and cash and tossed the remaining contents out onto the street. Kathryn considered calling Donna to let her know what her husband was up to, but she had more pressing matters to deal with. Maybe she would mail his driver's license to her with a quick note about how she had come into possession of it.

She had a good idea how to reach the interstate from where she was parked and ensured she drove the speed limit all the way out of Los Angeles so as not to raise the eyebrows of any police officers in the area. Kathryn turned up the radio, looking for a station that played classical music. She had put her baseball cap back on, tying her hair in a ponytail. Kathryn tapped her fingers on the steering wheel as she drove. All of it was a rush. Kathryn saw the city lights growing dimmer in her rearview mirror as she drove eastward to her destination. This might be the last time that she would see this city in her lifetime, and she was okay with that.

20

C ache woke to the sun beaming into her window, the smell of the salty ocean air filling the room, and one cheerful dog. She glanced over at a white enameled alarm clock with red numbers ticking on the nightstand and saw that it was just past two o'clock in the afternoon. Cache stroked Duke's head; she had fallen asleep in Vanny's guest room this morning after spending a few hours with Detectives Murphy and Johnston bringing them up to speed on what she had learned over the past few days leading up to the events of the prior night.

Similar to her father after she had left one of the ranch gates open at the age of five, Detective Murphy scolded her for not coming to them sooner with the information that she had discovered, and said her actions could have gotten her killed, a speech she had heard from her own parents through most of her life. She got up, showered and walked downstairs, where Vanny had her laptop open and was watching television on low volume.

"Any news?" Cache asked.

"About your friend or in general?"

"You know, you were never this funny in college."

"The news has aired a few times to tell viewers that Rachel Armstrong was found and that the police wanted to thank private investigator Cache Iron for helping bring her home safely to her family."

Cache dropped herself in a chair opposite Vanny and pulled her knees close to her chest. "They didn't say that, did they? They didn't say my name?"

Vanny snickered. "I hate to tell you this, but you're famous."

"Why?"

"You saved a woman's life and you may have solved the pinup murders; that's big news. I caught even the husband on camera wanting to thank you for all your help."

"Jonathan said that?"

"Yeah, and they said that woman Rachel would make a statement later, so she might even thank you. This is your fifteen minutes, girl."

"So why do I feel horrible?"

Vanny set her laptop down on the couch beside her, stood up and walked over to Cache, putting her hand on Cache's shoulder. "Because the villain in this case was someone you cared about."

"Have they found her?"

"If they have, they're not saying. Would you like a cup of coffee? I'm making myself one."

"Sure."

Cache grabbed for her smartphone. She had left it charging while she went upstairs and lay down this morning. She had received many calls. The first was from her mother, insisting she call her the first chance she got. Jake was the next call, insisting she call him the first chance she got. Her mother, addressing her by her first name, Julie, which she only used to grab Cache's attention, was the third call. The last call was from Detective Johnston, asking her to call when she had a chance.

At least someone wasn't demanding her immediate attention. Cache dealt with the easiest phone call first and called Detective Johnston.

The phone rang once, twice, and on the third ring a female voice answered.

"Detective Johnston, LAPD, how can I help you?"

"It's Cache calling, you called me?"

"Hey, how are you feeling? It must feel like you're living in a hurricane."

"I got some sleep and have been watching the news. Any word?"

"On Ms. Jamieson, nothing I can say officially, but if you were to come by in, say, a few hours, who knows what we might tell you."

"And Detective Murphy, will he be delivering the sermon?"

Detective Johnston laughed. "That's just his way. I can tell you there is some talk about giving you a citation for your efforts."

"Don't want it."

"Anyway, I know you were here until early this morning, but if you want to come back, I'm here until six o'clock and then I'm off for the night unless something further develops."

Cache hung up the phone and wondered what she couldn't tell her over the phone. Not knowing what had happened to Kathryn was driving her nuts, and she didn't think she could relax without knowing. She called her mother back, assuring her that she was never in any real danger and that she was all right. The phone got passed around, first to her father, who told her how proud he was of her and how happy he was that she was safe; next came her brother Tommy, who told her everyone in their small town of Hart was talking about it. After him came her brothers Cooper and Pauly, and then the phone went back to her mom, who wanted to know when she was coming home. After that call, she looked at Vanny, who had sat across from her with an amused look on her face and listened in on a rather intense conversation.

The next call was to Jake, who felt he needed to take Cache's mother's role and scolded her for being reckless and putting herself in a position that she had no control over. He wanted her to promise that she was done with it, but when Cache asked him when they'd gotten back together, that seemed to quiet him down.

When she hung up, she let out a gigantic sigh.

"That bad?"

"He thinks he's still my boyfriend."

"Maybe he should be."

"Don't start with that."

"What are you going to do?"

"I'm going to take Duke for a long walk, if you want to come, and then I'm going to head back to the police station; it's going to drive me crazy wondering what Detective Johnston couldn't tell me over the phone."

The two of them walked for about forty-five minutes down the boardwalk, stopping to talk with people whom Vanny knew. The beach was about half-filled and maybe a few dozen people could be spotted frolicking in the ocean waves as they crashed along the shore. They returned to the beach house, where Cache changed into her jeans and a T-shirt, wondering where her Def Leppard T-shirt had gotten to, and noticed that her duffel bag was missing. She then realized that after all that had happened the prior evening, she'd left it resting beside Kathryn's nightstand filled with sex toys.

———

It was about five thirty in the afternoon when Cache arrived at the headquarters of the Los Angeles Police Department. Cache made her way into the enormous building and asked a desk sergeant where to go and was instructed to go to the seventh floor. Eventually, after drifting around for about twenty minutes, she found the desks of Johnston and Murphy. Detective Murphy was out, and Detective Johnston sat at her computer keying information in from a file on her desk. Her desk was rather messy; stacks of papers and folders were bundled together in three separate piles. As Cache glanced around the room, many desks appeared similar. This differed from the army, where everything had a place and was expected to be there at any point in time. Detective Johnston looked like she had a tea—steam came from the top of a paper cup—with two protein bars to the side of it. A picture of her with a guy sat in a wooden frame at the edge of her desk.

"Is that your husband?"

"Yes, his name is Danny."

"How long have you been married?"

"About five years."

"It must be tough working all hours."

"Even more so since he's a fireman, but we make it work. So, you're probably wondering why I suggested you pop in."

"You got my curiosity up. Have you found her?"

"No, and we are not sure what we have gotten ourselves into."

"What do you mean by that?"

Detective Johnston looked around the room. A few of her fellow detectives were sitting at their desk or on the phone, but the room wasn't full of activity. She reached under Cache's chair and brought her in closer so they could talk more quietly.

"We found the entrance to the tunnel she escaped out of. It led to an alleyway behind the estate. We figured she left via that route. We got a warrant for camera footage in the area and caught sight of her in an alleyway behind a dry cleaner."

"What was she doing?"

"Talking on the phone to someone; you can then see her

throw the phone on the ground and kick it under the dumpster."

"Did you recover the phone?"

"Two uniformed officers found it this morning, broken in pieces. It looks like it was a burner phone used to call one number."

"Who was the call to?"

"Lunar Tradicity. Does it mean anything to you? Did Kathryn ever mention them?"

"No, never heard of them, why?"

"We called the phone number, and an automated voice message came on asking us for our consultant's number. So, we just kept pressing zero until we got a live attendant. We explained the reason for our call, identified ourselves, and they said someone would get back to us."

"And did they?"

"Yes." She motioned for Cache to lean in even closer. "The Justice Department called the chief of police about twenty minutes later, mentioning national security and charges of treason, and informing the chief that we were to lose that number and never speak of it again. We don't know who she called, but they have a lot of juice, so we can't pursue that angle."

Cache sat back and thought about all the things Kathryn had said to her and wondered if she knew who the person was that Kathryn had called.

"We got to thinking about a well-known, skilled cosmetic surgeon. Maybe her skills have been used by federal organizations in the past that now owe her a favor or two. So, we have no idea what we are up against trying to find her."

Detective Johnston explained that it was her opinion that the district attorney was not likely to want to take on a battle with the Justice Department if they didn't know what they were wading into.

Detective Murphy entered the detectives' department,

pulled up a metal chair and parked himself between Cache and Detective Johnston.

"Did she fill you in?"

"She told me about Lunar Tradicity."

"Shh, I wouldn't say that name too loud. I keep waiting for the feds to show up."

"Have you talked to Rachel or Freddy?"

Detective Johnston continued to key information into her computer as they discussed details of the case. Detective Murphy told Cache that Rachel was still in the hospital under a doctor's care and was slowly coming out of the catatonic state they had put her into with the sedatives. From what little they had been able to ask her at the present time, she remembered nothing about the abduction.

"Her doctors say she should make a full recovery, thanks to you."

"I have a gut feeling that she is still mixed up in this somehow."

"If your suspicions about her and Ms. Jamieson having a personal relationship are correct, then we will want to learn more about that. For now, her lawyers are hovering, telling the press that she will make a statement and not letting them know what their client is dealing with."

"What about Freddy? Did he lawyer up, or were you able to get anything from him?"

"Initially he wasn't saying anything without his counsel present, then when he learned he could face multiple murder charges and his aunt had flown the coop, his tongue seemed more cooperative."

Detective Murphy explained to Cache that Kathryn had made a copy of the key to the Armstrong residence once when they were out by pressing Rachel's house key into a block of wax that later could be used as a mold. Rachel hadn't changed her alarm code since the time she moved into Dr. Armstrong's residence, and most of her friends knew what the code was. She was also a creature of habit. Whenever she returned home after being out, she would go right to the kitchen and pull a bottle of white wine from the fridge and pour herself a glass. Knowing this information allowed Freddy to enter the home without setting off the alarm. He used a street drug called Wild Monkey and poured it into the open bottle of white wine and put it back in the fridge. That day he had somehow obtained the use of the van used by their pool company, and when Rachel returned home, alarm set, and spotted the pool guy out back cleaning the pool, nothing seemed out of place.

Then it was just a waiting game. He checked back periodically until he noticed Rachel passed out on the floor. He reentered the house, grabbed Mrs. Armstrong, put a section of pool hose around his shoulder so any cameras on the property wouldn't see him carry her out of the house or get a clear picture of his face. He then put her in the back of the van. There he taped her mouth shut and taped her wrists and ankles in the event she came to.

The rest of it was window dressing. He went into the house and grabbed the wineglass and bottle, poured the remaining wine out on the front lawn and put them in the back of the van for later disposal. He then went back into the house, opened a new bottle of white wine of the same label, poured out part of the contents and sat it down on the counter.

"I have to hand it to him. The plan was well thought out, almost genius."

"I'm pretty sure he wasn't the person who planned it."

The detective continued. Freddy had told them he took the glass out to the van, took the tape off Rachel's mouth and pressed it against her lips, and then retaped her mouth. He left tools that had been used in the pinup murders in the house and pressed her fingers onto the objects, which had previously been wiped clean of prints, so the only ones that would be found were hers.

They knew about Mrs. Armstrong's hiding place in her closet where she would keep drugs out of sight of her husband, and they planted the items there hoping we would find them. He then knocked the wineglass and wine bottle off of the counter so they would smash on the floor, turned over furniture throughout the house leading from the kitchen to the front door and dropped small drops of blood they had collected when Rachel had gone in for a surgical procedure.

Then he gathered everything up that could link him to being there, put it in the van, turned the alarm back on and left. He parked the van a few blocks away, snuck back to the house and broke the glass on the back of the kitchen door, causing the alarm to go off, and then snuck back to the van and left the area.

"And this would have just happened before I arrived?"

"Yes, he wanted the alarm company to respond and put things in motion. When no news came about the Pinup Killer, they dropped an anonymous call to the tip line suggesting that the abduction was payback for a drug debt. This forced us to enter the house with a K9 unit. We discovered the tools used by the Pinup Killer and presumed that this was not an abduction but a planned escape by the killer."

"You know, you should write a book about this," Cache said. "But do you know why they did this?"

"Not at this stage. I suspect, given his level of cooperation at this point, his attorneys want to see what deal they will offer for further cooperation. They are painting him as the pawn in the clutches of a supervillain."

"How is that possible?" Cache asked.

"He says they were sleeping together."

"What! Bullshit!"

"I am just telling you what he has told us. He's painting a

picture that she groomed him at a young age to do her bidding and she used sex to control him."

"I don't buy that at all."

"It's not you that has to buy it, it's the jury. They will paint her as the controlling monster, and him as just another victim."

Cache sat back in her seat, unhappy with the picture that Freddy was creating of his aunt. She wanted to know the why— why had a smart, intelligent woman gone down this path, killing four people and arranging the abduction of a fifth? This was not the person that she had gotten to know. Cache asked if she could pick up her duffel bag from the house or if someone could retrieve it for her. Detective Johnston told her that she would call the uniformed officers on the scene to allow her entry into the house, but they would need to inspect the contents before they allowed her to leave the premises.

Cache left the department and drove straight to Kathryn's home to collect her belongings. Vanny was insistent that they go out and have a good time now that she was home, but Cache felt like she needed to put some distance between her and Los Angeles and gather Duke up and head for home. She would encourage Vanny to come out her way in the coming months, as things like this didn't happen around Hart. Her plan was to spend another night with her college roommate and hang out at her place, get up in the morning, take one more long walk along the boardwalk and hitch up her trailer and hopefully make it to Oregon by nightfall. She'd stay overnight somewhere and then the next day would be on to Idaho and then across to Montana. As she approached the gates, a black-and-white cruiser was parked out front and a uniformed officer got out and checked her credentials. He then joined her in her vehicle as they drove up to the front of the house.

The house was still. The external lights had come on, flooding the exterior in a blanket of white light. The house itself was dark, showing no sign of anyone inside. The front door was unlocked; as they entered Cache flipped on the lights in the front hall. They walked down toward the drawing room and turned the lights on in the room. She looked at the large *Monja de Medianoche* canvas and thought the painting might have been making a statement to her the first time she saw it without realizing it. They left the room and walked down the darkened hall, turning the lights on in the rooms as they passed. She flipped on the lights in the kitchen, where they had had dinner together. The officer received a call and told Cache he needed to take this and stepped away from her.

Cache walked down the hall to the study. She had no reason to go there but felt drawn to the room nonetheless. The bookcase had been propped open with a box; the dampness of the underground tomb slowly had drifted into the study as yellow police tape blocked the entrance. She walked around the room and stopped behind Kathryn's desk, pulled out the chair and sat down in it. She pulled open the drawers to see what was inside. This was the first time she had been in the study with the lights on, and she stared at everything in the room. She looked at the pictures on the desk and a curious thought popped into her mind. Her mother was always writing details about photos on the backs of the pictures. Cache grabbed the one of the small cottage and pulled it out of the frame. Feeling the grainy texture of the photo in her hands, she flipped it over and it read *CLAYSON COTTAGE* in faded pencil. Cache grabbed her smartphone and took a picture of both sides of the photograph. She then grabbed the photo of Kathryn holding a small fish with her grandfather and pried it from the frame. The picture lacked the same grainy feeling and was smooth to the touch. Nothing was written on the back, but she could tell the photo was a photocopy. Cache put the pictures back together, returned them to their original positions on the desk and exited the room heading for the stairs. She spotted the officer in the front hall and pointed to the direction she was going. Holding up a finger to indicate she would only be a minute. She made her way upstairs to the master bedroom, throwing on all the lights. Her duffel bag was where she had left it, and she grabbed it and threw it on the bed. Cache glanced over at the table near the door leading to the balcony, reached for the photo of Kathryn holding a fish and pulled it from the frame. The picture felt grainy, and as she flipped it over, she could see a faded word on the back. She went into the bathroom and held the back of the picture up to the light as close as she could. In pencil it read, *PINE SPRINGS SILVER*.

21

Cache spent the night with Vanny and Duke. They ordered in pizza from a local shop, vegetarian for Vanny, meat lover's for Cache, though Vanny had only gone vegetarian since moving out to California. Cache had resisted doing anything with the name she'd found yesterday evening. She'd photographed both sides of the photo and reassembled the frame, returning it to where she had found it. When she'd left, the officer had inspected the duffel bag and asked that she turn out her pockets. The officer then went around the rooms turning the lights off and Cache drove him back to his cruiser at the front gates. She struggled with whether to call the police about what she had learned or just let it be, and if she left it alone, what would that say about her as a person?

The next morning, after a big breakfast prepared by Vanny, Cache began to load up her trailer. She kept thinking about Pine Springs Silver; when she couldn't let it go, she grabbed her laptop to run a search on the name. Very little appeared online. It seemed to be a small town of less than a hundred people that had once benefited from the silver-mining industry. On a map it was close to Big Pine, but what struck Cache as an interesting fact was that there was only a short stretch of road between Big Pine and the Nevada-California border.

"Leave it alone, Cache," she muttered to herself repeatedly. She looked down at Duke. One option was to go home via Nevada, but after what had happened in Arizona, she never wanted to put Duke in harm's way again. It had been reckless, and she knew it. No matter what, she wouldn't put him in danger. Cache checked the galley kitchen in her teardrop trailer and made a note of the supplies she had and the ones she would need to pick up while they were en route. She checked the batteries being charged by the solar panels; they were at 100 percent thanks to the California sunshine. Her clothes were all accounted for; she had borrowed Vanny's washer and dryer to make everything springtime fresh. Everything seemed to be there, she just needed to put Duke in the passenger seat of the truck and start what would be an hour-long hug with Vanny, with promises that they would get together more often and not let jobs, guys/gals or anything else keep them apart. Cache would call Jake from the road. She still wasn't sure about him, and if they got together before she left, it could lead her into doing something stupid with him.

"Cache, get in here!" Vanny shouted at her from the front door.

"What?"

"Get in here quick! They're talking about your friend Kathryn!"

Cache rushed inside the house and sat beside Vanny on the couch as she cranked up the volume.

"This is a Lightning News exclusive. The hunt for Dr. Kathryn Jamieson took an interesting twist this morning when police found a vehicle that she had carjacked at gunpoint from an accountant on the way home from work. Mr. Charles Willings of Malibu, California, came forward to report the carjacking after recognizing the woman who accosted him at gunpoint as Dr. Kathryn Jamieson."

Vanny started to ask a question of Cache, and Cache put her finger over Vanny's mouth as they continued to listen to the news story.

"Highway patrol encountered the vehicle this morning driving westward along State Route 14 and pulled it over to discover a male occupant but no sign of Dr. Jamieson. Police have taken the man into custody for further questioning. The police recovered a Glock 43 handgun from the vehicle.

"Unnamed sources inside the department suggest that the individual in custody may have been a victim of Dr. Jamieson, who stole his vehicle at a truck stop close to Cantil. We will have more information for you as the story unfolds."

"Can I talk now?"

"I'm sorry, what did you want to say?"

"She had a gun! She could have shot you!"

"I don't think she would have. Can I borrow your laptop?" Vanny told her it was on the kitchen table, and Cache retrieved it and sat down beside her. She called up the location of Cantil, California, on a map and noticed that if you continued along State Route 14, it would merge with US Route 395, which would take you up to Big Pine and then Pine Springs Silver.

"What does that mean?"

"I think I know roughly where Kathryn is."

Vanny got up off the couch, grabbed the portable phone and handed it to Cache. "Then call the police and tell them. That's what we pay them for."

"I can't."

"Why not?"

"I just need to do this for myself, for my peace of mind, but I need you to look after Duke and not say anything to anybody."

"You're going to do something stupid, aren't you?"

———

Cache went back and forth with Vanny for about an hour, going over the pros and cons of Cache's hopping in her truck, driving up to Pine Springs Silver and looking for herself to see if Kathryn was anywhere in sight. Vanny raised a couple of fine points: Cache had no idea where around Pine Springs Silver Kathryn's grandfather's home might be situated, if it still existed at all; she had already had a couple of close calls on this trip and she might not have nine lives that she could depend on; and last, Kathryn might not be in the area at all and it all could amount to a wild goose chase. Cache went on the internet to determine the distance between Santa Monica and Pine Springs Silver. Without factoring in traffic, she was looking at a journey of two hundred and seventy-five miles and it should take her a little over four hours to get there. Cache reckoned that if she headed out now, she should be there just before dinnertime. She could look around, see if there was any sign of Kathryn in the area and if not be back to Santa Monica before eleven. Cache had this feeling that she might still be able to bring Kathryn in without any harm coming to her, something she feared would happen if the police were to find her first.

Vanny knew Cache well enough to know that there was no point in trying to talk her out of it once she had decided to do something, whether or not it was advisable. Vanny made it very clear that she was to call her upon arrival in Pine Springs Silver and when she was leaving. If Cache strayed from this plan, she would call Jake and dump the situation in his lap.

Cache jumped in her truck and headed north out of Los Angeles. Traffic was congested near the major areas of the city but opened up once she left the city limits. Cache kept thinking about Vanny's point that they didn't know if the cottage in question still existed or where it might be located. Cache had a picture of the residence on her smartphone, and her only hope was to find someone who might recognize the photo and point her in the right direction. She had the radio up to half volume, listening to the music coming from a country station and trying to keep an ear out for any updates on the case that might come across the airwaves. After about an hour and a half on the road, she noticed several signs telling her she was coming into Cantil. According to news reports, the last place Kathryn had been sighted was Jackim's Truck Stop on the other side of Cantil. Cache looked down at her fuel gauge and thought it would provide her with the chance to fuel up and maybe get some answers as to what had occurred.

Jackim's Truck Stop was smaller than a lot of other truck stops she had come across. There were three large eighteen-wheelers parked to one side. There were separate areas marked out depending on whether you were looking for unleaded gasoline or diesel. Cache pulled into the gasoline section and got out and began filling up her truck. The stop had no areas marked for showers, but there were washrooms inside attached to the shop where you could pay for your fuel and pick up supplies for the road. To the left, a larger parking lot existed with a few cars and campers parked in various spaces marked out by faded white lines on the broken asphalt. The diner attached to the shop billed itself as serving all-day breakfast, and the signage suggested that might be all that was available here. Cache topped up her tank and went inside to pay. The man behind the counter looked to be in his seventies, wearing a baseball cap with the front lid bent upward, revealing a mop of white hair. He had on torn jeans and a white T-shirt underneath a long-sleeve shirt rolled up to his elbows. His right arm had two tattoos that had faded with age. When he spoke, you could see that he was missing two teeth, one on the top and one on the bottom, which may have been from a physical altercation as they were in proximity to each other. The shop smelled like oil and gasoline; the floors were peeling in spots and the countertop was heavily stained. There was a set of coffeepots off to the side, a microwave that looked like it hadn't been cleaned this year, and an old set of fridges carrying an assortment of sodas, bottled water and premade sandwiches.

"Hey, what pump number were you?"

"Pump number three."

"That will be eighteen thirty-five."

Cache handed him a twenty-dollar bill. "Hey, are you the manager here?"

"No, that would be Marty, he's not here right now."

"That's too bad. I'm an intern with Lightning News, they sent me to follow up about the guy that got his car stolen?"

"What do you want to know?"

"Can you fill in some details? I know the high-level stuff but none of the details."

"Didn't you guys cover all of this already?"

"Yeah, well, I'm new; they sent me up here to see if anything was missed or if anything new has come to light."

"Nothing new other than the cops were here asking similar questions. I'll tell you what I told them. The guy who had his car stolen actually had a van stolen, not a car. According to him, it was one of those old hippie vans. He picked it up for about seven hundred dollars to take him to Los Angeles to try to make it in the music business."

"Do you know the make?"

"No, you would have to ask him. Anyway apparently he came in that night and parked at the rear where other campers were parked. Met a woman a little older than him that he thought was groovy. One thing led to another and they were jumping on top of each other in the back of his van all night. In the morning, he came in here to get two coffees and some pack-aged pastries for the two of them, and when he got back to his spot, his amp, his guitar, and his suitcase were sitting where his van used to be."

"That is horrible. So how did he end up with a stolen vehicle?"

"On top of his suitcase there was a letter thanking him for the lay and a set of car keys. He figured out the vehicle it belonged to was worth more than his van, said it was fate. I asked him if he wanted us to call the cops for him, but he declined, hopped in the vehicle, and we didn't know there were any issues until the police called."

"So, he told you all this?"

"Yeah, came in to buy a few more things and told us the entire story. I thought he should report it, but he didn't seem to care, chalked it up as a story he would always remember. That's it, not a lot of details. I suspect if your news agency wants more details you're going to have to either talk to him once the police are done with him or find the woman who stole the van."

Cache thanked him for his time and agreed that might be the best plan to get the total story: find the woman who stole the van in the first place.

22

Cache had estimated that the journey would be four hours long. What she did not factor in was the hour and a half she had to sit in traffic before she could find her way to the highway to take her out of Los Angeles. She estimated that she might not make Pine Springs Silver until seven o'clock, and if she couldn't come up with the location Kathryn may have gone to, she'd be forced to find a motel, spend the night and get up in the early morning and continue her search then.

Once she arrived and assessed the situation, if she felt that there was promise to being in Pine Springs Silver she would contact the detectives and ask for help. If she felt it was a dead end that would lead to nothing, she would wrap the whole thing up, head back to Vanny's, grab Duke and her trailer and be off. She knew time was not on her side. Kathryn had reached out to someone with power and influence—Cache didn't know who for certain, though she had a suspicion—and that individual could help Kathryn evade justice by getting her out of the country.

This left an unanswered question in Cache's mind: what

resources would Kathryn have at her disposal? It was one thing to leave the United States through a regular airport on a commercial airliner—security would be tight and keeping a watchful eye out for her—but it was another thing to have access to a private jet that could land anywhere. Without knowing what Kathryn could access, every passing minute was potentially a chance for her to escape.

Cache listened to various local stations as she drove down the highway, which faded in and out, so she spent part of the drive listening to static. This route didn't have many fellow drivers on it today. There were a few transport trucks, but mostly it was an open highway. While the roads were clear for most of her drive, the delays in leaving Los Angeles meant that Cache could not pull into the tiny village of Pine Springs Silver until almost eight o'clock. She figured that she had about an hour of daylight left and the Traveler's Oasis Motel she had passed a few miles back in the town of Independence might be her best option. Cache drove around the tiny town for a few minutes. There wasn't a lot there. It was like many towns that had once seen a heyday giving rise to growth before something changed and people moved away. Cache came to the one major intersection, Main Street and Progress Avenue. She thought someone should have renamed Progress Avenue years ago. She noticed that there were a few streets branching off from these two major roads, but from where she sat, they didn't appear to lead anywhere. Some had stop signs, many did not. To her right there was a miniature strip mall, brown brick walls with a metal roof in need of repair. The strip mall contained four stores. The first two were dark with For Rent signs with a tele-phone number underneath in the windows, the next was a store that looked like a convenience store and post office, and beside it was a modest sized bank. There was a street beside the bank, and on the other side of the street a couple of offices for an accountant, a lawyer and clothing retailer. On the far left-hand side from where Cache sat, there was a full-service gas station combined with a mechanic shop. Everything looked closed except the convenience store. Cache pulled her truck up outside, turned off the ignition and went inside.

Cache remembered that Kathryn had told her that her grandfather's first name was Chet. The picture of the cottage that sat on Kathryn's desk had had *Clayson Cottage* written on the back. Cache went into the convenience store, the bells above the door clanking together as she entered. No one else was in the store. The air-conditioning felt like it might have been on max.

The kid behind the counter looked to be about seventeen. He had dark black hair hanging down over his forehead just over his eyebrows, tanned skin and a long shirt—dirty in spots, unbuttoned in the front—with a faded T-shirt underneath.

"Hey, can I ask you something? Do you know where Chet Clayson lives?"

"Who?"

"Clayson, Chet Clayson, supposed to live around here."

"Never heard of him."

"Have you lived here long?"

"Stuck here all my life. When I turn eighteen, I'm out of here."

"Where you gonna go?"

"Don't know, just ain't staying around here."

"Do you know anyone named Clayson?"

"Nope, sorry."

———

Cache purchased a soda, a bag of chips and two large-size chocolate bars from the store and walked around the small town. To the west were a few more office buildings, many with boards up over the windows and doors, paint peeling off, grass overgrown and protruding from cracks in the sidewalk. She walked over to the gas station and peered inside. A few vehicles sat in the mechanic's garage; the station hours were from seven to seven. The red neon sign saying *Closed* could be seen a ways back.

She walked down the street for about ten minutes, drinking from her bottle of grape soda. She loved grape soda; while her brothers were more orange soda and cola type people, grape soda was her thing, and it was becoming harder to find as it became less popular. In the distance, she could see someone sitting on a bench out in front of an old house that had seen better days. One window appeared to be boarded up, and the wooden front door had only a few splashes of red paint still visible in spots. There was a small garden out front with a few shrubs; the lawn grew long in some places and was bare in others. A small wooden fence separated the lawn from the side-walk, with boards missing throughout.

Cache walked up the front walk, and said, "Hello, I'm wondering if you can help me."

He had to be in his eighties, maybe even nineties. The old man had white hair along the sides of his head and was wearing a hat, so it was impossible to tell if there was anything on top. He smoked a cigarette that was burning in his right hand; it trembled as he held it and coughed into a red check-ered cotton handkerchief that he grasped in his left hand. The man was thin; his clothes screamed the seventies and he smelled like mothballs.

He looked at her and said nothing. Cache repeated her greeting and he yelled at her, "What did you say?"

Cache yelled back, "Hello, can I ask you something?"

He looked at her and fumbled for something in his ear. "Have to turn up my hearing aid. What did you say, young lady?"

"I said hello, can I ask you something? I just drove into town looking for someone and wondered if you might know them. Have you lived here long?"

He laughed to the point of coughing and then covered his mouth with his cotton handkerchief. He let the cigarette drop from his right hand to a collection of dead cigarette butts beneath his feet. "You see this house?" He pointed over his shoulder.

Cache said, "Yes, it looks like a very fine house."

"It's a piece of shit," he said, laughing and coughing. "It wasn't always a piece of shit. I was born in this house, that's how long I have lived here."

"And I'm guessing you're about fifty," she said, trying to flatter him.

"I haven't been fifty for forty years. Other than going off to war, my life has been in this town; used to own the gas station down the street. My son now owns it."

Cache smiled at him, pulled her hair back from her face and put it behind her ear. "I'm looking up a friend. Her family used to live here, and I was wondering if they might still have a place around these parts."

He looked at Cache and coughed. "Maybe. Not many people left here in the village, population is under a hundred people. Some have moved to Independence—it's a little bigger —or just moved out of the area altogether. Who you looking for?"

Cache told him she was looking for Chet Clayson.

He fell back against the back of the bench, breathed in and out deeply, and pondered the question. Cache waited and looked at him. "Do you know him?" His eyes looked like they were going to well up as he took his handkerchief to dab the corner of one.

"I knew Chet, everyone around here knew Chet. Chet's been gone a long time; I haven't heard that name in almost thirty years. Are you family?"

Cache said, "No, but I'm close to his granddaughter Kathryn. A mutual friend thought they had heard she was up this way."

"I don't know about that. You're the first fresh face I have seen come through town in a long while."

He reflected for a few minutes, searching his memory banks and muttering to himself something that Cache could not pick up on, then said, "You know, you don't need to go through town to get to the Clayson homestead, it's possible maybe she went straight there."

Cache asked, "Is the homestead still around? I would have thought it would be destroyed by now."

He cleared the mucus that had been gathering from his throat. "I know when Chet died his daughter took it over, used to come up here with her daughter, but as far as I know they never sold it; might still be back there."

"Back where?" Cache asked.

The old man motioned with his right hand. "You go up Main Street here a couple of miles. You'll see a dirt road splintering off to the left; that's what we call Seventh Avenue, 'cause there were seven families that lived off of it at one point, but keep a watchful eye out, there's no road sign, so you could easily go right past it. Take it to the end and on your right, if it's still there, you'll see a path going into the woods. Drive down it; there was an area where Chet or visitors would park. You then need to take the trail north for about thirty minutes, and if the homestead is still standing it will be there. Used to be a clearing, not sure what it looks like now."

Cache thanked him for the information and turned to walk back to her vehicle. The old man yelled out, "Missy, missy, you be careful going back through those woods. Not unusual to happen onto a mountain lion or bear in these parts; no telling what is back there these days. Just east of the homestead there used to be a dock on Millers Pond; animals may be attracted to it for the fish, so you keep a watchful eye. I wouldn't suggest you go in there in the dark. Best to wait until morning. You got a fella that can go with you?" Cache thanked him for his warnings but said that coming from Montana, she was used to dealing with deadly animals out in the wilderness and had a rifle in the back of the truck for just that reason; it was the other creatures she was more concerned about.

She made her way out of town as the sun was going down. Things were getting dark. She rolled down her window and shone her flashlight to her left as she drove down Main Street to ensure she did not miss the dirt road. Cache came upon it and stopped in the middle of the road. She could see no one for miles. The lights coming from the village had disappeared as if they had been a mirage in the first place. The old man was right: if you didn't know your way around here the road could easily be missed. She sat there in the middle of the road contemplating her next move. Common sense would have told a normal person to drive back to Independence, which was only about twenty minutes away; get a hotel room for the night; and venture back here tomorrow morning when daylight would aid her in her search.

She reasoned with herself that if Kathryn was there, time was of the essence; the longer she hesitated, the greater the chance of her slipping through the net. Cache knew from her internet search that Pine Springs Silver was about an hour and a half from the Nevada state line. From there Kathryn could move in multiple directions and be harder to find. If she wasn't there, if the homestead wasn't there, then Cache could drive to Independence, get a hotel room for the night and figure out what else she could do in the morning. She put her blinker on, turned left and rumbled down the dirt road for about thirty-five minutes. The daylight had been extinguished and the night sky surrounded her, looking like black ink that now covered a canvas. The road had large potholes in spots, and Cache bounced up and down in the truck's cab as the tires came in contact with them. There were no streetlights, no lights from homes; the only light available was coming from her head-lamps. She came to a dead end blocked by a large rock forma-tion. Cache put the truck in park and got out with her flashlight. She pointed the beam of light in all directions and saw nothing but an overgrown forest, until she spotted it: a set of indentations in the dirt just before the road ended. Cache walked over and kneeled down.

She pointed the flashlight at the ground and could make out what looked like tire tracks, and they appeared to be recent. Anything from too long ago would have likely been washed away with the last rainfall, but no, someone had been through here recently. Cache walked back to her truck, got in and threw it in reverse, and pulled out past the spot where the tire tracks were. She then put the truck in drive and pushed through the woods where the tracks entered. Branches crashed against the windshield as they broke from the trees, and she continued her path of destruction for about ten minutes, to an area where one could park one's vehicle. As Cache pulled into the clearing, her headlights caught the reflection of a pair of taillights hiding in the woods to the right.

She parked the vehicle, turned off her lights, shut the engine down and quietly got into the back of her truck to get her gun. She pulled the gun from its storage location, grabbed an ammunition clip from her ammo box and pushed the clip into the gun while keeping a watchful eye out toward those tail-lights. Cache reached down into the lockbox and grabbed a hunting knife in its sheath and attached it to her belt. She climbed slowly out of the truck bed, trying not to make a sound as she approached the taillights. As she moved forward, she could see the reflective lenses attached to a van, with a big blacked-out window on the side and a bumper sticker that read *Sex Is Better in a Van.*

Cache surveyed the vehicle, first approaching the driver's side, but saw no one in there. She put her flashlight to the glass and peered inside, but the lack of light made it difficult to see anything. She tried the doors to the vehicle, but they were all locked. Lucky for Cache she carried a metal strip in her truck and her brother Cooper had taught her how to use it when she was a teenager. She returned to the van with the thin strip of metal and pushed it down alongside the driver's window until she could unlock the door. Cache poked her head into the van and pointed her light all around. No one was there. The bed in the back looked like some activity had taken place there, but there were no clues to suggest Kathryn had used it other than the description the police had gotten from the owner.

She stepped back. There was a crescent moon that evening and you could see hundreds of stars in the night sky. Cache pointed her flashlight in front of the van and could make out a trail heading north. The trail was too narrow to take a vehicle down it; the rest of the journey would have to be done on foot. Cache shut the door to the van and took about twenty steps forward to the trail, then paused. She knew she needed to play both offense and defense when it came to Kathryn. While she doubted Kathryn could start her truck without the keys, she didn't want to underestimate her, and she certainly had the keys to the van. Cache turned and went back to her truck. Grabbing a bag from her lockbox, she popped the hood of her truck and removed the distributor cap; she then proceeded to do the same for the van and took the bag and put it at the bottom of the lockbox. As a last precaution she grabbed her smartphone and found an app that she had that would send your geographical location to someone. She called up Jake's email address from her directory, typed in a brief message—"Playing a hunch, maybe nothing"—and sent it off, then left her phone on and tucked it under the front seat of her truck and locked the doors. At least this way, if something happened to her, they would know where she was. Cache looked down at her handgun and thought about the old man's warning. She hopped into the bed of her truck and exchanged her handgun for her rifle and loaded it up. She then secured the lockbox. Cache then walked toward the mouth of the trail, with dense forest on either side, the smell of moss in the air and pockets of water dispersed among the bases of the trees. There was a pungent odor in the air, as if it was coming from something decaying in the forest. Ahead of her there was a path of flattened grass with hints that gravel had once been laid down here. Her flashlight beam gave her light for about fifteen feet in front of her, and then there was nothing to see. Cache could spot creatures against the night sky flying overhead, either birds or bats, she wasn't sure. She held her flashlight tight with her right hand, passing the beam in all directions, hoping not to catch sight of a set of eyes peering back at her from the shadows.

———

23

C ache walked down the trail in the dark for approximately twenty-five minutes. She would stop every few minutes to look at where she was, shine her flashlight in all directions and listen for any movement, whether it be animal or female. She wouldn't have put it past Kathryn to be lying in wait, but that would only be the case if she knew Cache was coming, so she figured she might have the element of surprise. After a few more minutes, Cache came to a clearing. For a property not likely visited for quite some time, it appeared to be pretty well kept. There was a mixture of grass and dirt in a large circle. In the middle of the clearing stood a wooden log cabin that appeared to have a couple of different rooms in it based on the shape. Cache crouched down and turned off her flashlight. How she wished she had better light to make her approach, but she was concerned that a flashlight might alert someone in the cabin to her presence. She walked around the cabin to have a look at it from all sides before making an approach; Cache began by walking to the right. She spotted the wooden front door. There was a small wooden deck with two chairs sitting outside but nothing that would suggest they had been used recently.

She moved farther around the house and noticed that the trees gave way to a dock. This must have been the dock on Millers Pond that the old man had told Cache about. Cache walked slowly onto the dock. The old wooden structure groaned and squeaked with each step. A few boards were broken in spots and she needed to be careful where she planted her feet. She reached the end of the dock and turned on her flashlight. Cache shined it around the pond, which looked larger than one would have imagined from the word *pond*. Cache could hear the sounds of crickets chirping as something broke the water's surface in spots, creating ripples on the surface of the otherwise still pond. She noticed that over on the ground beside the dock there was evidence that a canoe had rested on the banks, but it was no longer there. There were indentations in the dirt, and a large rock with a rope tied to it rested near the markings. Cache moved the flashlight back along the pond and noticed what looked like an inlet about twenty or thirty feet away, off to the right. Was it possible that this pond led to other waterways? Could Kathryn have ditched the van here only to take a boat to some destination farther upstream? Did the time it had taken Cache to disable both vehicles allow Kathryn to slip away into the shadows when she had no intention of using the van ever again? If Kathryn wasn't in the cabin, then most certainly Cache had missed her opportunity.

She was tempted to rush into the cabin and see what the situation was, but her training told her to scout out the building before making a breach. Cache walked away from the dock and continued to her right, sizing up the cabin. There appeared to be three rooms to the structure, one on either side of the main entryway. She noted that the back of the cabin was comprised of large stones, creating an enormous chimney extending above the roof to provide warmth during the winter months. Cache continued around the structure in the dark and saw nothing further to note. No movement came from the woods, and the thickness of the trees prevented any light from escaping. She crept slowly to the side left of the entryway. Close up, she could tell the windows had wooden shutters latched from the inside. Half a cross symbol had been cut out from each shutter so that they created the image of a cross when closed. This may have been used in the past as a gun port to protect the people inside from unfriendly foes outside or was simply a cosmetic addition to enhance the appearance of the cabin.

As Cache continued to make her way around the structure close up, she noted several other windows with closed wooden shutters. On the right side of the house she stood up and placed her face against one of the cross openings and could see that glass was behind the shutter. This room appeared to be a bedroom, with very limited furniture; a bed and dresser were all that Cache could make out. She quickly and quietly moved back to the other side of the house and peered in the window through the gun portal. This seemed to face onto what looked like a kitchen. She could make out a small stove and a round fridge left over from the seventies. The kitchen had no door and she could barely make out the fireplace in the other room.

Cache walked around the cabin and stood outside the front door. Her review of the structure suggested that this was the only door in and out of the cabin. She looked around and something slivery caught her eye leaning against the cabin wall behind an old wooden chair. She walked over in the dark to try to have a better look. It was a fishing pole, and the lure still felt wet. Cache pulled her rifle from her shoulder and gripped it tight. She crept back to the front door of the cabin and reached for the doorknob. She turned the knob clockwise and could hear the door squeal as she pushed it open.

Cache walked inside and looked around. She half-expected

to see Kathryn sitting in the dark waiting for her, maybe with a gun of her own in her lap; Cache could have walked in and been shot dead on sight. She wasn't there. Cache walked around the small cabin in the dark. She first walked to the tiny bedroom, but there was no sign that it had been used in a while. Cache then crossed what was likely the social gathering spot of the cabin, with an assortment of chairs and an old couch resting on a dirty matted rug next to the entryway to the kitchen but no sign of human life. She walked to the wood burning stove. A cast-iron skillet was on it; it was cool to the touch, but the residue in it tasted fishy when Cache ran her fingers through it and rubbed them on the tip of her tongue.

Kathryn wasn't there. Cache flipped on her smart watch to see that it was now ten thirty. As she saw it, she had a couple of options: she could try to hike back to her truck, hoping not to encounter any animals in the dark, call the police and let them know what she found out. She could then try to put the distributor cap back on in the dark and go find a hotel somewhere, or she could just stay here for the night and head out at sunrise. She had slept in worse, and while the night air was cool, it wasn't cold. Cache rustled through some drawers in the kitchen, found some matches and lit a fire in a kerosene lantern that was in the cabin. She was convinced that Kathryn had been here on her way somewhere else, maybe to get one last look at a place from her past, knowing that she might never return.

The cabin had a warm glow. Cache was able to get the fire going in the gigantic fireplace. She couldn't figure out why they had built such a large stone structure when the hearth was rather small, but it may have been to further fortify the structure against attack. Cache walked over to the front door and bolted it shut. She took a seat close to the fireplace so that she could feel the warmth of the fire and placed her rifle down across her lap. Cache wished she had brought her smartphone with her. She could have searched maps of the area to see where the waterway flowed; she might have gotten some idea of where Kathryn had gone next or whether any small landing strips were close by. At minimum she could have passed the time looking at social media or checking out her email, though the cabin lacked any electricity, so once her battery was dead it would remain that way until she charged it again.

Cache sat there for about an hour, rocking back and forth. The warmth from the glowing fireplace felt great. Her body felt bathed in heat, and the events of the day caused her eyelids to shut. The winds had picked up outside; she could hear them howl as they smacked against the wooden cabin walls. Cache closed her eyes and listened to the crackle of the fireplace and the noise outside. She could hear the old cabin moan as it was blasted on all sides of the structure. *Creak, creak, creak.* Cache just sat there rocking back and forth and listened. *Creak, creak, creak.* It sounded as if the winds had changed their direction and were now favoring one side of the cabin versus all sides.

Creak, creak, creak. Cache listened, trying to drown out any other noises, like the crackle of the fireplace. *Creak, creak, creak.* Cache in a moment realized where the sound was coming from: it was coming from behind her. As she opened her eyes and slowly turned around, she felt something heavy strike her at the back of the head. Her body fell forward and lay on the floor in front of the chair. Behind the chair Kathryn stood, with a wooden ax handle in her hand. A small stone doorway attached to the fireplace was ajar; it led to a small cellar underneath the structure where Kathryn had watched Cache from below from small holes in the floor boards lying in wait for the perfect time to strike.

Kathryn walked over to Cache and checked her wrist to determine if she had killed her. She was still alive. She dragged Cache to the bedroom and threw her onto the old steel-frame bed, which squeaked as her body hit the springs. Cache bounced up and then settled back down. Kathryn went downstairs to the root cellar, found some old leather ties and brought them upstairs to the bedroom. She first tied each of Cache's wrists to the bed frame above her head. She then pulled her boots off and tossed them to one side and tied each of Cache's ankles to the metal frame at the bottom of the bed.

"That should hold you."

Kathryn pulled Cache's belt from her jeans and pulled off the knife sheath she had attached there. She then went through her pockets looking for her phone but couldn't find anything other than her truck keys.

Kathryn took the knife, belt and flashlight and threw them into one of the boots; she took the truck keys and put them into her pocket, then went back to the sitting area to retrieve the rifle, walked down to the dock at the edge of the pond and threw the items in. First she grabbed the barrel of the rifle, and as if she were attempting to skip a stone across a still pond, Kathryn threw the rifle as far as she could throw it. She didn't see where it went in, but she could hear the splash. The next item to be tossed was Cache's boot with the knife in it and then her remaining boot. This would reduce Cache's threat level and keep her immobile while Kathryn made her escape. She walked back inside the cabin, closing the door behind her, and bolted it shut.

Kathryn then went to examine the head wound Cache had. It looked like it was more impact related, though there was a minor cut. Kathryn went back downstairs and returned with a small first-aid kit; she used antiseptic to clean the wound, and some gauze and bandage tape to cover the wound to help stop the bleeding and avoid an infection.

"Cache, Cache, Cache," she said, shaking her body to see if she would get an answer, but it looked like Cache remained out cold. Kathryn retrieved a wooden chair from the sitting room and brought it into the bedroom, with a lantern that Cache had lit and some old hunting and fishing magazines that had been stored downstairs. She sat there and flipped through the paper relics, looking at the articles and ads by the light of the lantern, waiting for Cache to wake up.

After an hour had passed, Cache woke in a groggy state. Her first reaction was to rub her head where she could feel something was attached to it, but her arms could not move. She tried to move her legs, but she saw they were secured to something as the room came into focus. Kathryn had put down her old magazine when she saw Cache starting to move about.

"What the fuck?" Cache said.

"Sorry about the bump on the back of your head, but I thought if I told you to be a good girl and lie down on the bed so I could tie you down, you might not be so helpful."

Cache realized that was why she could not move her arms or legs as she thrashed around on the old steel cot, which squeaked madly as she moved from side to side.

"How did you find me?" Kathryn demanded.

"Lucky guess," Cache said.

"You're telling me you happened onto a cabin in the middle of the woods, four hours outside of Los Angeles, near a village of less than a hundred people? I'm not an idiot, I want to know how you found me."

Cache lifted her head off of the bed to face Kathryn. "What the hell happened to your hair?"

Kathryn ran her hand through her long hair. She had taken the time to change her red locks to a soft brunette color.

"I'm trying a fresh look. I thought I would go with the Cache Iron color; do you not like it?"

Cache said, "I prefer the red, it better suits you."

"Well, that is the beautiful thing about hair dye; I can always change it back. And you are avoiding answering my question. How did you find me?"

Cache stared up at the wooden ceiling above her. She could

feel that the back of her head was sore and something was taped to it. "Tell me why."

"Why what?"

"Why are we here, why did you kidnap Rachel, why did you murder those women?"

"It needed to be done."

"That is not an answer. I want you to tell me why."

"Tell me how you found me and I will tell you why."

"Promise?"

"Absolutely."

She said, "I found the name of the village on the back of the old photograph in your bedroom where you had caught a fish."

Kathryn sat back in her chair. "Huh. You know, I would never have thought to check that. The picture and frame were a gift from my mother, and I don't recall ever taking it apart. Good for you. Now, did you bring friends that I have to worry about?"

Cache put her head back against the mattress. "If I'd brought friends, would I be tied to a bed right now?"

"Probably not, but that doesn't mean they couldn't be on their way. Any chance you want to run away with me?" Kathryn rose out of the chair, walked over to the bed and sat on the edge, putting her right arm over Cache's chest and placing her hand on the mattress to balance herself. "I have money, more than enough to look after the two of us for the rest of our lives."

Cache looked at her. "If I said yes, would you believe me?"

Kathryn, making a pouty face, said, "No, I wouldn't, but I wish you would say it anyway."

"So, I told you how I found you; now you tell me why."

"Nah, it's a boring story, I changed my mind."

"Kathryn, you promised."

"You will just have to sue me. Well, Cache, I think I have to be on my way; I have a place to be. I couldn't leave without seeing this old home one more time. I doubt I will be back; the authorities will be keeping an eye out for me for some time."

Cache looked at her and said, "And what about me? Am I to remain tied to the bed, lost in the woods, never to be heard from again?"

"My dear, I wish you would stop thinking I'm a fool. You found me here when the police couldn't, you discovered Rachel when the cops were looking elsewhere; I suspect you are more than capable of getting free, I'm just hoping these restraints will buy me the time to get away from here. You may notice that the property is pretty well kept for a very old cabin; I pay a young boy who lives outside of Pine Springs Silver to come here once a week to check up on the property and make sure everything is good. I will call him and ask him to come by in the next day or so, just so I know you're not still tied to a bed."

Cache said, "Thanks, I appreciate it. So why didn't you leave?"

Kathryn said, "Leave?"

"Yeah. leave. You had me tied to the bed; why did you just not pick up and go?"

"I had to make sure you were all right. I don't want that hanging over my head." And with that Kathryn stood up and exited the room to retrieve her bag from the cellar. She returned to the doorway and looked at Cache. "Last chance: hot sandy beach or steel cot, your choice."

Cache didn't look at her but stared at the wooden roof overhead. "I will take the cot."

Kathryn turned away and Cache could hear the door to the cabin shut. The room was quiet; there was no sound of movement. It was always possible that Kathryn was playing a game and waiting in the other room to see if Cache could free herself.

24

As the door shut, Cache knew the stopwatch had begun, and she had a limited amount of time. Providing Kathryn wasn't making a dash for her van in the dark, Cache figured she had maybe forty to forty-five minutes for Kathryn to make it to her vehicle, realize that it wouldn't start and return this way. Cache looked down at her bare feet. Where the hell are my boots? she thought, and surveyed the room and could not see them anywhere. She could see leather ties running from her ankles to the metal frame of the cot. Cache noticed that the frame was rusting in certain places, likely from being in this cabin for a number of years. She looked above her, where her wrists were secured, and then to the metal frame, where she saw even more rust around the curves. The top of the bed was closest to the window in the room, and moisture must have found its way onto the metal over the years and helped to generate rust. The rust points were the points of weakness in the frame. She looked to her right, and the part of the frame farthest from the window only showed small signs of rust. The frame to her left-hand side saw the most distress, and she determined that putting pressure on that area was her best course of action.

She pulled on the left side, the leather ties digging into the skin along her wrist. She could feel the metal frame give. Cache continued to pull with everything she had. The burning sensation along her wrists was painful, but she knew she needed to get out of there. She heard a crack at the top of the bed as the metal split into two. Cache slid the leather tie around her left wrist from the metal post, then reached over to her right wrist to free herself. She freed her legs and undid the leather tie that had burned into the skin of her left wrist. Cache looked under the bed and wandered around the cabin, but she could not find her boots, rifle or knife.

Cache went to the downstairs cellar. It was a small room under the floorboards of the cabin. The stone of the large fireplace extended down to the base of the cellar and formed part of the cellar's walls. The room was pitch-black and Cache made her way back upstairs. Light from the fireplace was the only source of illumination in the room. Kathryn appeared to have taken the lantern with her and Cache grabbed a piece of wood and lit it from the fire. She went back downstairs, hoping that no gasoline or kerosene was being stored there. Cache could see there were food, provisions and whiskey along one wall of the cellar. There was no sign of her boots or gear and no indication of any other firearms. She was unsure whether Kathryn might have had a gun with her or even Cache's own rifle. Cache made her way upstairs, surveyed the kitchen and stepped outside the cabin onto the hardened ground, from which rocks jutted.

"Ouch, that hurts," she muttered to herself as her bare feet pressed against the jagged rocks protruding from the ground. This didn't look good. She had no idea where her boots were and didn't like the idea of having to make her way back to her truck barefoot and in the dark. She tiptoed into the cabin and looked around. Underneath the couch in the sitting room was an old, dirty, thin rug that smelled musty and had seen better days. Cache thought that if she could cut strips from the rug, she could use the leather ties still attached to the bed to fashion something like a sandal. While not comfortable, it would protect her feet from the local terrain. She returned outside and dug out the dirt around one of the jagged rocks to loosen it, then took it inside to cut a strip off the width of the rug. Cache had to apply a lot of pressure with the rock to the carpet to make the cut, but when she had made a cut of about two feet, she found she could grab either end and continue to tear the carpet with her hands. She then cut the strip in half, folded the beaten carpet over and over again, and tied the carpet to her feet.

———

As Cache was preparing to make her exit from the cabin, Kathryn had made her way to the clearing and got into her van. She put the keys in the ignition and tried to turn the engine over, but it would not start. She tried again and again with no luck, and in a heightened state of frustration started smashing the steering wheel with her hands and began to cry. Kathryn sat in the driver's seat for a few minutes, tears rolling down her face. She thought she had done everything that she was supposed to do. Kathryn made her way back to her grandfather's cabin.

Upon his death, the cabin had passed to her mother and then to Kathryn, who'd kept it hidden from the world through an offshore corporation that she didn't think could get tied back to her. She had contacted Nina on one of the burner phones, and Nina had taken the headshot of Kathryn on the Dream Design website and changed the hair color through the use of software to match the brunette hair color she was now sporting.

Nina had gotten Kathryn a new passport through her contacts among the very people who issued the official ones to US citizens.

Two hours from Kathryn's current location, a small farm in Nevada had a private landing strip. Nina had arranged for a small private plane to arrive there at four thirty in the afternoon tomorrow. It would land, wait twenty minutes, and exit. If Kathryn wasn't there, she would miss her window. The small plane would take her down to Brazil, where Nina's contacts would help her disappear forever. Now the only thing that was stopping Kathryn from making her flight was this old unreliable hippie van that she had stolen. She wiped the tears from her eyes, looked around and spotted Cache's truck. Kathryn thought, Why did it not dawn on me that Cache would have driven here? Of course, her truck. That was the solution. She jumped out of the van and walked over to Cache's truck. The doors were locked.

Cache had told her how much she loved this truck and that it had been her grandfather's. Kathryn understood that connection. That was one reason she'd needed to go to the cabin one more time. Kathryn could leave the vehicle at the farm. She could leave a note inside advising whoever discovered the truck how they could contact the owner. Kathryn could even reach out to Cache once she was safely away to tell her where she could find it.

Maybe it was fate that had brought Cache to her; maybe fate knew that old van would break down, and this truck was the way to get Kathryn to freedom. She pulled the keys from her pocket and put the truck key in the ignition, but the truck would not start. Kathryn tried again and the engine would not turn over. She sat there and thought, What are the odds that both vehicles would not start? Pressing her tongue to the side of her mouth and thinking, she realized that Cache must have done something to both vehicles that would prevent Kathryn from escaping.

"That little minx," she muttered to herself, exiting the truck and slamming the door. She grabbed the lantern that she had placed in the truck's bed and made her way back to the trail to go back to the cabin for some answers.

———

Cache started down the trail in her new carpet sandals. She knew at some point she would come across Kathryn heading back to the cabin, thwarted by vehicles that would not cooperate in her escape. The problem with Cache's carpet sandals was they didn't repel moisture. As she walked on soggy terrain in the dark, the moisture absorbed into the old carpet fabric and squished against her bare feet. As she moved down the path, she tried to keep an eye out for any movement in the distance. After walking for about ten minutes she could see a white bouncing flicker swaying from side to side, moving toward her. She knew this had to be Kathryn. No one else would be out here and wild animals relied on their vision; none of them carried lanterns. Cache decided this was not the time for the confrontation. She needed supplies if she was going to be successful in restraining Kathryn and felt getting to the lockbox in the back of her truck was her best plan. There she could grab her handcuffs, a spare set of keys for the truck and her pistol.

Cache crouched down and walked off to the left, stepping slowly into the forest. She found some mud in a wet bog and smeared it over her white T-shirt, face and arms to help ensure that Kathryn did not catch sight of her as she passed. The coolness of the mud felt crisp against her bare skin and allowed her to blend into the darkness of the forest. The smell was something foul that was now all around her. She squatted down, trying not to make a sound, estimating that she was about ten feet from the trail and might still be visible to the lantern. As Kathryn passed her location, she stopped on the trail and looked to her left and then to her right. She might have sensed something in the forest watching her as Cache made every attempt to remain silent until Kathryn had passed out of sight. Cache looked down at her smart watch and waited for about five minutes to pass before she exited the forest back to the trail.

Knowing that Kathryn would reach the cabin and discover that she was gone, she picked up her pace, trying to avoid a situation where her foot might hit something in the dark and cause her to sprain or break a leg.

Cache made it back to her truck in the darkness. She rubbed the dirt from her palm so she wouldn't have a problem with the biometric scanner not being able to read her palm print. Cache rummaged through the lockbox, wishing she had a pair of shoes back there and making a mental note to keep a backup pair there in the future. She grabbed her spare keys from the box. Cache pulled the gun from the mounting sleeve in the lockbox, and rested it on the bed of the truck by her right foot. Cache didn't want to lose this creeping around the forest and rummaged through the box in the dark; she told herself to add a light to this sometime in the future as well in the event her flashlight wasn't available, as was the case now. At the bottom, she found her holster, shoved it down into the waist-band in her jeans and slid the M9 into the holster and secured it. Cache rummaged around the box, locating her handcuffs, and slipped them down into her rear pocket. She locked the box back up and hopped off the bed of the truck. Cache proceeded back up the trail to the cabin and stopped and looked back at the truck. Once this trip she hadn't carefully thought things out before acting, or maybe it was twice, she thought to herself. Cache went back to the truck and fished under her seat for her smartphone. She flipped it on to see a new email from Jake demanding to know what she was up to.

Cache typed out a simple reply to him, "FOUND KATHRYN AT THESE COORDINATES, BRING POLICE ASAP" and she included the GPS coordinates and pressed send.

————

While Cache had made it to her truck, Kathryn had reached the cabin. She opened the door and said, "That is not funny, Cache, what the hell did you do to the vehicles?" There was no response, just silence. She walked into the bedroom and noticed that Cache was no longer tied to the bed. Kathryn noted that the frame at the top of the bed appeared broken and the ties at the bottom of the bed were gone. She walked back into the sitting room and tripped over the rock that Cache had used to cut the carpet. Kathryn fell to the floor, picking up the rock and looking at the carpet. "You bitch, I should have just killed you like the others," she said as she gritted her teeth and threw the rock against the wall.

Cache was keeping her from her one chance at freedom, and for what? She didn't know the people that Kathryn had hurt. They were faceless strangers in a crowd. She got up and brushed the dirt from her pants. Kathryn hadn't seen Cache outside, and she knew the boat was gone—someone had stolen it, assuming no one at the cabin would miss it—which meant at some point they had to have passed each other. Kathryn reached down into her pocket, pulled out Cache's keys and looked at them. If she had a spare key somewhere, she could leave, racing to the nearest police station to tell them of her whereabouts.

"Shit!" she screamed. If she was left stranded out here, her only hope of escape might be to swim to the other side of the pond and try to make it on foot, but with few provisions, how far could she travel? And there was no way she could make the flight by that afternoon. At best, she would need to find her way to the local highway that led to Nevada and see if she could hitch a ride, but few trucks or cars took that route anymore and she could wait a long time until a ride came along.

"Damn it, every time I let someone into my life, they screw me over!" she yelled. She looked toward the ceiling. "What is it? Do you hate me? Can't you give me one fucking break? I have had to work my ass off my entire life and not once has anything ever come easy!" She took a couple of deep breaths; there weren't a lot of options. She needed to walk back to the clearing and see if Cache had left; if she had, she would need to continue walking and hitch a ride with a stranger if she was going to survive.

25

Cache marched northerly on the path. Her mud-filled carpet sandals clung to her feet and had started to cause her skin to itch. She had her gun for protection, but the lack of any light put her at an extreme disadvantage. Trying to get off a shot in the dark and hit your target was near impossible if you didn't know where you were supposed to aim.

Kathryn marched south, back to where the vehicles were parked. If Cache hadn't left yet, was there a chance she could reason with her? If not, it might get physical. Not like your typical catfight in a bar where two drunk women slurring their words spend a half hour pulling each other's hair and swearing at each other. Cache was physically fit—Kathryn had seen that up close—and while Kathryn had several years on her, her daily fitness regimen had kept her in good shape for a woman her age.

The two women approached each other on the path. Kathryn held the only light between them, and she could spot the sidearm that Cache now had on her waist.

"I gotta get out of here, Cache, you have to let me go."

"You see, Kathryn, I don't. You have killed people. I don't know what Jillian's deal was, but she didn't deserve to lose her life over it, and Emily Peeters, Gabriela Perez and Heidi Larsen, they were just innocent victims caught up in this storm that you created."

"I didn't want to hurt them, they had to be sacrificed for the greater good."

"What greater good?" Cache yelled at her.

"I am a surgeon, I help people, I help restore lives, I help people with new beginnings. They weren't a maid, a school-teacher or a librarian, they were women selling their bodies for sex, to a married man."

"But not yours. And what about Jillian? Was she a sex worker?"

"She was a threat like the others."

"To who, to you?"

"To Rachel. Rachel was afraid, she came to me for help."

"Afraid of what?"

"She thought he was having an affair."

"It looks like she was having one too."

"That's not fair."

"She could have divorced him."

"She was in pain. I couldn't let her be in pain, like I couldn't leave the cabin without knowing you were okay."

"Then why did you kidnap her, if you cared about her so much?"

"Because she figured out what I had done and instead of being grateful, she turned on me, said I would have to pay her for her silence. That was her idea of love, that manipulative little bitch."

"I can't just let you waltz off into the sunset, to sip piña coladas on some foreign beach beyond the reaches of the law."

"Cache, you are not hearing me!" she screamed. "I am not, I repeat, I am not going to prison! You don't cage a swan, you cage a pigeon."

"Kathryn, for some reason you see yourself as better than everyone else, but we are all held to account, and you need to be held responsible for what you did. If you had stayed out of it and let Rachel deal with it herself, Jillian, Emily, Gabriela and Heidi would still be alive, and you would not be facing down charges that could keep you in prison until you die."

Kathryn said, angrily pointing at her, "There, you do get it. I am in my fifties; I will never see the light of day again. I am not going away for a few years to then get my life back, I am going away forever, to be beaten by those who don't deserve to walk in my presence, to be raped in my cell by any guard or fellow lifer that wants to teach me a lesson. I am better off dead."

Cache stepped back and moved her legs out, so they were shoulder width apart, and pulled her gun from the holster. She clutched the grip with both hands and pointed the gun at Kathryn. "I need you to turn around, get on your knees and interlock your fingers behind your head."

"What?" Kathryn said. "Did you not hear me? Did some cow kick you in your head when you were little and scramble your brains? Cache, maybe you're all tits and nothing else. I am not going to prison."

Kathryn walked over to a large rock and picked it up in her hand. She weighed her options in her mind. There were only a few to consider. First, she could charge Cache wielding the heavy stone and Cache could shoot her dead. No prison sentence there. Second, she could make contact with her, and maybe Cache would get off a shot, maybe she wouldn't, but Kathryn might be able to incapacitate her and make Cache fix one vehicle, leaving her free to escape.

"Kathryn, put down the rock, I mean it, I am not playing around here," Cache said.

"You know, I shouldn't have waited around to see if you were okay. I should have tied you to the bed and left the door open hoping a hungry animal would walk in, and I would be gone."

"Gone where? Were you planning on walking to your next destination?" Cache said. Cache ordered her once again to put the rock down, but she also recognized the situation. Kathryn didn't want to hurt her, but she wanted to provoke her so that Cache would be the one to put her down.

Cache put up her left hand in a stop motion and holstered her pistol, putting the safety strap back into place. "Kathryn, let's talk about this. You don't have to go through this alone. I will be there for you."

"Are you planning on coming to prison with me to watch my back?" she asked.

"No, I am not, but I will be there for you through the process if you want me to. You don't have to face it alone, just put the rock down and kneel down on the ground."

Kathryn stood there looking at Cache, still holding the rock firmly in her right hand. She envisioned getting on top of her and bashing her skull in with the stone. Kathryn had been kind to this stranger, who in return had ruined everything. She once again assessed the situation. Kathryn didn't feel the odds were in her favor, but she refused to become a prisoner for the rest of her life, living on someone else's terms.

She bent down and put the lantern on the ground and stood back up. Kathryn would count to three and charge. She didn't see any other option available to her. If she didn't die and had to kill Cache, it would force her to try to hitch a ride with someone while she walked along the side of the road, but at least she would be free. She could just drag her body off into the woods and hope the animals would finish her off.

Cache stared at her. "I came here looking for you because I was afraid if the police cornered you, you would provoke them into shooting you, just like you're trying to do with me now. I want you to come in peacefully." As Cache spoke to her, she kept an eye on that rock and Kathryn's demeanor. Cache wondered what was going through Kathryn's head. Would she be compliant? Could Cache negotiate a peaceful outcome or was Kathryn trying to assess whether she could inflict harm on her with the rock in her hand? Cache concluded that no amount of talking would result in a peaceful outcome to their standoff. Very simply put, Kathryn didn't want to go to prison, period.

Cache bent her right knee to give her the ability to push off. She felt the best way to resolve the situation was to get the rock away from Kathryn and force her into a position where she could get the handcuffs in her back pocket around her wrists. Cache pushed off on her right foot, charging at Kathryn, who stood fifteen feet away. Her shoulder contacted Kathryn's ribs with the sound of a baseball cracking the windshield of a car. Kathryn swung the rock into Cache's back, making Cache feel as if the air had been forcibly squeezed from her lungs, as the two women fell forward onto the ground. Both got to their feet, with Cache landing the first punch to Kathryn's face, like a steel pipe smashing a wet pillow. Kathryn could feel the pain coming over the left side of her face, the bitter taste of blood in her mouth.

Game on, she thought. Kathryn responded with a series of blows to Cache's face. The first one was her right fist making contact with her cheek, the second her left fist smashing her nose. As she went in for the third strike, Cache delivered a driving blow to Kathryn's rib cage, like a freight train breaking through a barricade. The feeling of the hit caused Kathryn to miss her target, and she ended up grazing the bottom of Cache's chin. Cache fell backward, disoriented. She wiped the blood from her nose with the back of her hand.

The adrenaline was now pumping through both women, with different objectives: for Kathryn, to survive, for Cache, to dispense justice. Cache stepped forward, back within a short distance of Kathryn. Kathryn laid out another punch, striking Cache in the stomach.

The two women continued to exchange blows, slamming each other's faces with their fists and pummeling each other's chests when they left themselves exposed. As they came in close to one another, Kathryn grabbed the back of Cache's hair and drove her knee up into Cache's face. She staggered backward, lost in the moment. Kathryn mustered her remaining energy, like a wolf when its back is up against the wall and the way forward is its only chance for survival.

Kathryn pounced onto Cache and delivered blow after blow as Cache worked to block the incoming punches, drained of energy, like a flashlight that had been left on too long.

Cache grabbed Kathryn's hair and tried to roll on top of her. Kathryn would have none of it and mirrored the action as they rolled around on the ground. Cache managed to get her foot up near Kathryn's stomach and kicked her off of her.

She reached for her sidearm; this had to end now. She felt the strap that kept the gun in place unattached, and she panicked, looking all around her, from side to side. Where was her gun? "Looking for this?" Kathryn asked as she stood up about seven feet away from Cache, gun pointing right at her. Cache quickly fell back into negotiating mode. "We can talk about this, just put the gun down."

"Cache, the only person stupid enough to put their gun away is you. Who brings a gun to a fight without the intention of using it?"

"I didn't want to hurt you," Cache said.

Kathryn said, "That is where you and I are different. I didn't want to hurt you when it wasn't my only option, but if given a choice between hurting you and going to prison, well, my dear, then you just become another casualty in this story. Now, what you are going to do is get to your feet, and we are heading back to the vehicles. You are going to fix that truck of yours so I can leave, and if you don't, I will put a bullet in you and hope to flag down a passing motorist, and I will put a bullet in them. The thing about facing life in prison is it doesn't matter how much time they add; it doesn't change a thing. Whether I go away for fifty years or a hundred, I am still never seeing the light of day again, and you will be responsible for whoever I gun down with your gun, you stupid, stupid little girl."

Cache thought compliance at this point was her only option. She didn't like the idea of another innocent person dying today; better to send Kathryn on her way to deal with her another day. Cache came to her feet; her ribs felt tender from where she had been hit, and each breath caused a painful sensation in her chest. Her face felt battered and her nose may have been broken. She wiped the blood from her face with the inside of her T-shirt and started walking forward in the dark.

Kathryn threw her bag over her shoulder, gripped the gun with her right hand and held the lantern with her left. Cache could see her left hand shaking and she held her arms close to her chest. They walked for about ten minutes until they reached the clearing where the vehicles were parked. Cache headed to the hippie van.

"Where do you think you're going? I want your precious little truck for all the hassles you brought me by showing up uninvited. I may let you know where I leave it, or I might just pour gasoline on it and set it ablaze."

Cache didn't like the idea of giving up her truck; it was a close tie she had to her grandfather, but she knew he would rather see her alive than the truck.

"By the way, what did you do to them?" Kathryn asked.

"Do to them?" Cache said.

"To make them inoperable. I'm betting you weren't planning on leaving yourself stranded out here."

"I pulled the distributor caps off and hid them."

"Well, I have no idea what the distributor cap does, but obviously you do, and it accomplished your job. Now, be a sweet dear and go get it. I'll be watching from over here."

Cache hopped up on the back of her truck.

"Hey, what are you doing?"

"I put them in here," she said, pointing to the lockbox.

"Get down off of there."

Cache climbed down and off of the truck. Kathryn climbed up and looked at the lockbox. She noticed a palm-print mechanism on the top. "This is biometric, how am I supposed to open it?"

"You can't; I can."

Kathryn wasn't sure if there were any more weapons hidden inside but she also didn't like being close enough to Cache to watch what she was doing, as standing up on the truck bed, Cache could easily knock her off balance.

"Okay, back to the original plan. I'm going to hop down, you're going to hop up and if I see anything that looks like a gun or knife, I'm going to pull the trigger."

Cache jumped back into the bed of the truck and opened the lockbox. She knew all her weapons were gone. Cache pulled up the bag with the distributor caps with her right hand and kept her left in the air.

She hopped down out of the bed of the truck, holding the bag with her right hand.

"There are two in the bag. I need you to come over here with the lantern so I can see which is which," Cache said.

"Yeah, that is not a great idea," Kathryn said, setting the lantern down and walking back from it. "You can come over here to use the light, and I'm watching you."

Cache stood at the back of the truck, the bag in her hand.

She had hoped to get Kathryn with arm's reach so she could make a grab for the gun. Kathryn wasn't having any of that. Cache just stood there, trying to formulate a plan.

"I said fix the goddam truck!" Kathryn screamed. "Cache, I do not think you are taking this seriously; I think you're buying time hoping the cops are going to be racing in here, but I will not put up with your bullshit." And with that Kathryn walked closer to Cache. Cache thought her opportunity might be now, but Kathryn raised the gun and pulled the trigger.

The shot was loud in the quiet night air and could have been heard for miles. Cache Iron lay on the ground at the side of her truck, blood coming from a hole in her right leg.

She screamed, "You shot me, you fucking bitch!" as her teeth clenched and her leg felt like someone had poured gasoline all over it and set it on fire.

"Take one of those carpet strips off your feet and tie it around the wound, you big baby."

She looked at her; she could see the coldness in her eyes.

"Cache, you might think you have all the time in the world, but you don't. You have about three minutes to get that cute ass of yours up and fix the damn truck."

Cache took one of her carpet strips, caked in mud, soaked with dirty water. She could only imagine the parasites that would enter her wound; however, she knew if she died here tonight a parasitic infection would not matter.

"If you don't fix the truck, I'm going to put you out of my misery and put a bullet in that head of yours. I'm then going to yank that T-shirt you're wearing off and stick it in the gas tank of this old truck and light it with a match as I walk away. It will burn, you will burn, and it will take a long while for the police to figure out who you are. And you know what? I'm going to find someone before I leave who has a kid or something they love and I'm going to kill them in front of their eyes and tell them Cache wanted me to do it."

Cache could sense the desperation of the situation. Any goodwill that had existed between the two of them was now gone. She was dealing with someone who had an agenda and would do anything in her power to see that agenda be achieved. Cache, grimacing from the pain in her leg, picked up the bag and hobbled over to where the lantern rested.

She found the cap that belonged to her truck and hopped over to the hood on one leg. She opened the hood and stared into a black hole.

"You need to bring the light over here," Cache said.

"I'm not falling for that," Kathryn said.

Cache hobbled away from the truck.

"Look for yourself, do you think there is enough light under the hood for me to see what the hell I am doing?"

Kathryn walked over, keeping the gun trained on Cache, and peered in under the hood and couldn't see anything.

"Okay, maybe you have a point, but nothing funny. Remember, I have the gun and you have the bullet."

Kathryn walked over to grab the lantern as Cache jumped on her good leg over to the truck and braced herself against the front. She instructed Kathryn to hold the light at a certain angle as she worked away at reinstalling the cap. If luck was to come to her rescue, she might need the working truck to get herself to a medical facility, and trying to reattach it in the dark with a bullet wound in one leg would be a near impossible task. As Cache made the last connection, she noted that Kathryn seemed to be more interested in what she was doing than watching her.

Cache grabbed the hood and smashed it down on top of Kathryn's arms, causing the lantern to fall and the gun to hit the ground. Kathryn screamed in pain and fell backward holding her arms. Cache leapt for her, with her good knee hitting the ground, feeling like someone had smashed a hammer across her kneecap. Cache grabbed Kathryn's shirt collar and delivered multiple punches to her face. She didn't let up; she kept punching her as Kathryn's head would fall back and hit the ground and spring forward to receive another blow. After several blows, blood was running from Kathryn's nose and mouth. Her arms were in pain from the hood smashing on them, so they provided her very little ability to block the punches being slammed into her face. Kathryn's capacity to fight back diminished with each consecutive hit, until Cache stopped and rolled her on her front. Kathryn had not noticed the handcuffs Cache had in her back pocket as they walked back to the truck in the dark. Cache grabbed one of her wrists and pulled it behind her; Kathryn muttered some words, though Cache could not hear what they were. Her fight was gone. Kathryn had no more energy to resist as Cache cuffed her remaining wrist behind her back. Cache hobbled over to the truck and shut the hood. She then limped over to where Kathryn was lying and turned her over on her side. Cache wanted nothing to hinder her breathing. Cache then pulled herself up along the truck, got back into the bed and opened up the lockbox. A clean T-shirt that she had in there would make a suitable dressing for her wound, so she folded it up and pulled off her jeans caked in mud. She wiped the wound clean as best she could, and grabbing some duct tape from the lockbox, she taped the folded T-shirt over her leg wound.

The darkness surrounding them had given way as the sun rose in the distance. Cache retrieved her phone from the cab of the truck and saw a couple of texts from Jake. She texted back that she was fine and had captured Kathryn but needed help and was wounded. He replied that he was en route with backup and would be there shortly.

After about ninety minutes of sitting in the back of the truck applying pressure to her wound, the sun had vanquished the darkness. The clearing no longer looked like a scary place.

Kathryn had spent the time trying to make a convincing argument for why Cache should let her go, but nothing convinced Cache that it was a good idea. She watched as geese flew overhead, squawking as they passed, and the sounds of sirens grew louder with each elapsing minute.

EPILOGUE

C ache spent the next several days recovering from the gunshot wound to her leg, bruised ribs and a broken nose in the hospital. Her room was filled with flowers and get-well cards as news traveled throughout her circle of friends and family. Jake had taken time off work to care for her, a point that did not sit well with his current girlfriend and led them to take a break from one another. Cache called home to explain what had happened and why she would be delayed in returning to the ranch. Her older brothers were preparing to get in their truck and drive all night to reach her, but Jake assured them that she was in excellent hands and he would let nothing happen to her. He would come to her room at the start of visiting hours and they would watch television together as the nurses came by to check on her.

Kathryn had been taken into custody by the state police and transferred to Los Angeles County. They'd charged her with multiple felonies, including murder, conspiracy to commit murder and kidnapping. Freddy had struck a deal with the district attorney's office to reduce his sentence if he would testify that Kathryn was the mastermind behind the whole thing. She was now being held in the county lockup for women, and a judge denied bail when her attorney requested it, citing the fact that she was a flight risk.

They learned nothing further about Lunar Tradicity and all involved decided that given that the perpetrator behind the acts was caught, inviting federal involvement wasn't a road they wanted to go down. Cache received a bit of a reprimand from the Los Angeles police for withholding information about Kathryn's whereabouts and endangering her own safety, but the press had grown relentless in their pursuit of the story.

Cache and Jake watched the press conference being given by the chief of police for the Los Angeles Police Department, flanked by Detectives Murphy and Johnston in the background as well as several high-ranking uniformed police officers and the mayor. Nurses who knew of Cache's involvement had gathered in her room to watch with them. The crowd of reporters there for the press conference extended well beyond local and state media and included news desks for national news outlets from all over the United States and the rest of the world.

Detective Murphy was asked to speak as the lead detective on the case and thanked Cache for helping the police department with their investigation leading to the arrest of the killer and resolving the pinup murders. The extent of her involvement was not mentioned, but she knew her fans back home would get a kick out of hearing her name. Reporters seemed to be interested in who she was, how she had aided the investigation and why she was not present at the press conference.

Detective Murphy simply said that she was recovering from injuries at an undisclosed location and moved on to the next question, which had nothing to do with Cache.

Switching off the television, Jake looked at her and told her that she was now famous. Maybe the ranch would be a good place to head and lie low for a while.

In the days that followed, Detectives Murphy and Johnston

visited her to see how she was. They had been busy pulling all
the pieces together and getting answers from Freddy and
Kathryn. The fact that Kathryn said anything that might be
used against her surprised Cache, but Detective Johnston felt
that she wanted credit for everything that had taken place.
They learned that the brands burned into the victims' chests
was a way to tell the world that the victims were nothing more
than women selling sex for money. Rachel, when questioned,
said she'd used the word *whores* to Kathryn several times and
told her she felt that the women should wear something as a
reminder, though she'd never wished any harm to come to
them.

The pinup cards were from a set found in Kathryn's attic
and related to a game that she and Freddy used to play at
bedtime. She thought it was very clever. The police were of the
opinion that Rachel and Kathryn had once been involved in a
romantic relationship and that Rachel had used her influence
over Kathryn to help her deal with women involved in her
husband's life. Once she figured out what Kathryn had done to
the first three, she used it to blackmail her into dealing with
Jillian Douglas in a similar fashion.

Kathryn was of the opinion that at some point Rachel
would leave her husband for her, but once Rachel's competition had been dealt with, the prospect didn't sound so
appealing to her.

Kathryn, fearing the blackmailing would not end, had
framed Rachel as the killer and had planned on making her
death look like a suicide, with a confession note to seal the deal,
allowing Kathryn to put the entire ordeal behind her and move
on with her life.

The day had come when Cache could be discharged from
the hospital. Vanny and Jake did everything they could to make
her departure as easy as possible. In the days since the press
conference, the press, through its sources, had learned that

Cache had been staying with a college roommate and had descended on the beach house hoping to get a glimpse of Cache Iron.

News channels featured segments on the now famous rancher from Montana, interviewing people from her hometown and those she'd gone to school with. Her parents had stopped answering the phone as they were under siege from reporters eager to talk to the new heroine and get her side of the story, with lucrative offers coming in for her to sit down with various interviewers and share her story.

Cache wanted none of that and yearned to get back home to a simpler life. Vanny and Jake had loaded up her truck, put the trailer on, squeezed into the front seat with Duke and made their way to the hospital, trying to avoid being followed by the press.

They exchanged hugs and well wishes at the front door as Cache thanked all the medical personnel for taking such good care of her over the past several days. She made Vanny agree that they would spend more time together, but their next vacation would be somewhere they both could go together and wouldn't involve killers. She and Jake danced around the notion of what could still be for the two of them, and he promised to come visit the first chance he got.

She climbed into the seat of the cab, rubbing Duke's head; she was happy to get on the road and put as much of the chaos as possible behind her.

The journey home would take her about two days to make, as she chose not to drive through the night. She smiled when she saw the sign that welcomed her to Montana and found herself traveling down the highway that bordered the Iron & Sons ranch to the south.

The first happy sight for her was two large log homes with driveways off of the highway, both lit up with a lot of activity. Her nieces were running around on the front lawn of the first house, and her brother Cooper stood on the lawn of the second and waved at her as she drove by. Cache came to the driveway and turned in, driving under the big iron sign on two large pine posts declaring that you were entering the Iron & Sons ranch. She could see the main house was all lit up, and lights could be seen down in the barn. Cache stopped in the driveway. Duke sat up, whimpering and jumping up on the dash. She tossed open the passenger-side door; Duke jumped out and ran as fast as his four legs could take him down to the barn. Cache closed the door and looked at the beautiful evening sky hovering over the ranch that had laid the foundation for multiple generations of Irons. No one could have predicted the storm clouds that were coming on the horizon.

———

THANK YOU

Thank you for reading!

Dear Reader,

I hope you enjoyed *Hot Iron*. I have to tell you that I really loved developing the character of Cache Iron. What's next for Cache? Well, be sure to stay tuned. Cache will be back next in the book *Iron Proof*.

I need to ask you a favor. If you are so inclined, I would love it if you would post a review of *Hot Iron*. Loved it, hated it - I would just love to hear your feedback. Reviews can be tough to come by these days, and you, the reader, have the power to make or break a book.

Thank you so much for reading Hot Iron and for spending time with me.

In gratitude,

Alex Blakely

JOIN AUTHOR'S NOTES

Join Author's Notes

If you want to stay up to date on the latest work from author Alex Blakely, join his monthly newsletter called Author's Notes. There he will share with you behind the scenes info on his current and future books as well as things going on in his personal life.

You will get to see book covers before they are released to the public and get to download exclusive content created solely for subscribers.

To subscribe go to: https://alexblakely.com/alex-blakelys-authors-notes

ABOUT THE AUTHOR

Alex Blakely is a Canadian author who grew up loving works of fiction in the classic "who dunnit style." A university graduate in the study of economics, he spent a number of years working in the area of finance before embarking on his writing career. He lives with his family in a community, west of Toronto, Ontario.

facebook.com/AlexBlakelyBooks

twitter.com/alexblakelybook

instagram.com/alexblakelybooks

bookbub.com/profile/alex-blakely

goodreads.com/alexblakely

tiktok.com/@alexblakelybooks

ALSO BY ALEX BLAKELY

THE IRONHEADS

If you enjoyed this book consider joining our Facebook Group called The Ironheads to talk about all things about Cache Iron and future Books from Alex Blakely. To join go to: https://www.facebook.com/groups/theironheads

Made in the USA
Las Vegas, NV
15 April 2022